KING
A SUPERNATURAL TWIST OF FATE

By Justin Robert Harnish

Published by Tigerseye Publications
Printed by Lulu

tigerseye@xtra.co.nz

ISBN 0-476-01333-X

About the author

Justin Robert Harnish was born in Auckland, New Zealand on 23rd of December 1973. He has been writing for most of His life such as poetry and short stories, but never really did anything with it. Early in 1999 He started a book called Sirius Exposure – Dogs in Space, which was a satirical look at things to come. Sadly, that got lost along the way when a new interest in writing popped up. The spiritual world has been of great interest to Justin from the time He was very small so, with this new genre and some good ideas created the first pages of **KING – A Supernatural Twist Of Fate**.

The second book in the trilogy is **KING - God And Ghost** and the last in the series in **KING - The Amulet.**

This book '**KING**' is an expression of the artist's true passion in the genre and the first book in a series of three.

From the author

It's taken me many long, hard years to get to this point and it's not over. There are more books to come not to mention the next two books in this series. I would like to dedicate this book to my daughter Piper, my wonderful friends Bex, Cat, Shane my Mother and of course my partner Julia. The list of people I wish to thank could go on, but I think you know who you are. And thanks to you the reader for getting this book or receiving this book as a gift. You are what this is all about.

Blessed be!

Justin Robert Harnish.

Introduction

Just because you don't believe in something doesn't mean it doesn't exist. If you are a sceptic it's understood that the supernatural and other worldly happenings could be something to scoff at or ridicule, but when you're face to face with a world you've only ever read about, fighting it brings adventure to a whole new level. Detective Robert Kingly is thrown head first into a life He knows nothing about by a woman who thought She did. It's not silver jump suits and flying cars in the future, but desperation and the hunt for euphoria, which rule our lives. When the reality of the Universe guides the world it could only lead to a chaotic end if not for a handful of old souls and one man who realises that He is somehow different from the rest.

If you think the Universe is trying to tell you something you're probably right. This is what King discovers in the first part of this exciting thriller. The stories of the gods are true, and we have dismissed them as myth. We may have forgotten the gods, but they haven't forgotten us and it's time for a reminder.

Now, you wouldn't think that going from run-of-the-mill private detective to a spiritual guide is the kind of thing that sane people do to impress a woman, and you'd be right, that is until you meet me. It's not that I'm stupid, far from it, it's just that I take on this foxy blond that leads me around by the manly parts in the hopes that I can sort out Her life. There's money in it and of course the slight chance that we could be more than just client/detective. The problems start when it appears that this gorgeous woman is possessed - and that's the good part! Reality becomes mixed with the 'other side' and people's worlds get turned upside down. But hey, it's not like it wasn't going to happen, it's just that it happened to me, and I have to do something about it!

KING

By Justin Robert Harnish

I lit a cigarette from an old match that took a half hour to find. I quit smoking long ago, but times were tough, and I needed a hit. A plume of white smoke curled into the air accompanied by a few small smoke rings and the smell of stale tobacco that emanated from the crumpled cigarette hanging loosely from between my lips. I took a long draw inhaling deeply tasting the foulness as it stung my lungs in that familiar way. I spluttered a few times remembering why I gave up in the first place. I couldn't remember the last time I smoked and the nicotine affected me instantly making my head spin. I took a moment to calm down, get a hold of myself and wait for the feeling to pass.

Outside was cold and wet, and though the rain stopped nearly an hour ago a fresh smell filtered through the air conditioning. I walked over to the window and peaked outside. The lights from the buildings reflected on the glistening roads making the city light up like a Christmas tree. The neon signs hypnotized people as they walked around looking for opportunities. The druggies on the footpaths and in the alleys trying to get their meagre possessions dry. Small fights broke out all the time and there were the flashing lights from police cars and ambulances racing to their charges while hobos sat hunched over small fires. Stray cats and dogs were hiding in the shadows shaking and shivering against the frigid wind. This was a scene that you either got used to or moved to the suburbs to avoid. For me, it's what I know and have always known. I made my way to my desk and typed a few more words to finish the report I was compiling on the PC then clicked it into standby mode. Last week had seen me spy on somebody's lover, track down a missing person and catch some poor bastard at the slot machines after He swore black and blue to His wife He wasn't going to gamble any more. Not exactly riveting stuff, but it paid the bills.

But only just.

It must have been about ten PM on Saturday night. I don't own a watch and the clock on the wall was broken permanently boasting ten past three. Time was not an issue for me, money was, or the lack thereof; it was so frustrating. My stomach was growling when I got a chill down my spine like somebody just walked over my grave. A feeling of expectation that something was about to happen. Similar to cop instinct, but this was different. I closed my eyes and took a deep breath. Not again I thought as I got up from my desk and walked over to the liquor cabinet. Recently I had feelings that resembled what I was experiencing right now so maybe I was having one of my spells. I grabbed a pill from the bottle my doctor gave me last month. I poured a whisky and downed the pill with the malt liquor. It was carving its way down my throat when in walked this tall, fox of a woman. I swallowed in surprise and at that point everything around me stopped.

From out of nowhere She came. Her hair was a transparent blond, the kind you see in black and white movies. She had a creamy white complexion, a red silk blouse and a neat, black mini skirt. Her legs went all the way up and were skinned with dark nylons, which were finished off with stiletto heels. She was every man's wet dream. I didn't recognize the perfume She wore, but it was sweet, fresh and intoxicating. She was perfect in every way, and I guess that was the problem, She was just too perfect. She took over my senses and all thoughts of the outside world left me, so all I could do was watch Her walk up to my desk. She leaned over slightly putting both hands on my desk and looked me right in the eyes. I have never seen anyone quite like Her in all my years and now that She was here I knew that I didn't want to let Her to walk out of my office without at least getting Her phone number.

"I have a problem. How much do you charge?" She said simply.

***

My name is Detective Robert Kingly; most people call me King. The date is the twelfth of February 2100. At forty-five years of age I am a retired cop turned private investigator and up until this moment my life wasn't worth the space it took up. This is the story of how I went from being a run-of-the-mill private investigator to being a class 'A', demon fighting son of a bitch.

- 1 -

Anyone not fortunate enough to be born into a rich family found living through the twenty first century to be rather cruel. A fuel had been discovered that could propel a craft fast enough and long enough through space to reach the nearest star system within ten years, which quite literally changed the world. The physics involved meant the craft was unmanned and the desire to actually go to these far off places had died down along with the funding for such a project was damn near imposable to get. The technology had, however, allowed a fast track journey to the planets within our own system prompting the richer of the governments to fund outreach projects to realise the age old dream of inhabiting said planets. People fled the dying planet of earth like rats from a sinking ship and now, only the struggling masses remain. Mars has been teraformed and now there is a greater population on the red planet than that on Earth. Gaia has had the worst treatment in the last ten years than She has had in the history of mankind; nobody seems concerned about the state of the planet any more. Though the Earth is dying people are still being born and raised here. No longer is there such a thing as third world countries; this was just the third world. Off world trade still existed, not like it used to be, but it still existed. Products like anti-fire clothing and oxygen regenerators are the industries that remained to make up the struggling economy. The rest of the economy was made up of manufacturing companies producing various sundries like toiletries, food and household apparel. The US dollar had not surprisingly become the worldwide currency and inflation rose like never before.

First there was one of the biggest recessions history had ever seen where jobs were lost by the millions. Then the depression hit and it hit hard. Even a $20 loaf of bread was a half days work. The CBD was falling apart at the seams and there wasn't a damned thing anybody was going to do about it. The greenhouse effect was in full swing as the Earth started fought back to save itself from the plague of mankind, but we wouldn't let it. The outcome was worse than anybody had expected. As the polar caps melted the biggest industries of the world banded together to work on a strategy to relieve the symptoms of the rising waters. The idea of dykes was reanimated from the traditions of Holland and constructed around the dock sides of the major cities to sustain commerce and the industries that barely held the planet together. The money poured in form the most unlikely sources both on and off world as interests held in trading still remained between Earth and Mars. As the money ran out so to all hopes as the water subsided and followed the laws of physics rather than that of the doom sayers. Due to the density of ice compared to water, when the ice caps melted the displacement reduced and therefore instead of the seas rising as everyone was lead to believe they actually receded about ten meters from the shore and in effect concentrated the pollution in the dying seas. This sparked the worst acid rain in centuries and the overflow of casualties in the hospital wards reached critical. More plagues and diseases sprang up than there were cures for and the population dipped so dramatically that it plunged the remaining survivors into a deeper depression. Crime was rampant; the police and security companies were overwhelmed. Major crime syndicates where taking over areas where the money had evaporated to try and save their respective cities; whole metropolises where relocated to higher areas to take advantage of the cleaner air.

I, unfortunately, was one of those people who missed out on the good life of the upper class; I am a working class man. My parents were killed in a tragic accident that took me years to get over. To this day it still angers and hurts me. They were taking a holiday around the Pacific when, due to massive ice movements, their ship was struck by a rogue burg and suffered the same fate as the Titanic all those many years ago. They had little money saved and spent almost all of it on the trip. They died with nothing. I guess they figured, like so many others, that you can't take it with you. At the tender age of fifteen I left school to get a job at a supermarket on minimum wage to live in a dingy little inner city apartment. When, after years of struggling, I turned eighteen I applied to the police force. Not surprisingly, I got accepted. This was not something that I really wanted to do; it was something that my Father wanted me to do. He was a cop in a long line of cops through the family and I was just following tradition. As time marched on being a cop is something I wish on no one and twenty years after I started it was time to give it up. The Force wears you out like an old sock. So, I guess the tradition will end with me. I retired and used my pitiful payment to sit my P.I. certificate and rented a modest office in the heart of the CBD. It was cramped, but I figured that I wouldn't be there half the time anyway. There was a bedroom down the hall, a tiny kitchen as well as a small room near the main door where, when I got one, my PA could work. The main office had a drinks cabinet, perfect for me, with a slate tile surround. The rest of the place was decked out in a pleasing grey carpet designed, apparently, to bring on a calming effect. I managed to find a desk that fit nicely in the office which added some character. Smack bang in the middle of the desk sat my computer. I bought a small, steel filling cabinet which I could bury my cases in and display my few well-earned trophies on the top. I had my walls covered in all the certificates I had received while in the force including my PI certificate and many other various framed memorabilia that told of my history. This was going to be hard, but satisfying and it's there I have stayed, still without a PA.

Not long ago I felt my age catch up to me and started to experience things that, when I was younger, the 'lifers' in the force told me sarcastically I could look forward to. Then came the sleepless nights and memories of a life I don't even know. I must have blocked out a lot of my childhood and when I did manage to get some sleep I would wake in the middle of the night in a cold sweat and a racing heart. The nightmares were cruel and I had anxiety attacks through the day. There was so much time to spend thinking that I often became physically sick. Something in my past was haunting me. It was part of me. I was paranoid and sometimes delusional to a point where I couldn't face the day. There was virtually no work so the fear that I couldn't feed myself, much less house myself, gripped tightly. After getting major chest pains one afternoon I decided that it was time for a visit to the doctor. After months of visiting the quack He finally decided that there wasn't anything He could do so He prescribed some anxiety pills for me, which seem to do the job.

***

There are always people wanting something from you, whether you're living here on Earth or on Mars and sometimes it gets a little too much to bare. Amphetamines were often the answer, but there was a new designer drug on the market. This one is the pharmaceutical equivalent of the plague that a pocket full of posies just wasn't going to cure. These pills would have you addicted as soon as you looked at them. The drug crimes were out of control and those that couldn't get the money for their addictions would steal or kill for it. Those that could do neither killed themselves or got killed trying to cheat others out of theirs. This was nothing new to the underground, but the need for the euphoric drug had been brought into the real world. Consequently there were a lot of religious fanatics that re-established burnt out beliefs to bring the people into a sense of spiritual euphoria in a naive attempt to rid the world of the need for drugs. The problem here is the sense of Euphoria never lasted more than a day and people always reverted back to drugs, albeit weaker, to satisfy their intense need for a rush. Scientology had flourished since the early 2000's and was now the biggest religion on both worlds. One of the few re-born religions that started to catch on was that of spiritualism. Maybe it was because of the great feeling of belonging it gave you or maybe it was because it wasn't the least bit dogmatic.

Within the realms of spiritualism there were many forms from Astral Travelling through to such things as meditation and Reiki, but they all revolved around the same principle; you needed to get in contact and involved in the nether world, the spirits, both light and dark. For the uninformed I guess the only way you could describe it is energy. It's a big energy thing. The universe is made of energy. Everybody has it and everybody uses it. From the dawn of human intelligence we have known about this energy and learned how to use it to our advantage, but for some reason we stopped using it and just kind of forgot. In fact for the last few millennia most simply chose to believe it didn't exist at all because knowing about this extraordinary human skill would be sacrilege and could get you killed. Entire 'worlds' were lost in the mists of time and some of our greatest achievements became laughable beliefs. Let's step back from this heavy-duty stuff for a while and get serious. The energy is very real. This isn't any fucked up attempt to gain popularity with the girls or pretend you're better or know more that anyone else. The world we live in is not real; it is an illusion made up from information fed to our senses by that very same energy which is all around us. This is not, however, a computer game, but it is the only way we can learn about the Universe and ourselves.

Consider a rock. You see the form of a rock and you know it is a rock. You touch it and it feels like a rock and for all intense and purpose it is a rock. It is, however, nothing more than a bunch of molecules made up of a bunch of atoms. These atoms are not solid object, but in lay terms, they are microscopic balls of energy. By their very nature these tiny balls of energy take on the appearance and nature of a solid ball of mass. This is what we have come to understand and accept, so it becomes part of our nature to see and feel a rock as a rock, but it's nothing more than energy.

In about the middle of the twentieth century the western world found out about hidden pockets of people around the globe that practised what they called Witchcraft.

Because of the ignorance and the fear within the church at the time most of these people were killed along with many innocent people by finger pointing. The Witch trials as they were called. The ones that were left went underground and re-emerged around the end of the twentieth century to try and expand the cult and bring a sense of balance and harmony to the new world. Most still considered them crackpots, but this time, due mostly to massive politically correct uprisings, they were accepted. This cult became somewhat of a saviour though some followers became entangled in the darker side of spiritualism, they just got drawn into it.

There is a place the Nordics called Yggdrasill, within this place is a realm known as Midgard. Deep in the centre of this world surrounded by a huge, impenetrable block wall, is Asgard. This is the place we have forgotten, the place that we have stored in the dungeon of our minds. I didn't have much interest in the subject and never got involved though I had heard a lot of stories about some of the experiences people have been through and sometimes, so I've been told, the things from the nether world come through to ours. It's a bit far fetched if you ask me, so you could imagine what went through my mind when my new client told me that She was being taken over by demon spirits. 'Crackpot' was what I saw tattooed on Her forehead, so of course I didn't believe a word of it.

***

Fast forward about a week since that Goddess walked into my office and into my life. Her cool charm and Her vivacious looks had taken me in. She was only twenty-five years old and I thought She was the woman of my dreams. Yeah, I've said that many times before about many sexy women and as usual I thought this was different. Through the week our relationship, although at this stage was purely professional, began to grow. I had taken Her case because She had the money, but it soon got a lot more complicated than that. I began my descent into a world that I wasn't sure I belonged to…until now. I was about to become something of a third wheel in a very complicated love triangle that I couldn't get out of. Have you ever been in a situation were you thought to yourself 'Fuck, this is fucked!' that's how I was about to feel.

This is how it started. A couple of days after we met I got a call from Her wishing me a happy Valentines. I had learnt to kind of forget about that day after years of not having anybody to share it with. I always thought it was just another day for the retail lords, but with Her I was willing to make an exception. We agreed to meet up and have a couple of drinks, so we met at an out of the way café down by the old Devonport. I was sitting at a window seat on a tall stool just soaking up the atmosphere and sipping on one of their boutique beers when I felt a tap on my shoulder, I turned around and there She was. She was still able to take my breath away.

"Hi." She said with a smile.

"Hey, how are you?"

"Great thanks Babe, do I get a Valentine's kiss."

Was She kidding? Wild horses couldn't stop me from planting one on Her! I pecked Her lightly on the cheek and offered Her a chair.

"What are you drinking?" I asked

"I'll just have a dry white thanks." She answered.

I went to the bar and while waiting for Her drink I looked back to see how She occupied Her time. She seemed very nervous as if She had a hard time keeping back the tears. When She saw me walking back Her mood and attitude snapped back to the happy girl that walked in.

"Thank you. So, how are you anyway?" She asked when I got back to my seat.

"Well, I can't say that my life isn't exciting." I started with a smirk. "There should be a soap opera about my life, there really should. Maybe I'll pen a screenplay and see how it goes. For a start you've got my insignificant life tailed by numerous people wanting one thing or another."

I paused and looked at Her with a droll expression fishing for sympathy, but all I got was a pout.

"Strange as it may seem, but people actually come to me for help." I continued and got a smile for my sarcasm.

"Well, that's what you do." She interrupted.

Maybe the irony was lost on Her. I waited to see if She was joking or not, I don't think She was.

"Yeah, I know, I was being sarcastic. Anyway, then you have their respective lives and how they actually came to require my services. Maybe a chapter on each of those people. Then of course you've got the symbolic relationship between these people and of course the hero of the show, me. Wrap it all up and you have drama, intrigue, romance and a few tears along the way."

"Well, I can tell you," She said with a wry smile as She gently touched my leg with a finger tip, "I'm quite intrigued with the romance bit."

I coughed slightly and tried to smile without twitching and carried on.

"You have mystery and laughter, trials and tribulations, kissing and a couple of bloody good looking people. You have the drinks and the drugs along side the heartache and sorrow, the lies and deceit and that creepy guy who's always in those daytime soaps. Along side the manipulations and thoughts of angst and anxiety of the unknown and lonely world."

"Wow. I had no idea you were so poetic." She giggled.

"Nor did I." I laughed.

The night went merrily by as we joked about things we could use from everyday life to write the screenplay. By the end of the night we were both rather drunk and stumbling, so we left the café and hailed a taxi. Cabs are not the way I remember them. When I was younger you could see the driver from the back seat. Now, however, your lucky if you get one of those old cabs. Usually there's a heavy, bullet-proof, one-way mirror so all you could see was yourself. There is a keyboard and screen mounted on one side of the mirror where you tapped in your destination and they charge it to your account. It was so impersonal, but every now and then you can get one of the old type, semi-friendly taxis and it makes up for all the bad things in the city.

The trip to Her flat was a quick one and as we pulled up to the curb She asked me if I wanted to come in. I wanted to, I really wanted to, but I couldn't. She looked at me with sad eyes and all I could do was stare back. Then She reached over and kissed me on the lips. It was magic. My heart beat so hard that I thought I was going to loose my eyesight. I tentatively pulled back a little and She stayed, then I went back for more. What started out as an innocent goodnight kiss turned into a long, passionate kiss sending electric shivers through my body. I was still in a daze when She got out and said goodbye. I don't remember the taxi ride home, all I could think about was that kiss.

***

After a night of pleasure, comfortable numbness and clarity of thought the type you can only achieve with the consumption of copious amounts of Jack Daniel's, I had the misfortune and unwanted feeling of incredible sobriety. I felt so many different emotions streaming through my body fighting for a place in my mind. I'm in lust and it's a feeling that has grown since She first walked into my office that night.

- 2 -

THE EXPERIENCE

I'll never understand women. After spending time together and finding out all about Her I didn't hear a word from Her after that kiss for the next two days. I was feeling lonely and I bet She was to, I was hoping She was to. I couldn't forget that kiss. I felt like calling Her up, but I had nothing to say to Her, well nothing that would make any sense anyway. She came to me for help and I had to put away my feelings until this whole thing blew over. The weather has been the worst it's been for some time, I was basically trapped in my office board out of my brain. The roads are too dangerous for any travelling when the rains come, not that I would consider myself a bad driver, but everybody else is even as good as the modern cars are which practically drive themselves it's been the same since I can remember. People get more aggressive in the wet and still drive as if it's dry. I wasn't about to catch a train because those things make me nervous. Auckland had employed the use of a monorail system in the heart of the city, which is perched nearly fifty metres in the air and ran from one building to the next. Each building the rail came in contact with had it's own little quasi-station where people could get on and off. Some of the buildings had two stations, one on each side, which worked like an exchange system for commuters to transfer to a different rout. With the occasional exception it always seems to be filled with a mix of high powered business men and low lifers, the haves and the have nots, which makes for a very unstable powder keg, which I'd rather not get caught in the middle of. The only thing to do was to watch TV, so I was stuck inside on the two days off that I had needed for a long time. Restful though it was I found it very anti-productive, so I started to compose a journal on my smart phone that I could carry around with me and then PAN to the computer at a later stage. It didn't take very long, just a few notes on what She told me about herself and Her story so far. The pleasure of knowing that I had started this bizarre case was enough to keep me happy. For a while anyway.

Over the week we got to know each other we became very close. Not really knowing how to take this apparent relationship that had sparked in the first thirty seconds of us seeing each other got me thinking. It felt so right, so natural, almost as if we'd never been apart. Perhaps it's just that we were always meant to be together and I had this uncanny feeling I already knew Her. The difficulty lay in the fact that this angel was actually my client. She was paying me for my services to protect and help Her, so She was basically in my custody for as long as this thing lasted. My feelings for Her were very unethical and immoral, but I really didn't cared too much. We had so much fun going to the movies and watching holo-ray's as well as getting blind drunk at the local and playing pool. We generally enjoyed the hell out of each and all the while things around us were happening that brought us closer together in almost a coincidental kind of way. I got the impression a strange kind of cosmic connection was forming.

On one occasion we were just about to cross the street when She suddenly stopped and turned to me.

"What?" She said.

"Nothing." I replied mystified.

"I thought you told me to stop."

Just then from out of nowhere a car lost control and hurtled towards us, but managed to rectify the situation and carried on. I say cosmic because the scary thing is that if Sam hadn't stopped the car would have taken Her out.

"I could've sworn it was your voice right next to me telling me to stop." She said looking at me wide eyed.

I didn't know how to feel or what to think. Chills ran up and down my spine as the full impact of what had just happened dawned on me. The sceptic within took a step back looking for answers. I think I was learning a lesson here. It seemed that everything happening was supposed to happen, like deja vu. I learnt a lot about Her and the weird things going on in Her life, I even started to believe it. I was becoming a believer. I know I was falling for Her in a big way and though my average relationship really only lasts about as long as a Tic Tac, I really believed that on some level this would last forever. While sitting in the dark mesmerized by a picture of Her face in my mind and sipping on a rum and coke the phone rang and scared the b'jesus out of me. My hand jerked and splashed the drink on some files sitting in my lap.

"God damn it!! Shit!!" I yelled throwing my other hand in the air, "Man!"

I put the drink down on the side table and stood up to shake as much of the liquid from the papers as I could while wiping my hand, so I could answer the phone.

"H-hello?" I stammered.

I wiped the rest of the liquid off my hands onto my pants and tried and compose myself.

"Hi, King."

I froze not quite knowing what to do with the sound of Her voice.

"Hi." I managed.

"There is something that I want to talk to you about." She said slowly.

"You mean the kiss?"

There was a pregnant pause on the line.

"Well, no. But now that you mention it…" She started.

"Look, forget about the kiss." I said back-tracking trying to maintain some of my dignity.

"OK, if that's how you feel." She said sounding hurt.

"Um." I said not really knowing how to get myself out of this one. "What can I say to vindicate myself from what I just said?"

"You could say that you liked it."

"I did." I said finally. "I really did. It's just that…"

There was a long silence and I felt increasingly uncomfortable.

"Look," I said, "I gotta go. I'll talk to you soon." I said awkwardly and I hung up the phone.

***

I had more questions than answers now and what was it She wanted to talk to me about? My destiny was set in motion and I was shortly going to have one of the biggest secrets of my soul pinned to Her heart like an arrow buried in a bull's eye and Her secret placed firmly on my shoulders like a backpack filled with cement. The lies and passion would grow stronger with each day and not just with Her. When I met Her I had the feeling that She was very spiritual. I knew there were people that believed in a spiritual life or something which we can call on to blame if there's no way to explain a situation – an 'act of God' type situation. I never thought that I would be involved in it and had less idea of how big and how real it was. The full picture was yet to show itself though little nuggets of information Sam had given me made me realize that from that moment things were going to get very interesting. She had mentioned such phenomenon like astral travel, the after life and spirits which had intrigued me. This is not to say that I had previously been interested or involved with it, but I enjoy the accounts that people have divulged to me over the years and Sam opened the doors to my suppressed enthusiasm. I was intrigued by the theory behind it and found myself inadvertently being introduced to it as part of my job. The way She described the things that had happened to Her sounded as if the real world is now just a figment of everybody's imagination. It was like a dream that I woke from when I realized the things She told me could only be true. Not because I had proof, but simply because of the way She described them to me, the things She told me made absolute sense. Like a true believer. I followed without proof, without asking any critical questions. I had doubts about my own sanity as I was thinking this, but it would all come very clear to me soon, but for now I was blissfully in denial and happy to live life as I knew it. When more strange little things began to happen there would be nothing I could do about it and no way to describe it. Things just happened. Like I said, there is no proof and nothing has changed in the outside world to illustrate my thoughts, but they happened. It was a feeling that nothing is what it seems. Goose bumps. Light headed dizziness. It was a slow evolution, but the pleasure and the space, the immaculate whiteness and light that emanates from the soul is such that when you venture deep enough into the realms of your own psyche sometimes it is impossible to get out. That's why Samantha came to me. She had wondered into this other world and the consequences of Her actions have landed Her in a hole and it looks like I'm the one to dig Her out. Was She taking advantage of me? Was this all a plan to get as much as She could from me? I don't know, but something in me wanted to help, not an easy task when you have the hounds of hell nipping at your heels, so to speak, every second of the day.

Depression hits hard on planet Earth and the suicide rate is proof, but for some killing themselves is not the answer. These people, these lost souls, turn to the 'dark side' of life for the experiences that only the dark spirits, guided by their hunger for emotions to feed on, can provide. These are the tribulations that my young client had got herself into. With alcohol and drugs weaving vile roads through Her body She was lonely, tender and very vulnerable to whatever spirits decided to play on Her. Horrid creatures looking like they were from the pits of hell came into, and preyed on Her young mind injecting thoughts of grandeur and depression in obscene amounts as to totally confuse and disorient Her from the world and then take Her body like a rag doll and use it for their devilish doings. This has, in short, destroyed Her. Destroyed Her emotions, destroyed Her stability, and totally rocked Her life. In that respect She is stronger than most though Her flesh was weak. I know it sounds a bit OTT when I talk about demons and the likes, but its all true, every word of it. Not only our love, but our hate, anger and frustration cause us to manifest the energy into a metaphysical demon of our minds. When negative energy becomes intense enough the metaphysical becomes the physical and you're basically fucked. Even our own physical presence on this earth is a case of 'I think therefore I am.' That's the 'why and how are we here' question answered. We want to be here, so we are; believe it or not.

****

The third day after we met Samantha told me the story of how She came to be in the predicament She found herself in and I shall try to retell the story.

On an off chance She went out for some Friday night fun with a friend of hers and somewhere along the line they bumped into someone that Her friend knew. He was an older man, short in stature and podgy. He could only be described as unclean and He had a voice like He'd swallowed sand. They were introduced and got talking, that's to say He spoke and She just sat listening. He was like an unprovoked fortune teller and it seemed to be all about Her, but the things He was saying were uncanny in their accuracy. In a way She enjoyed it as long as He didn't get too personal, but then came the detailed impressions of Her life that He portrayed in His words, which were so detailed She became both mesmerized and uncomfortable. As He spoke the rest of the world started to fade away and while in this out-of-body type trance He took Her on a journey through a world that She would never forget. He told Her things that made sense to Her and took Her on a trip within Her own mind to places that She had never visited. She saw things that frightened and excited Her – this was Her dreamscape.

A dreamscape is a culmination of vivid images and disjointed thoughts that come together to form a totally new world. Whilst in this state She had seen a man who had shown himself as somewhat of a spectre. He was apparently a good spirit that She should follow, much like a shepherd. The old man, now Her guide, had told Her about the holistic nature of the universe; which is the very philosophy that everything is in some small way connected to everything else. This interconnectedness of all things had drawn Her, inexplicably, to the one person who was to show Her the way to exorcise the demons in Her life that had led Her astray. The ire and the angst that threatened to take Her very essence was compounded by the fact She had become very confused about the person She was. The most vague part of this whole ordeal is the man She saw knows nothing of Her and She knows nothing of him. This is where the story gets somewhat confusing the result of which would leave me completely drained both physically and spiritually.

I didn't know much about what this promiscuous princess got up to, but I was about to find out in a big way as more of Her story came out. She was a very up and down person that lived for excitement, to excite others and to live life on the edge in every part of Her world. When She walked into my office the night we met I got drawn into Her life in a way that I can't say about anyone else I have known. At the end of this account, you will believe me when I tell you that the road I'm about to travel is one filled with traps and snares, tears and joy and horror and not one bit of it is made up.

- 3 -

Way back in history there was a story told. It's a story parents told their children when they want them to behave. It's a tale about an unforgiving place, the darker side of the nether world and it's a place you go when you die if you have lead a bad life. This is a terrifying place of death, which is ruled by creatures and temperamental gods. Startling blackness and darkness like nothing else, terrifying shadows and soulless monsters with teeth that are so long and sharp a single scratch would cause a hundred years of pain. If that didn't drive you mad the restless infinity and infectious depression would definitely do the trick. The place was over-grown with noxious weeds and huge, black-wood tress. The animals that lurk in the shadows are evil and rat like and ten times bigger. Creatures of all descriptions; Phoenixes, demons, dark souls and ghouls all share their world with the gods and fallen heroes, warriors and the hoards of darkness. These are the places where even angels would fear to tread, but I walked into it foolishly with the thought that I was doing the right thing. It didn't happen right away, no. The devil in disguise, this temptress, the Goddess that walked into my life had forced my hand to try to recover some of the life that She had lost. This as I said, is the dark side. This is the place where those that cause pain to others for pleasure find themselves imprisoned. Some souls stay there seemingly throughout eternity. Perhaps they feel that what they deserve or maybe they still have a black heart. The darkness of Niflheim, the lower realm of Yggdrasill the Nordics were terrified of; once you go in you can't get out. Nothing is forever though and as the aeons go whizzing by they slowly start to understand that guilt can be vindicated and they can move up to higher planes of energy until they are once more joined to the combined consciousness. The gods were born and bred in Yggdrasill. They were created by the ancients to guard and protect what they felt was important to the minds that thought them up. Thus the energy platform known as Asgard was formed.

***

The last time Sam and I were together I could see there was something She wanted to tell me, but didn't because I screwed up. I tend to do that a lot with women. So, I called Her to meet for coffee once more, but this time it was at 'Tavern Café', which is a little coffee shop tucked away down a small alley in town. A lovely little spot and just right for talking about the money She was going to pay me for my work and find out what She wanted to tell me. When She walked in it was like all the angels in heaven broke into a chorus of song and shrouded Her with a veil of holy perfection. No such thing actually happened of course, but that's what went through my mind. Other things were going through my mind at the time like why was She coming to me with these ridiculous problems. I thought She was crazy, I really did and I guess that's why I took the case; it sounded simple enough and She had money. The thought that I might just get Her into bed had also crossed my mind, it then doubled back and crossed it again just in case it missed anything the first time and then decided to stick around to see what, if anything, would happen. Mistake number two was listening to this poor young girl talking about the spiritual world and me nodding vigorously as She spoke like one of those toy dogs in the back of some cars who's head moves to the rhythm of the road travelled, just so I could get into Her knickers.

It wasn't completely my fault. She had a body on Her like you wouldn't believe. A face that reminded me of every beautiful movie star rolled into one package. I think I was falling in love. It was like I was looking into the eyes of a hypnotist and falling into a deep trance accepting every little suggestion that was bestowed upon me and working only to please. I guess that's why I agreed to try the spiritual world just so I could 'get a little experience' as She put it. I didn't need to be asked twice. I also liked the thrill of the chase. The mystery about whether this girl really likes me or was She just playing? Or was it just in my own mind? I was about to turn on the ol' King Charm and draw this out as long as I could. If this was going to happen I'm going to enjoy building the sexual tension.

We finished up with the coffee and I paid the waiter with a tip that I didn't think He deserved and started to make plans as to where we were going next. I suggested that She might as well show me this thing now and if we headed back to my office we could get all those little 'experimental' things out of the way. After that we could move on to more pressing problems which in my mind was how to get a very sexual relationship out of this blond perfection. I had already established a short stated, semi-satisfying sex life with Her in my mind, so let me paint you a picture of my obsession. She was blond and tall, comparatively to most other woman I have met and She had a voice that was sweet and innocent with a tongue and forwardness to Her that impressed me. When She spoke it was as if music filled the air and when She laughed it was like the troubles of the day vanished. Blues eyes the colour of summer skies, skin the colour of creamy pick roses and a perfect complexion. She had the kind of body that you expect to see on aerobics instructors and She could drink any man under the table; my kind of woman. Her name was Samantha, aka Sam. This was truly the woman of my dreams, the goddess that would occupy my every thought, who would distract me from what I was supposed to be doing for Her and as a result I would almost get Her killed. She came to me like a bolt out of the blue and into my life like a myriad colours radiating from a prism. Even if I had known then what was going to happen, there wasn't a thing that I could do about it. Destiny had been set in motion.

We got back to my office and I poured us both a drink, She took it with thanks and skulked around for a while looking at the ornamentation that I have scattered around the place. She had something to say, something to show me, but perhaps She was deciding whether I could take it or not. Maybe She was wondering how much of it I would believe and what I would think of Her if She told me anything at all. I watched Her move around the small room. She was so graceful walking with almost no impact on the ground. I can hear the padding of feet on my carpet when anybody walks over the floor, but this time I heard nothing. It could be that I was perhaps hypnotized or too busy paying attention to the rest of Her body, but it almost seemed as if She glided around on a pocket of air which separated Her from the ground by only millimetres. I was lost in Her motion. She moved towards the desk and slowly sat herself down in one of the two chairs that faced my desk and finished Her drink.

The phone sprang into life and we both jumped, I breathed in deeply and gathered my thoughts before going over to answer it.

"Hello." I said as usual.

There was nothing.

"Hello?" I repeated.

"Who are you?" Said the husky voice on the other end.

"You obviously know who I am," I retorted, "so, the question is who the fuck are you and what do you want?"

"I suggest that you don't, for the time being, worry about who I am. I ask not of your name, but of your nature. I recommend that you stay away from the woman you have in your office right now. Don't get involved with Her problems. Please head my warning as you don't know what you're getting yourself into."

And then the line went dead. I put the phone down slowly and turned to the beauty.

"Who was that?" She asked.

I chose to ignore the call, but noted it in the back of my mind.

"Nobody, it sounded as if it was a prank caller. I'll ring the phone company in the morning."

She held out Her hand and asked me to sit down. I casually walked over and sat down in the second chair and clasped Her hand firmly as not to let Her go. She was quiet for a minute as She slowly closed Her eyes.

“We have to have silence for a little while,” She said finally, “otherwise we'll loose the mood in the room.”

As She continued I could sense something strange happening, like a blue spark I guess you could say, that constantly leaped from Her to me and back again.

“The air has no soul in it. I thought I'd better let you know that first so you know there is no danger of anything bad happening here.”

“Well, that's comforting, but I don't know what to expect.” I said foolishly.

“Quiet. Try not to expect anything. Just close your eyes and let it happen.” She said. “Breath in slowly counting to seven and then hold it for a count of seven. Then exhale for another seven count letting everything around you fade away. Then exhale for a further seven counts using your diaphragm and ribcage. It may seem a little hard to do at first, but it works. As you do this let your worries go and try not to think of anything. Then inhale normally.”

We did this and I relaxed a little more. There was another moment of quietness and then the most unreal feeling of peace seemed to fill the air. I started to hear things in the background that I had never heard before like the sound of the wind and the ticking of my clock. I was beginning to get lost in something. I have always been of sound mind and body and I always need to be in control, but now I seemed to be loosing that and I liked it. My eyes were shut so tight that I couldn't open them. Then something altogether different started to happen. I began to see things on my minds big screen. Wonderful things with no shape, but they had the most brilliant colours. Greens, golds, blues and reds the shades of which I have never dreamed about, but there they were, right in front of me. I forgot about the state of my eyelids and let myself be drawn into the perfect world that my subconscious had formed. I was easing more and more into total relaxation. I was so calm that all feelings of the natural world just dripped away and I felt fresher in spirit. Everything I saw and everything I was feeling, everything I was enjoying, started to fall apart. Like the death of a million little pinpricks of light. Like the melting of chocolate in a pan. Then suddenly everything was dark and my senses toward the outside world returned with a stunning viciousness and I immediately woke with a shout. Sam had broken the circle of hands and everything ebbed away. It took a while to calm down and to get my grip back on reality. When my heart rate slowed down enough for me to think about what had just happened I began to feel as though I had a new outlook on life itself and then She looked at me.

"You are now ready."

What She had just done was introduce me to the world of the spirits, the world on the other side, what we like to call the supernatural. I'll try to explain; it's like everything suddenly makes sense and the world has become a place where there is nothing to worry about. This is why so many people get drawn in, it's so peaceful. I was shortly to be proven wrong, but right now I was wanting to know more. If this was the kind of problem that Sam has been going through it was going to be a walk in the park. What I will tell you next, however, is the account She gave me in full, almost word for word about Her experiences with the nether world.

- 4 -

I just sat there staring at this beautiful creature as She spoke while thinking of the things I had experienced with Her. She made me feel alive. Even if She was full of shit, which I was beginning to doubt, I was enjoying it.

"I had had a few drinks, but I wasn't drunk," She started, "I wasn't even getting there, but I guess the alcohol put me in the right frame of mind to be able to go through what was to be the turning point in my life."

I was already hooked on Her, but as She started Her story I found myself almost at the edge of my seat waiting with baited breath to hear what happened.

"It was quite late in the evening, not sure what the time was probably somewhere around eleven or twelve and I was just having a little fun with a friend. Now, before you start to judge me, let me explain something to you." She said gazing at me with what looked like teenage angst raging against me the adult. "I had always known that there was something missing in my life. I latter found out that what I thought was missing was actually just my feeble way to try and fill a gap I wasn't even aware I had. I have, I guess you could say, a varied sex life. Some would call me promiscuous and by doing what I did I was able to, or more like failed to, fill the void that I was carrying. Anyway, to make a long story short it was the friend that I had gone out with that I was very keen on, but it didn't happen which I think was just as well. This friend of mine knew a lot of people, I mean She knew everybody and…"

"She?" I interrupted with a cough.

"Yes."

"Oh."

"Do you have a problem with that?" She asked in a short tone.

"Err…no. I guess I don't." I said trying to recover. "It just surprised me that's all. I mean what with you and I…" I trailed off.

She looked at me sideways, after all, there wasn't really a 'Her and I' to speak of - just those sparks.

"Anyway, like I was saying," She continued, "She knew a lot of people. This one particular person, a short and extremely ugly man had sneaked up behind me and said 'hi'. He scared the shit out of me much to the amusement of those around. My friend, once She stopped laughing introduced him to me and I instantly forgot His name. I was in my own little world for a while after that only snapping back to reality when I realized He was talking to me. Did I mention He was a fat man? He spoke like He knew everything. This man was ugly, really ugly and He smelt like stale smoke. I just didn't know what to think of him. How did He get into a place like this? His breath stank of raw onions or something like that, He had dark scraggly hair with the most evil looking green eyes you've ever seen and to top it all off He was a bad dresser. The guy wore a paisley orange shirt and bell-bottom pants for fuck sake!

"I wasn't really in the mood for this guy, so I tried to give him the cold shoulder, but it didn't work. I think it was encouraging him to tell the truth. It was kind of strange after that. He offered to buy us both a drink and I of course accepted. We finished them fairly quickly and started to feel the roses in our tummies, which I think He took as a signal to talk to me more. He started talking about my life, which kind of scared me because what He was saying was fairly accurate. He asked if I was at all spiritual and I replied that I thought I was. He then said that He could see a lot of potential in me for great things and I could, with proper care, get a great deal of relief from my torments. I swear I thought He was coming on to me, so I started to mentally back away. Then He said the classic come on line; well that's what I thought it was anyway. He said that He could show me what I was missing. I turned to my friend and made a face that She understood. He began to freak me out a lot, but continued talking. Some of what He had to say was uncanny and I felt too weird, so I told him to go away and get a life…obviously I said it with a few stronger words, but you get the gist.

"The next thing I knew my friend was asking him if He still did the travelling thing, He said yes and then She turned to me and asked if I would like to try. I of course thought this was a bit weird, but replied if that was all we were going to do then I didn't see any problem with it. Yes, I said, I'll come along for the ride. I thought He meant travelling in the car. You know, cruising the streets."

I had to but in then and get something sorted out in my own mind before She went any further.

"You had only just met this guy?" I questioned.

"Yeah, do you have a problem with that? I said that I was promiscuous, yes, but I also said that this guy was butt ugly…"

"You didn't say 'butt ugly'." I interrupted.

"Don't be facetious. He was ugly and I wouldn't touch him with a barge pole. Now is there anything else or can I continue?"

"Yes, there is something else." I said, playing with fire, "You went along with this guy on the pretence that you were going for a ride in a car?" I said with incredulity in my voice, but I was trying to make it sound as matter-of-fact as I could.

She looked at me and treated the comment with the contempt it deserved.

"Yup, just goes to show how naïve I was. Anyway, there we were driving along when we pull up to this huge house. Up the drive we go and all pile out. Now it's at this point that I start to get a little bit nervous about what's going to happen, but think that if my friend knows this guy and says it's all good, then it's all good. So, I go along with it.

"Outside was kind of dark and haunting like one of those houses you see in horror films. Inside was kind of Goth if you know what I mean. It was dark and the only real light was from that of the candles that where dotted here and there. It was pretty in a scary kind of way. I walked in and got this creepy feeling, but at the same time it was kind of a warm and inviting. Kind of hard to explain. Anyway, I'm standing in the middle of the foyer looking at the roof when I get the fright of my life as I hear this slight cough behind me. When I turn to see who it was this woman was standing right there, I almost fell dead away! Talk about your change of knickers time! She was very attractive, which made me wonder how She got stuck with a creep like the 'fat man'. She was average in height with long brown hair and brown eyes that could reach into your soul. Her face was drawn down, not long, just drawn down. This didn't make Her look bad, in fact it made Her look better because Her hair framed Her face. She looked like She was on the younger side of fifty and suited Her age. Like I said She was quite attractive, not my type you understand, but I could see that men would like Her.

"She put Her hand out to shake mine and introduce herself, so I said 'Hi, I'm…', but when I touched Her hand I immediately froze and lost myself. I got this electric chill which instantly turned to a peaceful lull. Her eyes widened, like really wide you know. She looked at the short man who was standing next to my friend and said 'My, we do have our work cut out for us'. The fat man smiled and nodded as She continued 'hi Samantha, my name is Rena. I'm what's called a spirit guide. I help people find what they're looking for and help fight their demons. Or try to at least. You have a lot of anger and jealousy built up in you. I think we can help.'

"I was stunned. Not only had I not actually given Her my name, but something inside of me just clicked. It was like yes, this is what I have to do. Again, hard to explain. Before long we were sitting on the floor quietly as Rena told us what we should be doing. Could I have another drink please?" She added at the end.

I was so engrossed in Her story that She had to ask a second time before I snapped out of it and realized that She was talking to me. I stood up and shakily walked over to the drinks cabinet. I Look back briefly to see She had a kind of vacant expression on Her face. It was like She was recalling the night She met this bizarre couple and She looked drained and tired. Her head was drooped and lazy, but gradually She lifted it up and stared me right in the eyes. They were deep and soulful, almost apologetic. All of a sudden, through Her eyes, I got the full blast of what She had been through. It was like She was trying to show me and I could 'see' what had happened. I don't know how She did it or if I had anything to do with it, but it was definitely something I have never experienced before and it rocked me. I saw the pain She had suffered and the joy that night had brought Her. I felt Her looking into my soul for guidance and help. It was at that point that I had the first clue as to what I was getting myself into. I felt something very real was going on here, something indescribable. It was like all of a sudden all the atoms in the room had simultaneously shifted a fraction in time and we were the only two people on Earth. I dropped the glass I was holding, and the noise that it made when it hit the tiles and shattered snapped me out of the unrelenting feeling of…of, well, it's hard to describe. It's like the deepest feeling of hollowness mixed with the highest feeling of fulfilment. My lust and adoration drained completely giving way to a felling of hope and nurturing. A feeling of love and compassion on a deeper level. A kinship had just began, a soul connection and something that would keep us together for a very long time. The type of bond that we started that night could not be broken. A bond that secretly I knew was somehow always there and I had mistaken it for something else. I could see in Her eyes that She felt the same way, no longer was She this beautiful woman now She was a beautiful person who could have been my Sister and the love that went between us was the same love that a Father would have for His Daughter.

My mind opened up and whatever it was that was happening between us enabled me to see and feel everything at the same time. I could look back and imagine the lives we may have shared together. Dreams of knights, horses and brotherhood. Memories of an Egyptian Faro and Her adviser. Pictures of Kings and Queens, rulers and conquerors. She may even have been my partner in the great battles that long ago were fought where blood was shed and lives were lost…then it all stopped. Something had just come over me like a blanket holding me down. I think I could see the truth. At last I could see where it all began and it was something I was far more involved in than I thought possible. I fell to my knees as it all washed over me and looked up into Her eyes. I totally understood what She had gone through and I wept unashamedly like a man who had just found His long lost Brother. I felt like I had been chosen to fly a suicide mission or something. She stood up and walked slowly towards me, crouched down and put a hand on my shoulder. I felt the pain sluiced away like a slow moving mudslide under Her gentle touch.

"You see it to. The truth. Now you know why I've come to you." She said quietly looking me in the eyes.

"Please continue your story." I said softly.

I steadied myself for the rest of Her account sitting next to Her listening intently.

"You could imagine how I felt at this point. The room was full of all kinds of expressions and experiences. Things that I latter found out were spirits and demons that were fighting for a place in my soul. I know it all sounds airy-fairy, but it was very real at the time. Like the last push by the spirits to take me and own me. I felt it, I truly did and this was the first time I had actually realized that there was something missing in my life which was being driven away by everything I was putting myself through. I fell silent, like totally silent and listened to what Rena was saying. She taught me so many things like meditation and the way to clear my mind to greet the good spirits in the room into my life.

"Once we were in deep meditation and things seemed to be settling down, Rena asked us all to hold hands. As we did so the shit hit the fan. As soon as the circle had been completed all hell broke loose and I saw for the first time right in front of my eyes the battle that was raging inside of me. I was frozen. I couldn't move. It was like I'd been hit by a train. It may just have been the most terrifying thing I have ever seen. Like a battle of good over evil, life over death. All my fears span in front of my eyes and I saw Rena standing there in front of me. But it wasn't Her as such, well it was Her just not in the shape and form that I knew. I recognised it as Her though, it was Her life force in the form of a bright light, Her spirit I think. She was my guide, my protector and everything that She did was for me. I felt a little more at peace. Darkness closed in for a moment or two then everything changed into a bright yellow colour. Someone told me, it might have been Rena, yellow is the colour I had been missing. Yellow is the colour of life and understanding. I could see the damage I had been doing to other people and the reason why people treat me like they do. The reasons my relationships with anyone never worked and all the hurt I had put people through. I felt so selfish that I had been telling the world it owed me something when all the time I had been loose with my thoughts, my body and my words. It all became crystal clear, but the yellow dissipated and turned into empty space again. I was terrified, lost in my own world created by my mind and I was horribly confused."

She stopped and wiped a tear from Her eyes then looked at me. I could see the confusion in Her heart and asked if She wanted to stop and carry on another night. She simply replied that there wasn't enough time and that She would be all right soon. I let Her continue.

"Rena and the short man, Ray as I was reminded, came up to me in my vision – I guess that's what you would call it - and grabbed an arm each. In the distance I could see my friend racing ahead. She had obviously done this before, but I couldn't move and felt like if they let me go I'd fall into an abyss and if that happened it would mean death. I didn't like the feeling I was getting with this, but I remembered these two were not about to drop me, so I began to relax again. After a while I started to enjoy the ride. I tell you, it was absolutely amazing.

I started to see some little black dots buzzing around me and I got a bad feeling about them. Ray told me that these were the surface problems – the little negatives in my life. Once I heard what He was trying to say I realized what it meant. In short I didn't think much of myself. I wasn't that bad of a person was I? Even with that tiny bit of positive thought some of the little dots evaporated. That was the secret. Unfortunately there were too many of them and I was trapped. Just as I was about to loose hope Ray and Rena said something to me. I can't remember exactly what it was, but all of a sudden the emptiness fell away and a green meadow appeared that stretched on for miles and it supported my weight. They both let me go and I stood there dumbfounded not knowing what to do next.

"Just as that thought entered my mind these dark shadows started to form in front of me. I turned to run, but they were there behind me as well. Rena shouted out that these were the demons that I had to fight. Great, what does that mean? This must have been a drug-induced dream or something. What were they talking about demons for? I'm not one for fighting demons and how was I supposed to even know how? I started to run, but my feet felt sluggish and I wasn't able to go very fast. Ray shouted at me to lift my spirits, but I wasn't sure what He meant by that. I realized, though, that I was still looking at myself as a person. I wasn't a person, not in this plane, I was a soul. I was a spirit. I glanced up at Ray and Rena who were quite a way ahead of me now. My friend was way off in the distance doing Her own thing and having fun. I pictured myself in the body I was looking at and imagined I was a bright ball of yellow light. I don't know how I came up with that thought, but the weight that the physical world had lumbered me with disappeared into nothing and I felt myself float up. Free as a bird I swooped around and enjoyed the exhilaration. I had forgotten the reason that I was running in the first place until I looked down and with a fright I saw the demons had taken flight. I yelped in shock and almost lost my new found flying skills though I managed to catch myself. I yelped again as I saw Rena loom back in front of me and Ray came up behind me. Their life forces were urgently beckoning me to go with them as the demons were gaining on me and I could feel their icy breath. Ray did the ultimate, His courage was greater than His ego and I started to cry when I saw what He was doing. He dived down onto them and fought my demons. He, of course, came out on top because Rena soon joined the fight. All I could do was watch helplessly. There were screams that just scared the hell out of me and suddenly Ray plucked one of them out of the air and hurled it down through the ground like a rock into water. My god, I was frozen. I had never seen anything like this before and it all seemed so surreal!"

She squirmed in Her seat as the memories returned.

"There were so many the sky was black with them. But when Ray did what He did the other dark spirits fled to fight another day. Rena said that they would be back, but our journey had at least started. We were then joined by five or six white spirits and I took to the air like a ride on a roller coaster in fast motion."

She stopped for pause and looked at me. She could sense my clueless stare.

"Do you know what I'm talking about? White spirits."

"I have a fair Idea." I shrugged, "Go on."

"We were speeding over towns and cities, trees and lakes, mountains and valleys." She continued. "Everything was so real in even the minor details. I could feel the cold of the snow on the mountains. I could feel the freshness of the water in the tropical islands. I could see the buildings in the cities and peoples faces that mingled in the small towns. Over such familiar land marks that I had only seen in pictures, Europe, America and Asia. I was speeding over these countries seemingly unnoticed. I wasn't actually there, but it felt so real and I was elated with the discovery of this New World. I felt so at peace."

She paused and thought for a while about what She had gone through, She sighed and continued talking. I was at a total loss for words, so I just sat there and listened.

"I felt so alive for the first time in so long. I was at peace and harmony with the world. Now I knew how to do it I could let myself enjoy the rest of the world knowing that at any time I could fight the demons that tormented my life. That was my mistake. You see the truth is, I didn't fight any of the demons myself it was Ray and Rena. Before we came back to our shells – that's what Ray called our bodies - they showed me something that had been following me through my entire life. I looked behind and saw this man just sort of hanging, or floating, or something – right there. The man looked so familiar, I knew him, but I didn't know him. This being, this person had been there in my soul all the time. He had been there since I was born and before. This was my soul partner, for the whole of time. In passed lives we have been together, but I just didn't know it."

This really threw me. Somewhere along the line She has been with a spirit together as one and She never knew it. They had never met, never actually seen each other until now. This was starting to make a little sense.

What was I thinking? What was I talking about? This is just a load of rubbish. This isn't happening! I've been lead down a fantasy path by this beautiful young lady. For what? So I can get into Her knickers!! That's it, King, enough is enough! You have been through some kind of hypnotic session. You've got to pull yourself together and do the job that you have been paid for. That shouldn't be so hard as this girl is quite clearly nutty!

"This is the problem I've gotten myself into." She continued. "I thought I could handle this by myself, so I tried it at home, alone. I can't really say any more, but I need your help to get me out of the trap that I've fallen into. Please come with me, together we can take it on, I think. There is so much at stake here and I can't do it alone."

"You're nutty." There, I said it.

"What?"

“I said, you’re nutty. Totally out to lunch. You don’t seriously expect me to believe all this do you?”

“But you’ve seen it for yourself. How can you not believe it?”

“What I experienced could have been the result of you spiking my drink when I wasn’t looking. I don’t know!” I stopped to think what it could have been. “There are lots of explanations for what I just went through. I don’t want to take your money when quite clearly your bananas!”

“I’ll double it!”

“What about Ray and Rena?” I asked rather confused.

“That, unfortunately, is impossible. If you accept to help me with what I need, then I’ll show you why they can’t help. Please don’t ask now.”

“But, why me? What can I do?” I reasoned.

“You, because we have made a connection, I can trust you. You’ve seen what’s going on and you are very strong spirited. It has to be you.” She replied gravely.

I didn’t like the sound of what She had said, but She was right as far as I knew if Her story is true.

“So, what am I supposed to do? Just accept what you’re saying and let you lead me into something that I don’t know anything about? Into something that just might kill me? Are you out of your pretty little mind?” I found myself saying.

Then She looked at me in a way that made me instantly regret saying it. I was guilty about my own insensitivity.

“You have to, it’s your destiny.”

“Who are you? Obi-Wan Kenobi?”

“It’s you that’ll make everything right again. You and only you can bring me back to the real world that escaped me. I’m willing to show you how to do what I do. You have to say yes.”

“Now you’re a fucking Mills and Boon?”

"Yes, I am out of my mind, thank you for asking. That's why I need you. It will all become very clear soon. You need to keep the faith. You need to believe."

And with that, She got up and left the room without another word. I reeled in what I had just gone through wondering if what I had just experienced was real or just a dream. She was right though, the attraction to the spiritual world is buried in the fact that to survive each of us needs to believe in something. Thoughts of the supernatural world, gods, spirits, angels and demons were whizzing around my head. Anyone who hasn't experienced this can't even begin to understand what life is all about. Nor can they understand or even contemplate the fullness of life and the fundamental interconnectedness of everything. There is a downfall to everything and in this case it's the 'come down'. Without knowing this, none of what Sam went through will make sense.

Fate is the here and now. Fate is how you got to where you are now. Whatever happens as time ticks by and we walk through life as every door opens and as every path is taken; it's all fate. The journey is destiny, between the start of life and the ultimate outcome of our lives. Fate is just the steps we take to follow destiny. Destiny is basically the line of our life, the map by which we travel, but cannot read until we reach the end. Our lives are set and the choices that we make are the choices that we have already made, the choices that take us to our destiny, which is the sum of all the little bits of fate. It has already happened and all we are doing is playing out our lives. No matter the road we travel, no matter the path we take it is always the right one. The only one. There was a theory I was putting together in my mind; if we try and do things our way, the way that we think we should it's like going against the universe and things start to spin out of control and life seems to slip away from us. If you go where the universe takes you and do what you feel you should rather than what you think everything will go the way it's supposed to. Trust me, it's harder to master than what it sounds, but once you get the hang of it things seem to fall into place. That's when you look at yourself and feel happy and satisfied with life. Like I said, it was just a theory. As I sat contemplating I thought that destiny and free will or even the saying "we choose our own destiny" are all now contradictions in terms. The ultimate paradox! The concept of free will is just a futile attempt by our own imagination to conjure up illusions of grandeur and choice. It's possibly to hide the grim truth that we are all just pawns in the great game of life. Mere actors on the great stage we call life playing out the story of the ultimate outcome. If this can be understood and accepted then life and all its facets becomes a pinnacle of the Earth, a smile from God and a peace from the heart. It all sounds a bit far fetched I know, but life and the journey to our destiny can be as happy or as sad as we make it. Perhaps in the greater scheme of things we once had the choice. Before we were born, at a stage when we were part of the combined consciousness we chose what we were going to be going through during our lives. That would give back our free will I guess.

I could see what She was saying, against my better judgement, was something I could do nothing about. Looks like I was in this till the end and I'm not sure if I can handle all this new information.

- 5 -

As soon as I woke up the next morning I knew it was going to be one of those days, it already started with the obligatory bad day burnt toast. The water cylinder had switched itself off in the middle of the night again, so I had to have a cold shower; perfect. As with any day that starts this badly I usually just give in to it, hope it gets better and I treat myself to some breakfast at a nearby coffee shop. Well it usually does the trick. This particular day was much worse than I had first anticipated and it didn't look like it was getting any better. First my car wouldn't start. It's not unusual for my car, but still it didn't help this morning. Next was the taxi; or the lack thereof. I ordered a taxi, but not only did it not arrive, but when I called them back to see what the problem was they said that it had been and gone and that I should have been in it. I told them that no, I was not thank you very much. They said 'Your welcome' and hung up. To top the morning off was a run in I had with this strange young man who just appeared from the crowd of people that were walking the busy street. He seemed to know me, I didn't know him, but this didn't seem to bother him. He was about 5'8" or 5'9", a muscular physique with blond hair and blue eyes. If I were one to judge these things I would say He was handsome. He looked no older than twenty-five and had the arrogance to match. He tried to start a conversation with me and I thought I recognized His husky voice, but I couldn't place it. It was weird, He lit up a cigarette and started talking at me.

"You see the thing about this girl you've taken as your client, She's bad news. You don't want to get involved with Her no matter what She's told you, or what She's paying you. She will turn your thoughts around so you think you can control the situation and then bring you down like a lead brick. She's into a whole lot of mumbo jumbo, voodoo type shit that you want to stay away from." He said.

"What?" I said in a stunned manner. "What are you talking about?" I got closer to him, right in His face. "Who are you to be telling me about my life and who I associate with?"

"You know what I'm talking about. I'm just here to warn you."

"Have you been following me?" I questioned.

"All I'm asking is that you understand. You are getting yourself into a whole pile of shit."

"Well, not that it's any of your business, but She's 'into' spiritualism," I defended, "and quite frankly I'm fascinated by it. I do know you don't I? I can't quite place it, but I never forget a voice or face. Who the hell are you and why are you bugging me?" I added.

"Pah!! Spiritualism my ass. That's what She's leading you to think. If you want to know the truth She's a waste of your time and She could get you killed."

And then, just as He appeared from the crowd, He disappeared back into it. He had pushed my buttons and I felt like punching him in the mouth. That kind of thing doesn't happen every day, so I made a note of it in my PDA.

***

The day ended much like it had started and I didn't really get anything done. That night I lay in bed and just couldn't get to sleep. I didn't know what to make of what Sam told me yesterday. What had happened to Ray and Rena? I guess the answers to those questions would come to me over time, but I was kicking myself for not knowing now. Was what She showed me real? I got chills when She told me Her story, and what happened when She looked at me and I got all those weird feelings? But nothing I have experienced is as bad as She's making it out to be, surely. Not yet anyway. I pride myself on being a very perceptive person, but this was beyond me and I had no control. I tossed and turned for most of the night having hot and cold sweats. I started to see things in front of my eyes, startling pictures and scenery like Sam had described to me about Her night of travelling. I could feel the fear that was moving through Her that night and I could actually see Her. She was looking at me and crying, trying to say something that I couldn't make out. I urged Her to move closer and then suddenly She was right in front of me and I started to shake. It is almost impossible to describe the way I felt then. A grief lifted and a veil of peace and harmony landing softly on my aching body. The thoughts that occupy my mind are scrambled, but somehow make sense. A high you could almost say, a natural feeling of purpose perhaps and the thought that somewhere along the way everything will be all right.

I've looked at myself sometimes in my darkest hours and thought there's nothing left to do and nothing left for me in this life. These are the times that test my mind, heart and soul, and stretch them beyond the limits of human understanding. When words mean nothing and speech is impossible. When a tear falls down my cheek and I have reached the bottom; this is what Sam was going through only worse. This is when I have to look for solace in my soul and it all seems to become clearer instead of the unrelenting murk that is my life. That's what She needed from me, clarity. For now at least I can say that those days are almost over and I have found myself as a drifter looking for a place to hide and rest. Away from the demented crowds and the artificial life that so many of us lead. I can see the reality of why we are here because of Her. We can't do anything about it, so I sit back and accept this is the way it will be and a light appears at the far end of a tunnel. It's a tunnel so long it twists the very limitations of my mind. It's a journey that is not impossible, just extremely difficult and perilous, but obviously the choice to make and the road to follow. So, there I lay wondering, not for the first time, what I was worried about. Truth and justice, to coin a phrase, will prevail and I'll achieve the goal I want so much and the light will beam upon me until I am surrounded with the brilliance. All this from one look, without a word. She kind of hovered there for a moment in front of me like a spectre on a cold night and I shared these thoughts with Her. She opened Her mouth and started to speak, this time Her voice carried for a long way and sounded like She was speaking into my ear.

"Don't be scared this is not a dream. I've been able to come to you as you slip between the realms of sleep and wake and I am asking you for help." She said.

I was shaking more and my heart was going bananas. I saw from the corner of my eye strange dark things moving in from far below.

"What's happening?" My voice was weak.

Before She could answer a wisp of darkness the speed at which I couldn't comprehend took Her away from me and She shouted.

"Help me, it was my fault, but…" and Her voice trailed away as the darkness took Her.

I woke, sat bolt upright and started to seriously sweat and shiver.

***

This was all too much for me to take and I needed a drink. I padded down the hallway and into the small, dusky room and over to the drinks cabinet feeling the cold of the tiles that surrounded the cabinet on my bare feet, which had somewhat of a calming effect. Suddenly pain shot through me from my left foot. I yelped and looked down to see a bloody mess and realising I had stood on a piece of broken glass that had once formed part of the whisky tumbler I dropped. The memories of what Sam had said to me came rushing back. I steadied myself and reached for my pills and managed to pour a drink, downed it in one and poured another. Something flashed in my mind like a premonition or something making me want to call Sam just to see if She was all right. I padded over to my desk trailing bloody footprints behind me and found the piece of paper She wrote Her phone number on. I picked up the receiver, waited for the dial tone and shakily punched in the number. I didn't actually expect Her end to ring, but it did and my heart started to thump thinking of why I had the sudden urge to call. Holding my breath I steadied my self for the answer and a funny sensation fell over me that something just wasn't right, not too sure what it was and I'm quite certain that I didn't want to know. Still the phone rang and still there was no answer, so after a very optimistic thirty rings I decided that enough was enough. I had to go to Her place to see if She was all right though I knew something terrible had happened, I could feel it.

I put on my coat and ran down the hall and when I got to the door I grabbed my keys from the small table that sat next to the front door knocking over the small table lamp. There didn't seem to be much time and I felt an overwhelming need for Her and that She desperately needed me. I opened the door, took the stairs three at a time to my car which I had parked outside the building. Fumbling with the car door for a few seconds I managed to get myself in and drove the forty-five minutes it took to Her place.

- 6 -

As I pulled into Her street the feeling of urgency that dwelled deep inside me strengthened. The closer I got to Her block of flats the stronger the feeling became. It's nothing that I could describe. Perhaps the closest thing that I could relate it to was the feeling of depression coming at me from every direction, a visual manifestation. I felt my jacket pocket to make sure I had my pills, there was a reassuring lump. I pulled up to Her drive and the feeling was screaming to get out and every hair on the back of my neck was standing on end. Something was terribly wrong and I had to get to Sam immediately. I jumped out of my car and completely failed to stand up crashing to my knees with a pain inside me that was worse that anything I've felt. I steadied myself and looked up with tears streaming down my face. The flat was surrounded by something so black I could see the outline of the night around it and my heart sunk as I saw what was unfolding before me. The terror gripped me and I couldn't breath. The pain in my body reached exquisite tenderness and I passed out.

***

I didn't know how long I was out for, but when I came around the night had somehow grown blacker; so black that the lights on my car couldn't break through the night. I was blinded by the darkness. I stood up and felt my way towards the flat using the cold concrete of the steps under my hands for guidance while yelling out for Sam. The pain I had before was still with me, but I was able to block it out. The blackness must have shrouded only Sam's flat or just in my head because my shout was not answered by Sam, but from Her neighbour telling me to keep it down, so I yelled back at Her and told Her where She could put it. There was a disturbance coming from inside the small, ground level flat. Some sort of screaming or fighting like the noise the wind makes on an extremely stormy night, a kind of wailing. A battle, that's what it sounded like. It literally sounded as if there was a war going on inside. My heart was pounding faster than a galloping horse and I sweat poured off me like I had just stepped out of a shower. I stumbled down the small path to the door yelling Her name all the way, but still no answer. All I could do was feel my way down like a blind man through unfamiliar territory. I was still sightless and my eyes showed no signs of adjusting; it was just too black. I managed to make my way to the door. The noise coming from inside grew in intensity as I scrambled for the doorbell which refused to be heard, so I started thumping loudly. Still no answer. I felt a rage ripping me up from inside; I had to get in. Yelling again and again, and again there was no reply. I decided to try for the handle once more and strangely enough it gave to my efforts and sprang inwards. I fell into Her small flat and everything stopped and went deathly quiet.

There was nothing.

No sound.

No screaming.

The silence was more deafening than the rage that encompassed what seemed like the whole neighbourhood. But now, at least, everything was still.

***

I flicked the light on. The flat was made up of a lounge, kitchen, laundry, bathroom/toilet and a single bedroom. The decorating that Sam had done to it made it seem a lot bigger than what it was with soft angled furniture of stark colouring that opposed the cream coloured walls. There were very few pictures around just the odd photo of a relative or friend. A large picture of two dolphins swimming together hung above the TV and there was a Van Gogh print hanging next to the hallway door. In one corner having almost pride of place next to a big bay window was Her computer. Not the cheapest computer I've ever seen either. It had everything you needed a computer to have and more. It was where, I assume by the expense that went into it, She spent a lot of Her time. The carpet was thin and off white, so thin that it really didn't give too much when walked on. The flat looked empty while at the same time being very comfortable carrying a taste of a post-modern personality and youth. The kitchen was scarcely decorated, less so than the lounge. All the appliances must have been hidden in alcoves and cupboards probably plugged in and ready to go when extracted from their various lairs. The whole effect seemed to suit Sam down to a 'T'.

There was a feeling of coldness in this room and the sickly smell of something rotting. I've heard stories about bad odours in haunted houses and the likes, but thought it was bullshit. I called for Sam and at last heard Her groan from the bedroom. I raced in and saw Her lying on the bed shivering and sweating like She was suffering the effects of pneumonia. I walked up to Her and crouched down laying my hand on Her forehead feeling the deathly cold of Her body. I was suddenly ripped from my trance when Her eyes sprang open. The fright made me stumble backwards and narrowly avoiding a crack on the head from the wall behind. I just sat there as She turned to me and looked into my soul. These were not Her eyes. It was Her body, but not Her eyes. They were black and dead. The kind of black you get before you put the milk in coffee, the same kind that surrounded the house. They're searching for something. If the smell and my paranoia were anything to go by I'd say that whatever I was looking at was not Sam, but a demonic thing from another dimension. I just couldn't bring myself to believe it, but that's what I was looking at. The fear grew in me. She opened Her mouth and the voice that came from within was not hers. It was like a thousand demons screaming for a place to be heard from the pits of hell.

"You got my message did you?"

My chest tightened and I could hardly breath. I fumbled for the tiny plastic bottle in my jacket pocket. I managed to muster up some courage.

"Who the hell are you?" I yelled.

The smell became more pungent in the room and tears stung my eyes.

"I am the one they call master. Thor bows down to me and now I will take this shell and you will follow me to the shafts of death. There you will see your destiny with me that we share."

"Wh-who are you? Where did you come from?"

Was I imagining this? Was I going to wake and sit bolt upright in my bed with sweat pouring off me like those horror movies? God I hope so.

This is what it said.

"I am the one that came first. Of all the gods and heroes, of all that manifests itself in the here and now, I created it all; I am the God of all. The Father of all and you will kneel before me as my own and together we shall rule with zealous fervour."

I thought I was asleep having some kind of nightmare that I wanted to wake up from, I tried, but I couldn't. The eyes stole my thoughts and once again I was plunged into unconsciousness.

- 7 -

I woke to the sound of rain tapping on the window and found myself crouched next to the bed cradling Sam's head and holding Her hand. The rain was like the cleansing of the world drowning the terrors of the night before and washing away the anxiety which gripped me so tightly. The little light that the sun offered on this wet morning struggled to get through the curtains to shed its warmth on the situation. I stood up looking down at the sleeping beauty. She looked like She was at peace, resting well, which was more than I could say for myself. My legs were shaking and I felt a great hollowness. The smell from the night had gone and was replaced with a damp musty smell, but the room still felt cold and lifeless. I peered over the bed to look at the alarm clock, it was eleven thirty AM and the day was already half over. Where did the time go? I slowly removed my hand and gently rocked Sam until She started to stir then left for the kitchen to fix something for brunch. From the kitchen I could hear Her in the bedroom with the normal rustling of getting dressed and washing up. I put a couple of slices of bread in the toaster and fished around the fridge for something that resembled a breakfast drink. The fridge was a collage of health foods; this girl looked after herself it was just a pity about all the other stuff She did to Her body. I managed to find some orange juice and turned to go back to the kitchen table only to find Sam standing there which scared the shit out of me. For the second time I dropped my drink.

"Don't *DO* that to me…do you realize what kind of a night I have had?" I barked.

"Not a clue." She said plainly. "I'd like to know what you are doing in my kitchen, though." She said looking a little bit confused.

"I take it you don't remember what happened last night?" I asked already knowing the answer.

"As far as I was aware…sleep. But now I'm not so sure." She said with a raised eyebrow. "Did we go out for drinks or something?" She asked innocently. "I mean we didn't…you know?"

I shook my head and looked down, all I could do is shut up and make the brunch. The smell of the coffee I brewed myself and the cooked bacon was comforting. As soon as we finished eating I brought up the subject of the previous night. I explained the strange things that happened as best I could. Her face visibly dropped and I could see the worry start to crawl across Her brow. It was almost like She was expecting something like this to happen, but probably thought that She would at least be part of it. Unfortunately She was more a part of it than She realised, it was just a pity that She wasn't in the right frame of mind to deal with it. I could read Her mind from Her expression, which disturbed me as I was hoping I was the one having the bad dream.

"I want to show you something." She said. "Something that happened to me yesterday morning. I don't know what to make of it. Pass me that spoon." She pointed to the small teaspoon sitting beside my cup.

I reached for it and passed it over. I swallowed hard and rubbed my eyes – this is what She had been talking about and I didn't believe Her. There was no camp-fire, no marsh-mellows, no stoned dude trying to scare the shit out of us; this was real life and I started to shake. I tried to keep an open mind, something that I think is going to become easier as time goes by.

"What?" I asked dubiously.

"Just watch. Maybe you can tell me what's happening to me."

She closed Her eyes and held the spoon with Her forefinger and thumb just below where the ladle began. She drew a deep breath and started to softly rub the spoon with Her finger and thumb.

"What are you doing?" I asked.

"Shhh." She hissed. "I don't know if I can do it again. You'll see if it happens."

I let Her continue without a word wondering what exactly was supposed to happen. I was starting to grow impatient when She opened Her eyes and looked directly at the spoon. It happened right in front of my eyes. Something I had only seen in those magic shows, something that psychologists have always said was a hoax, a fraudulent trick of the light. The top of the spoon started to sag like it was melting over. There was a smell in the room like the smell after rain. She caught Her breath and dropped the teaspoon, which made a clinking sound as it hit the table and made me jump. I could only stare at the spoon; I didn't know what to say.

"Well? What do you think?" She asked with a confused look in Her eye.

"I don't know. I have never seen that before, well, not unless it was on TV."

I picked it up and by involuntary response immediately threw it down again. The thing was red hot.

"What's going on with you? Has this only just started to happen?"

"Yes." She replied.

"I just have to know," I started, "how did all of this come about?"

It was my job. I had to get to the bottom of it all. I had to find out though the bottom wasn't really where I could picture myself happily getting to, but I was in this thing now, so I may as well figure out what the hell is going on and what, if anything, I could do about it. So She sighed, sat back in Her seat and folded Her arms.

"Are you ready?" She whispered.

"I think so." I whispered back locking eye contact with Her.

There was sudden clap of thunder from lightening that I hadn't seen and the rain started to fall once more.

- 8 -

THE POSSESSION

Samantha opened the door and walked shakily out of the house She was taken to. This day will forever be remembered as the day She had Her first travelling experience. It was an old style villa with new extensions – a second level, a new room that was attached to the left-hand side of the house and a garage on the right hand side with an additional room on top. In the darkness She couldn't make out any colours, so the paintwork looked grey. The door was white and the decorative pillars were a darker shade made from highly sanded 2x4's. Somehow the air seemed a little thinner, a little cooler. Maybe it was the fresh night or maybe it was just because of what She had been through. Perhaps, She thought, it was even a little nicer smelling like jasmine. Her soul, if that was what She felt was filled with a longing for more of what She had just had and Her heart was aching for what She now knew She was missing. It was like She had just stepped out of a fairy tale and back into reality. She was walking away from the real world and back into ignorance with the difference being that She now knew the world She thought She belonged to was the fairy tale. There was a man, She remembered, that came to Her in Her vision. He was middle aged, about forty or forty-five with greyish brown hair. He was maybe 5'8" with a slender frame that showed of years of training and exercise. He had eyes that told a lot of the life they had led. His face, apart from His eyes, was slightly out of focus, so She couldn't say who He was for sure, but the face was wizened. It was a face that spoke of intelligence and good old-fashioned hard work. It wasn't, however, a happy face although it had seen laughter. It was a serious face, which somehow gave rise to the gravity of the situation She was about to face. She had tried to touch him once in the vision, but when She reached out Her hand went straight through as if He wasn't there and it made Her feel lost and afraid when the mist that made up His face faded into nothing. When it was all over She believed She hadn't had Her fill of this new and exciting discovery and wanted more; this gave way to a hunger. It was the type of hunger that She, with Her addictive personality, couldn't resist. This hunger was the type that Ray and Rena had seen before. There were dangers that only they could see, but due to certain universal laws they couldn't tell Her or warn Her about what She would be up against. Mistakes are to be made and learnt from and all they could do is watch and be there for Her when She needed them. This usually meant they would be picking up the pieces when it really hit the fan. They had been through it all before, but they thought that Samantha was different; they should have known better. Her life was so full of sneers and traps that it could, in effect, kill Her. Her mind and soul were so complicated that they couldn't solve all of Her problems on the first session and probably not for several sessions after that. They knew She was going to continue on Her own no matter what they said to Her, they feared the worst and with good reason. The troubles in Her life and the skeletons in Her closet that may manifest could turn Her into a mindless vegetable or even kill Her if She tried to do anything by herself. Samantha walked through the cold night air with Her friend, Lorraine, in toe. They got in the car and with Lorraine driving they headed for Samantha's flat. Not a word was said through the trip home, but Samantha started to get a little light headed as She recalled the taste of the supernatural She had just bitten. She thought about the wonderful sights, sounds and types of creatures that She had encountered and beaten. A shiver ran down the length of Her spine at the thought of the demon spirits that played on Her mind. She remembered the meadow and how at peace She felt when She could touch the grass under Her feet and the weightlessness as She took off into the sky created from Her own mind. Why had it taken Her so long to find this world and to understand what She could do with just Her mind? Not even the drugs She had used in the past gave

Her quite the same euphoria that this experience gave Her. These were the things She wanted to experience again, but right now She was too tired and all She wanted to do was crawl into bed for a good nights sleep.

Lorraine stopped at the top of Samantha's driveway and then looked over as Samantha opened the door. Before She got out She looked back at Lorraine for a second without a word then reached over and pecked Her on the cheek whispering 'Thank you'. Lorraine touched Her and asked if She was going to be all right, Samantha nodded, got out and stretched Her legs. She said goodbye, closed the door and made Her way down the path. She was still sensitive to the fact that it felt like She was walking on a cushion of air. Her head went a little swimmy, but She made it to the front door and reached inside Her handbag to fish around for the keys. As She felt around for them She heard a sudden sound that startled Her, the horrible sound of a foot on dried leaves, a kind of crunch. She froze for an instant of silence. The seconds ticked by and She could hear and feel Her heart pumping the blood through Her head making Her sight slightly blurry. She blinked a couple of times and the fright She got finally abated, so She started to relax a little though Her hands were still shaking. She finally found the keys and fumbled around with them until She found the one that She was looking for then tried to find the keyhole; an act that proved almost impossible by the darkness and Her shaking hands. The night air seemed to get colder and then again the sickly crunch of dried leaves, this time a little closer and followed by the cracking of a twig on the ground which made Her jump as though the devil himself had put a hand on Her shoulder. She let out a little shriek and grappled for the door handle that eventually gave to Her persistence and She fell into Her flat. She floundered for the light and was relieved that the power was still working as the bulb shone its radiance on the empty flat. A bead of sweat rolled off Her brow and into Her eye causing it to sting with the salt, She winced and fought to get Her sight back. Looking around the room everything seemed to be in place, so

She made a b-line towards the kitchen to fix herself something to drink and calm the nerves. She sat down on the couch with two large vodka and tonics. She sculled the first one before She allowed any thoughts to enter Her mind then slowly She began to allow herself a thought about what had happened trying to make sense of it all. She realized, with a little embarrassment She was just being paranoid when She was outside. The noises She heard were more likely from the next-door neighbour's cat on one of its mouse hunts rather than that of angry spirits, but She couldn't stop herself from shaking. Still, with the things that She had been through tonight nothing would surprise Her now. No, She thought, that was a stupid thing to think. The smallest of noises was likely to scare the shit out of Her right now to be quite honest, She could expect anything to happen and She would be surprised; surprised, but expectant. This didn't comfort Her at all and She took a long draw from the second glass. A minute later She had drained the glass and decided to get some sleep. The day ahead of Her was the first day of a two-week holiday and it was starting to look promising. She was thinking that after tonight with the peace that She had been settled with She could start fresh and look forward to the rest of Her life come what may. She now had a goal ahead of Her and She thought She knew what was missing from Her life. She could work on that and see if She could fill the void that plagued Her life with confusion and fence sitting ever since She could remember. It seemed to Her at that point life was getting way too short and She should just not worry so much about things. But She also felt She had wasted a lot of Her life on one thing or another and She also knew that contrary to everyone's opinion there was still plenty of time to settle down and find that special someone. She was in no hurry.

There was just one thing stopping Her getting what She wanted, it was the thought that She had let the best part of Her go. Maybe She would never find anybody like him again and that scared Her. The fact that this was deep down in Her subconscious made Her think that She was going to be alone for the rest of Her life. But now She had a whole new faith in fate, or destiny, and hoped that what everybody said about it was true and that She wasn't just wasting Her time. All just because She had been shown that little glimmer of something better. All these thoughts were going through Her mind and the fleshy bits of Her soul were starting to expose them selves. The seed had been planted and the demons were waiting hungrily to feed on the emotions of Her weak heart and feast on Her torments.

Waiting.

All the time waiting. When the time came they would pounce on Her like a tiger. They fed Her thoughts of anger and resignation and could see the fear building up inside, the time was slowly approaching and She was getting vulnerable.

- 9 -

Samantha's anticipation of the start of Her holiday had gone completely sour. The day had not been a fulfilling one and quite frankly a little boring. Nothing had really happened and the only excitement was the phone call She received from Her x-boyfriend. They had become so close that when they broke up they suddenly became best friends. The phone call had felt so natural to Her for the simple fact that they could both talk the hind legs off a donkey. He was full of good ideas about life and He was more than happy to divulge a few of them when She asked. He knew, of course, most of what He told Her She would never follow through with, but some of it really stuck in Her mind. She told him about a week ago that She wanted to break up and He took it a little light hearted, but listened to all the reasons just the same, which is why She still loved him. He was really quite upset, but didn't want Her to know about it. He knew about Her sexuality, but accepted it because it really didn't make a difference to him. The way He saw it was that if He was to be dumped for someone else then it made no odds as to the sex of the other person, it had still happened. In truth She had ripped His heart out. She, on the other hand, thought about it thoroughly and felt that She wasn't going to be rooted to one spot and without discussion had decided that She didn't want to put him through the kind of lifestyle She lead. She was very sexually active and couldn't handle cheating on people. Now, however, She started to regret Her decision and thought She had burnt Her bridges. The real problem was that He was interested in any kind of relationship at all no matter if She was playing the field or not. He just wanted to be with Her even just to be in the same room with Her. She never let him speak and He was in mortified shock when He finally replaced the receiver. It cut him up badly. In His mind She had ripped His heart out and it would be a long time before He would talk to Her again. That was what He felt then, but no more than two days had gone by when She called again and they started talking. Perhaps *He* was what was missing, but Samantha, at that time, didn't have the faintest idea. And now She thought She would never know.

***

She sat down heavily on the sofa with a vodka and tonic and started to sift through Her life piece by piece. It was early in the evening and nothing more could be done with the day, so it was time to relax and try not to think. It happened anyway and it was always a little dangerous when Samantha was alone to think. She remembered that Rena and Ray taught Her how to meditate and maybe this was the best way to relax and not think; She had nothing to loose. She downed the drink and put the empty glass down on the wooden table beside the fruit bowl. The table itself had the 'old used' look to it and this is the reason She liked it so much and besides Her Mother had given it to Her for Her twenty-first and there was no way She was getting rid of it. The alcohol was already starting to climb up into Her brain and She felt the warmness of Her blood flowing through Her head. She made herself comfortable and started to meditate. Initially this was only for relaxation purposes, but something unexpected began to happen. She started to see snippets of Her past and it stretched across Her vision, memories and pictures, good and bad. She just sat there and concentrated on working through them all. The focus of Her visions seemed to be Her best friend; this was not good. All the feelings of guilt and anger flooded through Her and She knew She had made a terrible mistake. Although He let it go She just couldn't. Other people started to loom into Her sights, Ray and Rena. They weren't doing much just sitting there watching over Her, so She felt a sense of peace and tranquillity as She lazed into a calming mood. It was almost as if the two where trying to tell Her something. They would let Her know, She thought dismissing them, if it was important. They slowly disappeared and Samantha's mind went black. All thoughts She had slowly melted away and Her tension left. She lay back and let it all happen. After a while She felt like another drink, so She stood up and went to the kitchen. She was thoroughly relaxed and could face the world thinking things would continue to go Her way. She sipped away at Her drink thinking about that part of Her that was missing and in the morning, She told herself, She would start looking. Samantha didn't really know what She was looking for, so She may need some help. A missing piece is just that; missing. Perhaps the yellow pages would help, but what was She looking for? Spiritual guidance? The Church? A private investigator? She drained the glass and felt the tiredness sneak up on Her and Her senses began to deteriorate. Samantha was getting sleepy and decided it was time to go to bed, so She headed for the bathroom after which She padded off down to Her bedroom, red half a page from a dog-eared book and fell into a very deep and rich sleep.

- 10 -

The night brought much needed sleep for Samantha and although She woke a little confused She felt fresh and ready for the day ahead of Her. She couldn't decide whether it was the two drinks She had or the meditation, but She was thankful for the rest though She still felt like more rest was needed. She got up and padded around the small flat for a few minutes before preparing some breakfast. It was the first day of Her two week holiday and She knew She could use today to just waste away on rest and relaxation, so after She had done the washing up She headed back to Her bed and fell almost immediately to sleep.

When She woke up again She went to the kitchen and as She walked in She noticed something was wrong, but She couldn't put Her finger on it. Some food and a fresh glass of orange juice latter and She felt it was time to start the investigation. Samantha sat down at the computer and waited for inspiration to hit. Using the mouse expertly She opened up a new document and headed the page with the title 'The Missing Link'. That's about all She could manage because after that Her mind was blank, so She wrote down the date and tried to let Her fingers do a bit of walking, but all She managed was 'I am lost'. Those three words described what She was feeling perfectly. It occurred to Her to write down what had happened when She was with Ray and Rena, which ended up being ten pages long. From there She could gather facts and add them later and the only place to find the facts if you didn't know what you were looking for was the library. So, off She went with a brief stop at the local coffee shop to arm herself with a caffeine hit. When She got back in the car there was something wrong, but She decided that She still didn't want to deal with it right now. Driving the twenty minutes it took to get to the library went by quickly and the sudden arrival at Her destination stunned Her because She wasn't really paying attention and the entire journey seemed to have been forgotten. It was almost as if the twenty minutes had never happened and She had appeared at some random place decided upon by Her own autopilot. The library building was an old, post-modern type which was not matched by the books inside, they were ancient. There was no funding for the library as there was very little use for them apart from storing the bound works of art from years gone by. There wasn't anything new in print that you couldn't find online, but that's technology for you. Some of the most interesting facts and fiction has been written only in recent times, but very little had made it to the physical media. The shelves had stayed the same since 1997 when they had actually seemed quite new and modern, but now they had fallen into the category of just plain worn out. There were very few e-books and only one e-reader and the whole place was shrouded with a musty smell and the different sections were scattered throughout the library seemingly with no rhyme or reason. She had no idea where to start, so She had to ask which brought Her a new and interesting problem. She only had a vague clue about what She was looking for, but didn't have the faintest idea of what to ask for. When She finally found someone to help Her She floundered to find the right words. Samantha explained the situation and the experience She had hoping the librarian knew what She was on about and didn't think She was totally nuts. It turned out that what She was on about was, in a word, spiritualism, and yes the librarian could help Her. After having the correct section pointed out to Her She went over and saw that everything She wanted to know about the spiritual world could be found right here. After skimming through a select few books She found that things haven't changed over all the hundreds of thousands of years of human culture. Our beliefs had remained the same through time though there have been influences that have curved faith and teachers that have added new information over the years. The most impressive thing She found was a book about Asgard; the world of the gods. On one page She found a list of all the gods of Asgard, all the spirits that could be found there, good and bad, light and dark, and She couldn't help thinking that some of these names sounded vaguely familiar. Of course to find out any more She was going to have to go travelling again to experience it first hand. This at least was what She justified to Her self, but it made Her happy as the memory of the last time was still fresh in Her mind especially the way She felt after the experience. So, it was time She headed home to try it again. The trip home was like the trip there, uneventful and boring. Samantha's spirits were starting to get a bit low as the high from the other evening began to wear off and now She was more than ready to get Her fix of adrenaline.

As soon as She walked into the flat She had that funny feeling again. Something was still wrong and it took Her a little while to figure it out. The heaviest atmosphere seemed to be in the lounge where She was now. The closest She could describe it as was a complete lack of anything. There was no feeling, no nothing. It was so thick. Thick with nothingness. In a word it was soulless. She didn't know when this happened, whether it had been like this all the time or if it had just started, but it was here now and it freaked Her out. Travelling is what She came home to do, but She wasn't sure if She should or could do it without the help of Rena and Ray or even if it was such a good idea with this strange feeling in Her place, but She was going to try anyway. It just seemed like the right thing to do. She downed two drinks, the speed of which brought the effects on hard and fast. Perfect, She thought, this was going to be easy. It was logical to, She justified. When She first did this whole travelling thing, She was still not able to figure out exactly what to call it, She was more than a little tipsy, so it just followed that She'd have to be in the same state for it to work again.

Samantha walked to the bedroom, closed the curtains and got changed into something a little more comfortable. She let herself relax and breathed in deeply through Her nose as Rena had shown Her, held it for a moment or two and then slowly exhaled through Her mouth letting all Her worries out with it. After doing this a few more times She felt She was ready to start the meditation. She lowered herself onto the bed, got into a comfortable and relaxing position then started to calm herself completely. As She Lay there She listening to Her heart and as She listened She heard Her heart rate slow down, so She meditated on that thought for a while until Her pulse was at the desired level. This was one of the more impressive party tricks Rena had taught Her, how to control Her heart rate. All She had to do was picture herself in Her own body and concentrate on the heart or in fact any body part She wanted to manipulate. She had to imagine She was actually inside and truly watching Her heart as it pumped blood in and out at the same timing willing it to slow down. The next step was to gently lay the first three fingers of Her left hand just above Her right eyebrow and do the same with the respectful right hand, left eyebrow. This, Ray told Her, let Her control the electricity and aura that circled Her head and body inside and out. It was designed to get the whole body in sync as the blood and electric pulses are joined by the most sensitive part of the head with the most sensitive part of the hands. It closes a circuit in the body and the heart, soul and mind start to move together as they should. This is the start of deeper meditation and a completion of the body's neural pulses and chemistry to clear all stress. That's what Ray had told Her anyway and She didn't really understand it, but as long as it worked She would do it. As the electricity flowed through Her hands She could feel the thoughts of Her life rush around Her head, but She wasn't clear as to where it was taking Her. Yet again She had visions of Her x-boyfriend, which was something that She was getting a bit worried about. She felt there was something that needed to be done. Unfinished business of some sort, but She didn't know what. Samantha tried to think of all the things that they had done as a couple and how She may have treated him. She was looking for some kind of clue, but it just didn't make sense. She thought She did the right thing. Perhaps He was, somehow, putting Her through a massive guilt trip and

She was looking for vindication. Then She made a mental note that She probably wasn't going to follow up on; to give him a call in the morning. She dismissed the thought of him from Her mind and almost immediately Lorraine wafted in. Now this wasn't good. What was happening here? Yes, She thought, Lorraine was somebody She would like to get to know intimately, but maybe Lorraine was trying to get a message across also. Was everybody trying to get a message across or was it something as simple as a concerned thought towards a good friend? Maybe She was reading too much into it. Paranoia gripped Her so tightly that She had to take several deep breaths to control it. With all the faces that passed Her by it was like an episode of 'This Is Your Life'. She allowed Her worries to show themselves in many different colours and decided to dismiss other thoughts in order to concentrate on something more important. Ray and Rena had suddenly appeared in Her mind. She was comfortable thinking about these two as She had no ties with them and didn't think things would get too complicated. They were still there when the man, or spirit, or whatever He was appeared. This was the person that was missing according to Ray and Rena. It occurred to Her that He probably wasn't the only thing missing in Her life, just one piece in a huge jigsaw of what She was supposed to put together. As this went through Her mind things started to happen a little unexpectedly, but She welcomed it. Every thought dripped away and She was able to relax completely.

Everything turned black.

Pitch black.

It was a heavy, mounting blackness that enveloped Her whole body, mind and soul. It wrapped Her like a blanket and all Her senses of the real world left Her bit by bit while fear sneaked in. She was under the spell once more and was ready for anything. As soon as She had imagined the green meadow it appeared to Her once more and it was as real as if She was actually there. She could smell the fresh, green grass and bent down to put Her palm flat on the earth to feel its cool softness. A breeze blew through Her hair and She felt like She was one with the earth and on a deeper level with the universe. The blackness above folded in on itself and became the most beautiful summer sky like the type of sky you get when you're out at sea far away from the disgusting land. Looking up She could make out wonderful, graceful creatures that started to fill the sky. It was one of the most beautiful sights that She had ever seen and the sky looked like it was alight with them. She somehow beckoned with Her mind for one of the creatures to come down. Off into the distance one of them started to grow larger as it headed towards Her. As the creature got closer She could see an orange glow from its body. It excited and frightened Her as the impressive beast flew closer and as it did, so She could make out its form, its body. It was huge, truly enormous. Its wings must have had a span of over thirty feet or more and this put a fear of the unknown through Samantha and excited Her even more. She started to back away. Her nerves buzzed and Her head span at the sheer size of the thing. As She got a better look the creature slowed down and She could quite clearly see that its wings, or at least its feathers, were not what they first appeared to be. It became obvious that this creature had wings and a body of fire. Lavish oranges and vivid reds of all shapes licked the air and set the sky was alight with its brilliance. The creature in all its greatness swooped down out of the sky and just as it looked like it was going to crash into the ground where Samantha was standing it caught itself and reared up to showed Her the full grandness of a creature that had all the arrogance of the world in its flaming body. A feeling of unbarring, intolerable defencelessness flooded threw Her body and set Her legs shaking. She collapsed to the ground and all She could do was stare at the massive bird that brought narcissism to new heights. It was almost as if it hovered, or even floated there for a short time and then as quickly as it had arrived it reared its head and took off into the darkening sky. Something that Samantha had not noticed before was the sheer openness of the meadow giving Her a faint feeling of agoraphobia. It seemed to stretch on forever, almost as if it didn't stop.

Something was happening, something terrible. Not for the first time a chill spun through Her body and down Her spine. Staring off into the horizon it felt like all of a sudden the entire world that was created out of Her imagination turned a fraction. It wasn't even a fraction, more like a fraction of a fraction. Everything went slightly out of focus and then span another fraction of a fraction back. But this wasn't where She had just been. The meadow had gone, the beautiful blue sky had disappeared and the light had deserted Her. What She was standing in now was a totally different place, a more frightening place. The sky was dark and foreboding. The ground no longer spread out with the freshness of grass, but was covered in thick, sludgy mud. There was a feeling all around of negativity and helplessness. All Her power left Her and She fell to the ground shaking and fearful. Her soul was weakening.

- 11 -

Samantha stayed very still and silent for quite some time. The cold started to bite, so She hugged Her legs to keep warm, but it was all in vain as the coldness grew heavier upon Her. She collected Her thoughts and decided to stand up and see if there was anything She recognized. She didn't know what else to do or what to expect. She looked around for a while, but that turned out to be fruitless as She couldn't actually see anything. There was a complete and absolute absence of noise and this put the fear of all hell through Her and She shivered again.

She seemed to be totally helpless and unable, no matter how hard She tried, to get back to reality. This was getting really serious and She no idea what to make of the situation and a tear fell down Her cheek. Then She heard something so subtle that at first She thought it was in Her head. She listened harder and it started to become a low rumbling sound like that of very distant thunder. Maybe it was more of a feeling than a sound, so She crouched to the ground very nervously and put an ear close to the mud. She could just make out the slight baritone sound, but couldn't place where it was coming from. She stood up ever so slowly, so She didn't sink too far into the mud and took another look around. The blackness was still such that She couldn't see very clearly anyway, so She just stared out at the horizon until Her eyes adjusted very, very slowly. When the feeling started to turn into a faint sound She saw it. It caught Her a bit off guard, but there it was. Off in the distance and along the horizon was a long line of complete blackness. The line stretched its way over almost 180° and was as thin as a hair. All She could do was watch and the fear in Her started to grow rapidly like a balloon expanding in Her heart. The line grew in height and with it the low, rumbling noise which became clearer and clearer. A little shriek escaped Her mouth as She realized what was happening and stood there agape. She mouthed some words, but nothing came out. Then like the passing thoughts of spirits She could hear the airy sound of Irish pipes way off in the distance. A sound that She hadn't heard since She was back home in Dublin just a little girl listening to Her Father play His pipes that had been in the family for over a hundred years. She quickly snapped out of that thought when the line had grown big enough to make out what She was actually looking at. The darkness of the line formed itself into thousands of individual figures that started to heave and thrust getting faster and faster making their way towards the now frozen Samantha. Her knuckles where white as She clenched Her fists against the cold and the fear. Closer and closer they got and She could quite clearly make out the forms. The hoards of darkness were stretched out forever. So many of them, too many of them the darkness of which Samantha had never seen before and they rode their steeds like one was part of the other. The heavy beating of hooves on the ground and the pipes wailing a mournful tune got louder and louder until it was almost unbearable. Steam shot from the mouths and nostrils of these great, black stallions and the demons on their backs drew their swards. Samantha could do nothing, but watch and cry.

She opened Her mouth and let out the most terrifying scream that was heard through the nether worlds, the type of scream that sets the hearts of demons racing and the blood of the dark spirits bubbling. She screamed out for help, for anyone, She screamed out the names of Rena and Ray, She screamed out the name of Jason. She screamed until Her throat was burning and raw. The demons on their horses grew closer and She could smell the retched, acrid breath of the devil himself. The demons were faceless like they had no spirit; just pure evil. Upon the wind She heard a whisper, just audible, and there in front of Her was the image of Ray and Rena slowly churning into the darkness and taking form in the God forsaken land. Beside them, the form of Jason. It wasn't the Jason that She knew, it was His form, but not His spirit. It was an empty shell void of any soul it was Her mind trying to calm Her that brought this image and the form could do nothing, but stand beside Her and comfort

Her. Swards appeared in Rena and Ray hands as if they had willed them into existence. They prepared for the fight knowing well that this was not going to be a victorious battle, but they had to try. They knew how to use the universe, but so did the inhabitants of this realm. The demons rode on and not even the likes of a powerful spirit like Ray could fend off this many assailants. It was useless to even think about. Samantha had lost herself to this world even before She entered it and now She was going to loose Rena and Ray because of Her pig headed stubbornness. They put up a good fight for Her slaying beast after beast and standing up to the most hideous creatures this universe had thought up. One by one, to the amazement of Samantha, Ray and Rena hacked through and chopped up beast and demon alike. The furry of steel flying through the air, the piercing sound of sward hitting sward and the sickening, wet thud as blades scored their prey. As each demon and horse fell another rose up to take its place; Samantha was frozen with fear and could help nobody. Soon the numbers grew too large and before long the demons on their horses had surrounded them. One of them grabbed the ridged body of Samantha before She heard the blood-curdling scream of Rena as one then two then four of the retched beasts managed to get through Her defences. Ray was losing His grip on the sward He held as the black blood of the demons ran down the blade and onto His hand. All at once there were six of the great demons on him and He felt the pain of their swards on His flesh again and again, then the excruciating heat as one of the blades found His heart. The agony was heard for miles as Ray and Rena went down in a battle of honour and glory. Time and time again the poisonous swards of the demons found their mark whittling away at their life forces. The sound of sward hitting flesh continued long after the cries of pain ended. Even the empty form of Jason gave way to the darkness and disappeared. She had been defeated thoroughly and completely and now She had to face the fate that this world was going to play on Her.

- 12 -

The beast that grabbed Samantha, seemingly effortlessly, hoisted Her up on His steed. His hands were enormous and cold grasping Her so tightly that more than once She had lost Her breath to it. The huge creature carried Her off into the unknown. She couldn't tell up from down and certainly couldn't see ahead, let alone see the ground. She saw nothing, but the hooves of the stallion beneath Her as each beat brought the powerful hoof close to Her face. Tears streamed down Her face as the wind whipped Her body and Her wet hair lashed at Her face. So many miles and what seemed like days, years, She travelled with these horrific beasts of hell. The fear gripped Her tighter in a way that would leave a god crying and that is what She did. She cried and screamed, but could do nothing. The power and strength that She felt in the hands of the demon was overwhelming and She could only wait. It seemed now they were climbing up a hill perhaps, a mountain maybe, they were definitely getting higher and Her spirits plummeted further than they already were. Pain spiked Her stomach as the beating of the horse pumped through Her mid section with every step. She could barely stand it, but She had no choice. She couldn't loose consciousness either, not in here, not in the world of Her own mind.

***

She thought about Jason and tried to picture him in Her mind. He wasn't spiritual, but She believed She could form His image in front of Her even if it was soulless and empty She felt better to see him. She closed Her eyes and pictured him standing there and when His image was clear enough She opened Her eyes and there, in front of Her, stood Her lost love, Jason. It wasn't much, but that thought took away some of the physical pain and replaced it with a more tolerable pain; the pain of loss. Perhaps if

She wasn't so stupid She could have kept this truly great person, one who stood by Her and let Her do what She needed to do. She felt He knew Her looking back anyway and that He could sit back and let Her make the mistakes She was going to make and just be there for Her when She needed him. Perhaps He thought that sooner or later She would see the error of Her ways and come back to him. In an immense shock wave She had more than realized that She wanted him just to hold Her, to touch Her. She closed Her eyes and remembered the times they had together. She hoped that when She opened Her eyes again She would be back at home in Her bed and He would be right there beside Her just waiting for Her to wake up and say good morning with that glorious smile of His.

***

When Samantha opened Her eyes She saw nothing of what She had hopped. What She did see was the ground. She could quite clearly see it in fact and it brought all the pain and fear thundering back to Her. There was an airy light creeping its way through to the sodden earth. The ground had stopped moving, more to the point, the horse that She was on had stopped, so too had the pipes. Now She could only hear the raucous of the demons and their laughter echoing through what sounded like a great hall. Before another thought entered Her mind the demon that had grabbed Her now grabbed Her forcefully again and dropped Her to the ground. She hit the muddy ground with a wet thud and pain swept through Her body. The demon got down and roughly gagged Her and tied Her up. She rolled over to have a look at the place where She was. It was a hall, a massive hall, filled with the repugnant smell of roasting flesh and hot sweat. The walls from what She could see at this distance were made from the trunks of trees that were lashed together one on top of the other. That posed a problem that nobody in the hall seemed to notice or care about. The trees that formed the great walls had not been prepared for the job they were performing, they were just lashed together how they came and this meant that there were holes in some areas where the tree had twisted this way or that. At some places along the walls the trees were supported by the knotholes which set the whole wall off in a strange lopsided nature, but was then corrected a few logs up, this caused more gigantic holes. Scattered across the great hall were a random placement of what looked like massive park benches. On these sat the mighty dark spirits along side dark demons. This place terrified Her and when She tried to scream the gag muffled the sound and it blended in with the cacophony of noises that filled the hall. She couldn't move too much as the ropes that bound Her were masterfully tight. She looked up to see the roof, but couldn't. All the sweat from the beasts and the smoke from the fires and the pungent smells had wafted towards the roof and created somewhat of a cloud that hung several hundred feet up preventing any clear view of the roof for Samantha to be able to see anyway.

"FREYR!!" Roared a deep and husky voice from within the hall.

She craned Her head around in the direction of the voice to see who or what it was.

"It is I, Odin. I have brought your bidding." Roared Freyr equally as deep, loud and husky.

Samantha could do nothing, but listen to the apparent godly duo. Within Her soul dwelled the image of these creatures from storybooks and ancient legends that up until now She had never believed in. She knew now where She was. This was the mighty hall of Valhalla. A merciless meeting place of gods and spirits and those who had fallen in ancient and forgotten battles. This place, the hall of Valhalla was in Asgard, ruled by Odin the Father of the gods. Now She was His bidding whatever that meant.

"Bring Her to me." Ordered Odin.

***

On the outside world Samantha's body jerked and shuddered as if being torn apart by a pack of wild animals. Her body had no life inside, but continued its seizure with vehemence. The noises that came out of Her mouth were inhuman and filled every inch of Her small flat. Rivers of sweat poured off Her lurching body, which then started to vibrate with such unprecedented intensity it looked like She would explode. Then a giant shock wave hit Her body making it go rigid, then another and another and then Her body stopped and slumped to the bed completely still, lifeless and empty. The room went deathly quiet as the last of Her body heat steamed away into the night air. The only sound left to be heard was a death rattle coming from deep inside Samantha's throat and the last beat of Her blackening heart. The room echoed with silence as the air froze. All the moisture in the room sunk to the ground creating a thin mist that covered the floor like a morbid swamp.

***

Freyr bent down and grabbed Samantha by Her bound hands and pulled Her across the ground towards Odin. The hall was full not with demons, but with mighty gods. She couldn't recognize them and She wouldn't know them if they came up to Her, but She knew they were gods. All were wrapped in the skins of various animals and each stood at least seven feet tall. They wore great helmets with horns and each god carried a different kind of weapon. The gods had been gifted by the ancients with a power they could use at will, but wisely, to watch over and protect the world of the living. A protection that was no longer needed and the gods were growing increasingly restless. These gods of immense power had control over the world as nothing else did and nothing could stop them. The hoards of darkness, the army that had captured Samantha were obviously, at least in part, owned by Freyr.

As they came nearer to the Father of the gods of Asgard She could see another figure sitting next to him, smaller in stature to the rest of the gods, but just as menacing. This She guessed must be Frigg, Odin's wife. Sitting next to Her was, She guessed by His attire, Forseti the Chair of Asgard. There was definitely something amiss, but She let it go as all legends have their truths and their exaggerations.

"You have served me well, Freyr. Your Father will be proud of you." Congratulated Odin.

"Thank you, Lord. I live only to serve you." He said on one knee, bowing to the all Father.

"Please leave Her with me and you may go reap your reward." Said Odin and dismissed the Lord of gods.

Odin looked upon Samantha for a moment to see if She had anything to say. When nothing was forthcoming He edge forward in His great seat.

"My dear child," He said to Samantha, "you have come to my world and expect to live? I ,in turn, will let you live, but only if you do my bidding."

He paused reaching for His mighty goblet and drank deeply before turning His attention back to Samantha.

"I own you now and wish to use your vessel as a means to get back the power I have lost. My army of darkness will take you where you are to be."

Odin was one of few words and that was the extent of His conversation with Samantha. He lost interest in Her very quickly and turned back to the rest of the congregation with a dismissing wave of His hand. She felt Her self weaken as heady vapours of the great Hall of Valhalla were ripping Her senses apart and the noise that bellowed from all directions was thudding into Her skull. The beast standing behind Her forcefully grabbed Her by the hands once more and dragged Her off to the side out of Odin's way. Odin clapped His hands three times and the sound of an enormous gong reverberated around the room beginning the celebrations. The gods were seated and the fallen hero's followed shortly thereafter. They all began to feast on the roasted flesh that was once wild boar.

Odin clapped His hands twice more and Samantha's head erupted with the sound of a rubbish truck dropping Her rubbish can outside. Sweat was dripping from every inch of Her body drenching Her bed and drying Her mouth. She had awoken from the terror that had grasped Her mind and still She was in shock. She could do no more than just sit there and let it all wash away.

Something had changed.

- 13 -

Samantha got up and raced to the toilet just in time to lift the seat and catch the bowl with a mighty push from Her solar plexus and diaphragm. The broth from Her stomach came churning out in a colourful display of food and drink. This was not caused by any food poisoning nor alcohol poisoning, this was the direct result of stress and tremendous fear. A shudder ran through Her body as the next wave of nausea caught Her and sent another stream of revolting mush past Her mouth and into the toilet bowl. The acrid taste fouled Her mouth and She coughed violently. Thoughts of what She had just been through came rushing through Her mind like a frightening collage of photos. Like a snap shot out from reality, like the terror somebody feels when an icy hand touches their shoulder; this and many more feelings thrashed about Her body looking for a way out. Her senses were numbed and She felt disoriented and couldn't think and could hardly breath. The shock of the night had fully gripped Her, She was just too shaken up to get a good hold on reality at the moment.

Her nerves were shot and Her legs didn't want to work, so She just fell back and let herself relax for a while until Her strength returned and She could get up and walk. Her whole body was shaking, this time it wasn't from shock, but from coldness. Her flat was all carpeted except for the bathroom and toilet. This was decked out in Italian tiles which were as cold as ice. Samantha was still wearing Her modest, thin, silk pyjamas, which let the cold right in, but She couldn't move. Her mind was a mess with an array of shimmering landscapes and black halls. The coldness was welcome to Her aching body and besides it would probably freshen Her up a bit and snap Her out of the state She was in. The sweat dripped from Her forehead and into the toilet bowl making little high pitched plopping noises that filled the tiny room and reassured Her that She was back in reality.

***

With Her power returning She decided to try standing up. Slowly She got Her balance and grabbed hold of the toilet bowl hoisting herself up. She stood there, legs shaking for a while to compose herself and when She thought She was ready She started to walk. This worked if She took it slowly. The kitchen was the closest thing to Her at the moment and the room that held promise of an ice cold drink of water, so She headed down the hall and into the kitchen where She reached for a glass from the cupboard. Filling the glass with cold water from the fridge She downed the cool liquid in a matter of seconds and the awful taste of the stomach acid seemed to melt away, but not completely. She downed a couple more glasses of the metallic tasting fluid and got rid of the last remnants of the acrid taste. Her strength had returned almost fully, so She decided to seek the advice of Ray and Rena. She made Her way to the phone, which was in the lounge and fumbled with the receiver for a while with Her shaky hands, but managed to steady herself and regain a bit of control over Her extremities. She dialled the number from the back of the card Ray had given Her and waited. The phone at the other end started to ring as She heard the tone in the receiver, but it was not picked up. Not even the answer-phone kicked in. She put the receiver back then decided to try again, but got the same result. Samantha wanted to try a different approach, so She reached for Her phone index to look up an old number; Jason, Her x-boyfriend. On reflection it wasn't really an old number She had spoken to him nearly everyday for the last five days it was just that He always rang Her never the other way around. She picked up the phone and dialled. This time, after the third ring, the phone was answered. This kind of surprised Her as She didn't really know why She was calling him, so She hesitated a bit before speaking.

Jason listened to Her while She recounted as much of the dream as She could before She broke down and sobbed. Jason asked Her if She would be all right and seriously questioned Her sanity. She said that She would be if nothing more dramatic happened. Because of the sort of things that She had been through, She wouldn't be surprised if something did happen. It would be nice to have someone there. Jason said that He would be right around and hung up the phone and started seriously questioning His own sanity. Samantha dropped the receiver onto its holder and let everything go, She just slumped down and cried.

***

It took less than twenty minutes for Jason to get to Her house. He knew the way pretty well and He sped for most of it. When He got there He could do nothing, but hold Her as She wailed into His shirt. He rocked Her gently and cooed reassuring tones into Her ear with 'It's OK' and 'Don't worry' and other clichéd phrases from His repertoire. Slowly She started to calm down. Once She was silent enough to speak He sat back and just looked at Her. She continued where She had left off on the phone telling him about the whole experience She had been through and the terror She felt. He, of course, didn't think that it was such a big deal and just a bad dream. Sure that's all it was, He had them himself. Maybe not to that extent and as real as She had made it seem, but He had them. That was the only thing He could say. She seemed convinced of the fact that She had actually gone through this torment and He just didn't understand, which was true. The fact is She had someone to talk to whether or not He believed Her was not the issue, She had someone who listened. Even if He didn't have the answers and even if He thought She was slowly going out of Her mind He was there and that was all that mattered. Samantha started to feel tired, but too scared to sleep. She asked Jason to stay for a while and just lay there in His arms, which gave Her so much comfort. She didn't dare drift off to sleep in case She slipped away again, so She just lay there. There was nothing Jason could do and He tried to tell Her this. She understood what He was saying, but She needed some answers and Ray and Rena still wouldn't answer their phone.

She wasn't up to going to a Church or anything as dramatic as that and thought if She ever set foot in one of those places She would probably be struck by lightening or something and Jason chuckled at this. At least Her sense of humour was still intact. She decided to look for someone who could help Her. She felt She was no longer able to help herself, but She just didn't know where to start. She needed someone who could look at what She had been through without bias and without judging Her. Someone who could do all the looking and find out what it was She could see and perhaps even find the missing connection.

Samantha seemed to perk right out of Her slump just then and grabbed the telephone directory and thumbed through the pages. Jason saw that He could do no more for Her and She looked as if She was taking control of herself yet again, so He kissed Her forehead and let himself out. Samantha continued to be absorbed in Her search for something though what She was looking for She still didn't know. She stumbled across the Private Investigation section and stopped. Could it be that simple? Following Her index finger down the page She came across an advert that caught Her eye. That is precisely what it was designed to do. The words themselves didn't mean much, but somehow the ad jumped out at you when you weren't looking and made you take notice. The words were shadowed and kind of out of focus which was the bit that made you concentrate. The letters themselves were fractionally bigger than any others on the page.

It read 'KING'S INVESTIGATIONS'. She jotted down the name, address and phone number deciding that first thing in the morning She would give it a try; there was nothing to loose. It dawned on Her at that moment that Jason had let himself out and gone home. Fair enough She thought and relaxed into the couch and allowing sleep to catch Her without any more fear.

***

The morning greeted Sam with warm weather which always made things look more promising. After the obligatory morning stretch and visit to the bathroom She picked up the phone and called Jason.

"Hello?"

"Hi babe, me here." She said rosily.

"Hi me. You all good now? Is everything all right? Sorry I left you, but you seemed to have everything under control again." He said sounding quite concerned.

"Don't be silly. I just wanted to say thanks for coming over. I really needed that."

"No probs babe, you know I'm always here for you, any time day or night."

"Yeah I know. Anyway, thanks again."

"You got it." He said trying to sound cool.

"Well, I'll give you a call tomorrow."

"Jeez, Girl, that would make it three times in two days – you alright?" He joked.

"Yeah, fuck you." She replied.

"Yeah, see ya. Love you."

Samantha put the phone down. He always said that and She couldn't bring Her self to say it back. She was scared that if She did He would get the wrong impression. She did love him though and She hoped that He knew it. She went back to bed and read, but She didn't get very far before Her mind started to wonder, so She gave that up and switched the TV on instead.

After a restful sleep the night before Her fear of being over taken in Her sleep again crept up on Her. She knew it was irrational, but She had good reason. She also knew that it was probably all in Her head, but it didn't stop from being a real fear. All She could do for now was fight off the tiredness and try to make it through though eventually sleep would come for better or worse.

The day whittled away into night and the night carried on to the morning. No matter how hard She tried She just couldn't hold Her eyes open. It became a terrifying struggle to prevent any sleep coming over Her and She was loosing. Finally, at around five AM, as the light started to flicker into Her bedroom, She gave into the force that swept over Her and She fell asleep.

- 14 -

At first there was nothing. Then almost infinitely slowly things started to show themselves; things without shape or form. The time went by the seconds ticked and the aching for something to happen became unbearable. The little pockets of light, the infinitesimal shapes that wound around each other like snakes waking from a deep slumber, a hibernation, started to take the form of distant men, animals perhaps. Sounds, pinpricks and snippets of sounds began to be heard like distant thunder or the beating of hooves. The familiarity of it all caused a little anxiety, nothing too serious, but memories flashed and the fear those memories held came seeping in like water that found it's way through plaster walls.

Without any warning the shapes and sounds came thudding to the foreground and wrapped themselves around Samantha's vision like a cloak making themselves fearfully real. It was Odin that appeared to Her sitting where He had sat when She was first here. Before She knew it He was talking to Her in a deep, husky voice that made itself instantly familiar.

"Welcome back, I am so glad you made it." He said patronizingly.

"Not that I had any fucking choice you son of a bitch!" She found herself saying.

Where She got the voice She wasn't sure. It was as if all of Her terror had dripped away and She had become immensely strong willed or perhaps the fear inside of Her had reached a plateau and added to Her anger making Her feel invincible. In any case the shock of finding herself back in Asgard hadn't sunk in until the stale smell hit Her as more of Her senses returned. The ground was hard and moist and the vaporous cloud still hung. She was in Valhalla. There was a cacophony of sounds that filled the damp air as god and beast roamed freely. Samantha realised a great feeling of familiarity, almost a warm belonging to this place that now haunted Her sleep.

"Ah, so we do have a voice." Said Odin. "What of this voice then? Is it like your will, strong? I feel that over the years, over the very many years since I have seen you last it has weakened. But this we shall find out."

"What the fuck are you talking about you ugly runt of the litter?" She said.

She was mustering all the spunk She could before the fear could sneak up on Her almost as if it was some kind of competition. Somehow, She thought it may just be. There was something inside Her that made Her try so hard to show no fear, almost as if that would be the worst thing She could do. It was like an instinct.

"SILENCE!!!" Roared the ruler of Asgard and the mighty hall fell silent.

The fear found Her once more. She felt the eyes of the underworld on Her now and saw Odin grow angry and then calm down.

"Such bravado, but is it well founded? Could we at least continue this dialogue with none of that Anglo-Saxon linguistic angst? Your will was so strong when last we met, how is it now? You were different then. You out-shined me and didn't let me out of this forsaken world. You seem to have lost something by the way. Have you recovered from the wounds of self-mutilation yet?" He said coaxing fear out of Her.

The room returned to its feverish noise while Samantha breathed deeply. Before She could answer He grabbed Her by the lapel and pulled Her so close to His face that She could smell the fetid meet that had stuck in His teeth. The stench was overpowering, but there was nothing She could do about it as His strength was enormous and She couldn't move. She looked into His eyes and saw something that chilled Her all the way to Her bones and didn't let up. It was like staring into an abyss of nothingness, looking into the past and seeing the universe created. In Her mind She could see life being brought to the gods and Asgard churning into existence. All the tales that She had been told, all the stories of ancient Greek and Roman gods thudded through Her mind like a freight train. Complete paralysis settled on Her as She saw the future and past, life and death, souls and spirits. His eyes told a great many things about this place and all in the black of nothingness, but She could see it. When He spoke His voice told of eons and unfathomable wisdom, terror and anxiety shone through like a highly polished diamond and She was instantly hypnotized. Through an aggressive, gravely voice power and ease of destruction was conveyed.

"You are not so strong as I first thought. This will be an easy task. I shall now be able to see your world through your eyes. I shall be able to change the future and the history of your world and I shall be able to rule once more. All through your eyes, through your vessel." Said Odin.

An evil laugh escaped His lungs and rocked Samantha like a boat on the water.

"When the next full moon shines on your world it will all be mine. Your pathetic race made us who we are, but then you left us to our own devices and forgot about us. It is now time for my revenge. Soon both your world and mine will be under my command."

Odin pulled Her a little closer and whispered something to Her that She couldn't make out then His eyes came alive like the fire of a thousand suns, like the torment of a thousand souls. The power flowed like treacle into Her eyes and corrupted Her soul. Her mind and body were somehow being overwhelmed and overpowered, taken. Possessed by the power of the gods of Asgard. Her will crumbled away like old masonry on an ancient castle. Immense pain ripped through Her body and every muscle tensed at the sudden harassment. Her back arched and Her eyes widened. She tried to scream, but nothing came out. Then darkness.

- 15 -

Driving around Auckland was something only the brave can do. The traffic is always backed up and drive-by shootings are not at all uncommon. Both the ground level roads and the skyway, where the elite make their way around in machines that seem to defy gravity, where always packed to the gunnels. The emergency vehicles are always scooting around at a high rate of knots and there are never any parking spaces when you finally get to where you are going. She normally took public transport as Her job paid for Her to get to and from work, but She wasn't working today and couldn't afford the taxi fare. Driving a taxi had been classed as a dangerous occupation now and this sent the prices sky rocketing.

Samantha woke up to a very strange day. Nothing seemed to make sense to Her from the very start. Something was wrong, something was different and She had no idea what. Driving through Auckland didn't help matters and it was the first time in quite a while that She had the balls to do something so stupid, but then the last couple of days had seen worse things that made driving in the big city pale by comparison. For some reason She had no recollection of the dream She had that night which, in it self is rather unusual because She always remembers Her dreams. In fact She remembers them so clearly that She writes short stories from them.

But not this time.

This time She was totally at a loss as to what She had dreamt. There was another unusual occurrence; She kept thinking it was Friday, but when She bought the morning paper the date showed Saturday. It just felt so much like Friday to Her that it began to spook Her and when She drove past a murder crime scene it didn't help matters. Obviously Friday was Yesterday, but She had been too high on alcohol or something to remember and that always bugged Her because now She had lost a day. She thought of the dream that She couldn't remember. Everything about the dream was forgotten, but She had a idea it had something to do with the feeling of being a day behind. A thought flashed in Her mind, a memory of what She had planned; She was going to see a private investigator, which snapped Her back to the present. As per usual parking was impossible. Samantha almost felt like maybe it wasn't worth it today. She had left the piece of paper with the address and phone number of the PI on the kitchen table and was still quite disjointed with the reality of it being Saturday. But She persisted and drove around the block for the forth time dodging screaming children and angry mothers, hobos and bums, ambulances and police cars. She drove past the murder site yet again and shivers ran up and down Her spine. There was a string of plastic, police crime-scene tape surrounding the area and chalk outlines of different parts of anatomy scattered across a fifteen or twenty foot radius. This type of thing doesn't normally stir up emotions with Samantha, but it just felt too close to home and there was something vaguely familiar about the whole thing. She saw from the corner of Her eye a parking space and when this happens you have to move fast. She slammed on the brakes and came to an abrupt stop forcing the driver behind Her to slam on His brakes stopping just before colliding with Her. With the wailing of His horn and the yelling out of His window She shrugged Her shoulders and flipped him the bird. There was no such thing as politeness on Auckland roads just road rage and plenty of it. In fact it was probably due to road rage that some poor bastard was now in many different pieces within the crime scene tape. She scooted into the parking space barely missing a parking warden and jumped out of Her car.

She stood for a brief moment wondering what Her next move was, but then spotted a telephone booth. Locking the car was a job as Her hands were still shaking violently and Her brain was mush. Not thinking properly She had inadvertently left Her window wound down. She headed for the booth and hoped that the phone book or at least half a phone book was still there. In this part of the city most of the phone booths were vandalized beyond use and the council never did anything about it because most people had mobile phones and the use of a public phone was something you only did if you enjoyed the heady vapours of some stranger's urine. This time, however, the book was needed, desperately needed and it was only to find an address. This particular one, as Samantha breathed in relief, did actually have a book. It was a bit rough looking and dog-eared, but it was readable.

***

The office the address led Her to was right in the heart of the city which made Her a little nervous. She didn't like dealing with central workers because they were all a little on edge and unpredictable and She should know She was one of them. But She was here now and She needed help, so She committed herself to going in. The building was one of the last in the city with the old Victorian fascia. The pillars that held up the overhanging roof clashed totally with the rest of the glass high-rises in the city, but this just seemed to add to the look and feel of it. There was a short, cascaded set of stairs that led up to the huge timber door, which had been painted white to match the rest of the building. There was a yellow-grey tinge to the paint, the colour of age. She walked up the flight of stairs and entered the squalid hallway where She stood looking for signs to tell Her where to go. At the opposite end of the hall was a set of very old looking stairs with the same paintwork as the outside just a little older. On one side was a single door that led, at a guess, to the office that occupied the ground floor. On the other side there was a large, embossed explanation of who belonged to each floor. On the top floor was some kind of legal firm dealing, presumably, with the scum of Auckland. On the ground floor was a government funded doctors surgery; it was closed for business. The first floor was the one She wanted, so She headed for the rickety looking stairwell thanking Her lucky stars that there were no elevators in a building this old. There was a very musty smell that made Her feel a little seedy. If She were honest it made Her feel that She didn't want to be there. Mind you, She thought, She didn't. The stairs made Her feel nervous as She started Her ascent. They creaked every time She moved, so She tried to keep as close to the wall as possible where the wood that made the stairs was the strongest. The only effect that had was to make slightly less noisy sounds. She came to the door and thought about knocking on it, She also thought about how stupid this was and She should just turn around and go back home. This floor had the same décor as the ground floor, but didn't have quite the same smell. The door that She was standing in front of had been painted lately in a dark forest green and for some reason it actually fit in with the rest of the colour scheme. She felt like an explorer of ancient tombs as She stood there imagining when the building was alive with business. There didn't seem to be much life here now and a cautious feeling stopped Her in Her tracks.

There was a tarnished bronze plaque about head height and on it were some faded letters that stated who worked behind the door. She reached for the handle and turned it slightly pushing tentatively and it slowly swung open to reveal the small hallway inside. She held Her breath and walked in closing the door behind Her. She continued past a small room that had virtually nothing inside and down to the end of the hallway past the kitchen and into a smallish office with a medium sized desk. Sitting behind the desk was a middle-aged man, about forty or forty-five with greyish-brown, shortly cropped hair. Was this the guy that She had seen in Her vision? He was quite attractive and carried His age well. On first impression He appeared to have some money, but clearly when She looked around He didn't, though He knew how to look that way. She liked what She saw, so far. His eyes were slate colour and He sat there with an air of wisdom, but when He looked up His expression changed to one of disbelief, like He was stunned by something that She couldn't see.

She walked up to him and said simply,

"I have a problem. How much do you charge?"

- 16 -

THE AWAKENING

Samantha was clearly distressed about what was happening to Her, so I offered to stay for a while and let Her gather Her thoughts about what to do. I couldn't figure out whether I believed Her or not, but She obviously thought it was real. As She told the story I got goose bumps and I really started to get drawn into Her fantasies, I guess I was thinking like a psychologist more than a private investigator. It was also true that I was treating Her a little differently than any other of my clients which, was understandable because She was gorgeous. From Her story I tried to piece a few things together. This was going to be a first for me with all this supernatural and godly stuff. I stood up scrapping the kitchen chair along the ground and strolled over to the coffee pot to make another caffeine hit and attempt to wake myself up. At the moment, without knowing very much about this subject I was at a complete loss about what to do. There had been no training for this type of thing in the Force and I didn't know the first thing about spirits or gods or energy flow outside of what I had learnt in my very recent experiences; but that wasn't going to stop me.

"I'm going to take you to my office, so I can keep an eye on you OK." I said trying not to sound like a parent.

"I'll be fine."

"My ass you will. I'm not one for taking no for an answer and your not exactly in the right frame of mind to argue." A weak attack, but it worked.

She looked at me with a frown.

"Look," I continued, "you're tired and confused and you look like you really don't know what to do with yourself, so you're coming with me to my office." I said bravely. “I have a spare bed you can use. I can look after you and make sure nothing else happens to you.’

“I give in.” She said simply.

***

It was a welcome relief to walk into a place that didn’t feel like it had been dragged through hell and back. That nice feeling of homeliness or at least I thought so. Sam seemed oblivious to everything, but finding a place to sit down. My feelings for Her had changed so much and She was more like a Sister to me now and I didn’t want anything to happen to Her. Being an only child myself I'm only guessing that is the reaction of a Brother to a Sister anyway; I didn’t quite know how to handle it, but I guess I would pick it up along the way. It was such a rich and fulfilling feeling of belonging and I didn’t want to loose that. My life had been a lonely one with nobody to care for, but me and now I find I just wanted to wrap Her in cotton wool and protect Her against the world. She touched me with Her story and set the little parental bells going off in my mind.

I fixed us both a stiff drink and grabbed some chips from the kitchen cupboard, She smiled and thanked me then sat there contemplating life. I sat right next to Her and tried to transmit my energy into Her, which I didn’t really know how to do. She looked so drained and after what I have heard didn’t surprise me at all. It was unfamiliar territory for me and I only hoped that She knew how to draw from me because I was feeling a little sheepish trying to waft energy over. She smiled and looked into my eyes which filled me with a wanting desire so intense and passionate that I dismissed all thoughts of brotherhood and kissed Her tenderly on the lips and to my surprise She didn’t pull back an inch. My heart was pumping and my loins were tingling. I pulled back and shot a look at Her which I hoped would portray the thoughts and questions about ethics and brotherhood and whether we should be doing this type of thing or not. All She did was give a small nod and reached forward cupping Her open hand around my neck and kissed me deeply. It was all too much for me too resist, so I stood up, bent over and picked Her up in my arms and headed down to my bedroom.

Arms and legs were everywhere on the bed. Clothes flying off and landing in confused disarray on the floor. We were so deep in the throws of lust and yearning that any pause in the proceedings would fill me with such anxiety that I would probably explode. This had been building for some time now and the tension was thick in the air. Even when I was tearing Her clothes off I felt I was taking too much unnecessary time. When we were both totally naked I started to caress every inch on Her luscious, creamy body following every touch with a tender, but firm kiss until She started to squirm underneath me. Her skin felt so soft and tender that I wanted to take a bite out of Her. She was warm on my lips and I tasted the salty liquid of Her sweat that had mixed with mine. She arched Her back as I brought Her to the edge and over; licking off the sweet taste of passion that adorned Her thighs and moved up towards Her perfectly formed breasts. I gently wiped away the beads of sweat with the tips of my fingers to the accompaniment of soft little sighs that escaped Her lips. I moved up further and played my mouth over Her face and lavishly kissed Her mouth as She took my tongue playfully. My full weight pressed down on Her and with the unstoppable force of billions of years of reproduction we became one. The feeling was incredible as the rhythmic motion of Her pelvis joined my own passionate pulsations. The air was filled with the musty smell of sexual liaison and the muffled moans of the two of us. The moment carried us both away as the tempo increased and our juices mingled. I could feel Her squirming sensually below me and suddenly She tightened and let out a low gratified moan, which prompted me to an almighty climactic release.

- 17 -

The night had come and gone leaving us both physically drained, but, not surprisingly, incredibly satisfied and spiritually filled. The guilt, however, started to plague me bit by bit, stronger and stronger. At first I thought I could handle it, handle the moral wrong of it. I thought I could handle the feeling that I was taking advantage of a girl that was emotionally distraught and someone with whom I was so close to that I felt, as I have already said, like She was a Sister. We hadn't known each other that long and the bond was already incredibly tight between us. Maybe that's why last night was so damn good. Maybe what I just discovered was the one. Somebody with whom I could see as my lover and best friend, which is what we are all hunting for isn't it? She was just so young and really didn't know what She was doing. This Sister thing disturbed me though. I didn't know how to treat a sibling, but I knew this wasn't the way. I got up and walked slowly into the bathroom to look at the mirror and into the eyes of a sinner and perhaps try to repent some of my terrible actions. I couldn't think straight, so I went back into the room and told Sam to get dressed.

"Why, what's wrong?" She asked.

"This whole thing is what's wrong." I started angrily.

The frustration of the whole damn thing got me a bit riled up.

"We can't do this, we can't let it go on. You mean too much to me to carry on this type of relationship. It's not fair on you and it's definitely not fair on me." I said.

After a moment I realized that it wasn't over, not by a long shot. There was still so much unfinished business with this angel.

"Maybe when this whole thing is finished we can start over again if the feelings are still there, but at the moment we have far too many important things to think about to screw it up with something that will cloud our judgement. I can't let that happen."

I couldn't believe I just told Her all that drivel! I really didn't know what to think, so I said what sounded good with no real thought to what was coming out of my mouth.

"Do you have a friend that you can call to pick you up? I need to get to the library to look through the archives and hopefully learn something new."

"Well, I suppose I could call Lorraine to come for me." She said sadly hoping for a reprieve.

"Good, you do that while I go have a shower."

With that I headed down the hallway and into the bathroom. I didn't hear Her go due to the water, but I was alone again. I had no intention of going to the library or anywhere for that matter.

I had to clear my head.

I was incredibly fatigued and needed some sleep myself, so I got out of the shower, dried myself and headed on back to my bedroom to lay down. It didn't take long before the power of sleep overwhelmed me and I fell into a slumber that lasted for half the day.

***

So many things have affronted themselves over the last couple of weeks and it's all been quite frightening. How can I cope with all this stress? I thought this was going to be so easy. I thought I could stand back with an empathetic observation to see everything and judge accordingly. I thought wrong. All this time it was I who was being judged. When I thought I was doing the right thing it turned out to be totally wrong. It was as if there was a cloud hanging over my head that fogged my vision and stopped me from seeing the trouble I was getting into. Now I can see things will have to change. My old life was over and the new King was taking control. I just didn't know what to make of the situation.

Samantha was probably the best thing to happen to me, the best thing in my life. I feel so comfortable talking to Her and I can be totally honest with Her. I think I may have given Her up too easily; what a fool I was. I should have fought. It brings a tear to my eye when I think how good the relationship could have been.

So, I have to face the fact that I am going through, or have gone through, some big changes within my self. Most of it is due, in no small amount to what Samantha has shown me and told me. I've been having day dreams and sometimes nightmares, I've discovered things about myself that force me to take a second look at the world as I knew it. I think the images that I've seen could be more than just random. My gut tells me it could be my past or even my future, which is a scary thought. It started with the first time Sam took me on the journey through my mind. Some of the flashes were about Her and I, but most of them were incomprehensible and felt like dying memories. Out of the ashes, as it were, comes new life and a discovery that I perhaps I have been many different people. I think I can feel the spirits talking to me sometimes and they are talking about Samantha. As stupid as it sounds and I know it sounds stupid, since the time I met Sam something inside of me has opened up and I have discovered a whole new side to myself. Could I be developing powers I never thought I had? The signs are telling me She is my destiny, so now I have to do something about it. If I could hear myself think I'd be booking a room at the Padded Inn.

I pulled away from the most important person in my life and for what? A warm fuzzy feeling that She's my Sister? If I keep thinking things like that as far as I can see it's only going to get worse. All I have to do is wait for those stupid feelings to pass. Maybe I'm trying to be someone I'm not and all of a sudden I'll see who I really am. I think I need to be who I actually am, but that is perhaps the hardest thing for anybody to do because when we think about it, who are we? Once in a while we all need to reinvent ourselves. All this cock-eyed thinking was making me dizzy, so a siesta was in order, so I slumped down and closed my eyes.

***

The sleep I got was badly needed, but now I feel restless. The shit has hit the fan now that the whole PI/client relationship was at risk and I had seen what I was in for; God, I needed a cigarette. I slumped back on my chair and stared at the ceiling trying to hold back my tears. I found the soft carpet with my feet and lifted the rest of my body up. Just standing there for a second I thought I spotted something from the corner of my eye, but the observation was so fleeting that I didn't know where to look for it again. It was probably nothing, so I ignored it and made my way to the kitchen to fix something to eat. Sam had long gone and in a strange way I kind of missed Her, damn it, it wasn't a strange way at all. I missed Her and I wanted Her. I couldn't get Her out of my head. Sam, the glimpse of whatever I saw, Asgard; it all seemed so surreal and dreamy. I fixed a bowl of four wheat biscuits to take to my room. I stopped halfway down the hall and began to stare at the large 16th century Lotto. That was one of the most expensive and totally ostentatious purchases I have ever made, but it was kind of me and I liked it. I've never made much money and never really needed to, but one weekend when I was in the Force some of my numbers came up in the lottery and I couldn't think of anything better to spend the money on. It was pointless also, which made it was an even more stupid buy, but it made the office look complete. Candinski once said, 'It is clear that the choice of object that is one of the elements in the harmony of form must be decided only by a corresponding vibration of the soul.' It means so many different things, but to me it is that which defines and influences us, that which we are. The office always held that confused, but controlled look; controlled chaos you could call it. A mixture of the old and the new, the traditional and the modern, something that Lorenzo Lotto carried off with ease. As soon as I saw the painting my heart melted and my soul started to flutter and I remembered the words of Candinski. I had to have it. It wasn't the original of course, but it was a damn good replica of 'Portrait Of A Married Couple' dated about 1523, and it summed up the feeling of opposition of the times we find ourselves in. The message portrayed in the painting went thus 'A good widower will never find release from turmoil in sleep: He will always remember His lady.' – Like man and Mother Earth how it was about a hundred years ago when there was still some hope.

- 18 -

I was cursing myself for letting Sam go with the sudden realization that I was supposed to be protecting Her. I grabbed my keys and headed for the door. To hell with how I feel about Her or how She's going to treat me now. To hell with the sex and the great times we had. I don't know where all this sudden attitude change come from, but after what I experienced She needed to be protected and I was the one who took the job. After hearing myself think, as it were, I began to get the feeling I was buying all this bullshit. I wasn't thinking and wasn't watching where I was going as I hurried out of my building I nearly bowled over a kid of about five.

"Ah, sorry kid!" I said apologetically.

"That's alright, Bob." She said smiling at me.

This kid, this little girl, I never met before. I was just frozen as She smiled at me and skipped away down the street. Nobody had called me Bob for about thirty years. Now I was getting more than a little paranoid. I snapped out of the daze when I remembered about Sam. I had to get Her, so I rushed to the car and took off like a scolded cat in the direction of Her house. This day had started well I thought sarcastically. Now I couldn't get that little girl out of my mind. Was it just a guess? Did She think I was somebody She knew? Was it just a coincidence? My journal, I forgot about my journal. I clumsily searched my pockets for my PDA swerving all over the road and into oncoming traffic. I tapped my top pocket and found my pills, so I grabbed them out along with the PDA. I corrected my driving while trying to dial Sam's number on the car phone and swallowing one of the pills. Who says men can't multi task?

Around one bend the sun hit me right in the face; I could see nothing and then a glint of metal reflected a shard of light directly into my eye.

- 19 -

"Welcome back." It was a deep husky voice.

My head was killing me and when I opened my eyes a series of painful thuds shuddered through me making everything go blurry.

"It's been a while my friend."

"Who – who are you and where the hell am I?" I said weakly.

There was a smell, a terrible smell. I knew that smell, but I don't know where I knew it from. It was so familiar, but I couldn't place it. Things started to come into focus with shapes, and forms. The acrid smell was invading my nose like a militant manoeuvre, something that you could never get used to. My head pounded with the heady vapours of the old and warn out. The ground was hard and damp and my eyes were slowly getting used to the light. I could make out a figure. The figure was sitting on something throne like and noises polluted my senses. The harshness of sounds made my ears ring with confusion and the sight of this figure made me nervous. Where was I? It all seemed very familiar.

"I have brought you here because I have been concerned about you getting in the way. You're a thorn in my side Vali." Said the voice.

"What are you talking about? And you didn't answer me. Who the fuck are you and where the fuck am I?"

The figure started to come further into focus and He was huge. Enormous, god like. He wore some sort of fur coat that looked like it had never been washed, perhaps that was the smell. And then I remembered. Sam had mentioned something like this, but She said it was a dream. Was I dreaming?

"You're memory is not what it used to be my son. Lest we forget how we stood in battle together against evil. Fought along side each other in the face of death and built our world upon the wasteland of our ancient home." Said the voice.

“Is this some bad movie that I’ve just walked into? I have no idea what you’re on about and I would appreciate you telling me who you are and where I am.” I said in a bold manner.

Well it didn’t quite come out that way, but that’s what I was attempting. I felt weak and disorientated.

“I am your Father and this is your home. And once more, my son, you have become the bane of my life. I wish you would stay out of my business and let me do what I have to do! Fulla is mine and She is doing what I have told Her to do, so leave it alone!” He said angrily.

“Look *‘DAD’*, I don’t know what or who you think I am, but I have never heard of this Fulla and you still haven’t told me where the fuck I am. You don’t want to get me pissed off, so tell me where I am, so I can get out of here!” I was starting to heat up and this guy was not helping.

“Vali! You insolent mortal! You are home in Asgard as if I should need to remind you. Why is it so hard for your time to keep track of all your lives? Thor!”

“Yes, Father.” Came the response from behind me.

“Sit our Vali up will you, we need him to remember.”

It was like the arms of a forklift grabbing me from behind. I was dumped on a big slab of oak trunk as my body was jarred with pain.

“Get your big ass hands off me you oaf!” I yelled to Thor who answered with a thump to my head that almost knocked be back off the stump.

“Ha ha ha, this banter, this wonderful sibling rivalry how I miss it.” Said the mysterious Father figure.

“Could someone tell me what the hell is going on?”

“Vali, my son, you have come home to me. This is not the homecoming it should be. You have disgraced our world and family and now you must pay the price.”

“I still don’t have the faintest idea of what’s gong on.”

My eyes were starting to adjust to the meek light and I could just make out what I was looking at. This guy was ugly. He had a long, grey-black beard with one of those barbarian horned hats. He was huge, massive! The room I was in was bigger than I could guess and apparently made of logs strung together in a random procession of untidy lines. The smell was like burning flesh and my olfactory nerves had still not gotten used to the stench.

"I am your Father. Come now Vali, I know you are not stupid. I know you remember. Please don't let me repeat myself, I hate that. You have come back to us and I welcome you. Or I would like to. But you have brought us shame and you must vindicate yourself or be brought to a swift justice by your Brother."

"Look, all I would like you to do is tell me where I am, who you are and let me get the hell out of here. And who the fuck is Fulla?"

"I am Odin, Father of the gods. You are home, in Asgard and Fulla is your Sister."

"Are you trying to tell me that I am sitting in the hall of the fallen worriers and gods? Are you trying to tell me that I have a Sis – wait a minute, are you trying to tell me that I'm a god?"

"You do remember – Thor, pick him…"

"Wait, wait. No, I don't remember. Is this…this must be a dream right? This cannot be real. This is the kind of stuff we were told about in school. The kind of stories that the Nordics told their kids, so they could grow up to be rapists and pillagers. I never heard of any Vali or Fulla. I'm an only child and my Father was a cop who drowned in a shipwreck. You haven't really done your homework now have you."

"VALI!!!! You are trying my patients…"

"Oh, just shut the hell up you pillock! You have no idea who…"

Just then there was an almighty crash of thunder and before I know what was happening I got a blast of rotting meat as Odin was in my face faster than I could blink.

"You would do well to keep your mouth shut. Forget about everything you have ever learned or experienced. You are in the real world now, my world. Anything that has happened before now was just a dream. A figment of the mass imagination. Nothing was real, understand? You are home with me now and I have a deal to make with you."

OK, that worked. The monstrosity of flesh and stench cut my thoughts short. My heart flipped and I couldn't catch my breath. I felt like I was about to faint, so I took a few sharp breaths and let my fear grow as I realized that this may not be a dream after all. So, this may be my Father. I may have a Sister and…I'm a god?

"A demi-god." Said Thor, as if He read my mind.

"What?" I ask shocked.

"A mortal god, not full blood." Answered Odin.

"Yup, it's official. I'm lost."

"You will meet your Sister, you will meet your whole family even those you brought to shame. You are half mortal on your Mother's side. She is, I'm sorry to say, dead. But I am still alive!"

"M...my Father was a cop! How can you claim that you, a god, the Father of the gods are my Father?"

"I was in the mortal realm for a couple of millennia. Are you to tell me that you don't remember any of this?" He said with sad disappointment.

"Let me think about that...no. Not even when I was learning about you in school. Not a glimmer of a memory, nothing. You're having me on aren't you? I don't get it."

"You will remember Vali, you will. Many life times ago you and I were on the same side. Your Mother was a fool, so I see you have inherited something from Her after all."

"Wait a minute. What you're saying doesn't make sense." I started, then a thought occurred. "From memory you have a wife. What was Her name? Ah, is Her name...Frig? That's it. You're telling me that you had an affair with my Mother? I always knew that I was a bastard, but that just tops it doesn't it."

There was silence as Odin composed himself against the truth. He knew what He had done those many years ago and I guess I wasn't making any friends here. That's if what He was saying was true. I couldn't believe it. All this time my Mother and Father had lied to me. It can't be true. I was completely confused about the situation.

"Vali," continued Odin, "there are some thing's that you don't need to know and this is one of them. Lets just say that it's because of your Mother and I that you exist in the first place, so lets not argue over the circumstances." It was as if He was reading my mind.

"So, why have you brought me here? I'm not entirely sure that I follow what you have been saying or asking or whatever."

"That girl that you're seeing, I want that to stop." He said matter-of-fact.

"Who, Sam?" I snapped?

"As you know Her, yes."

"Oh, don't you even go there."

"How dare you threaten me! That girl is mine. Keep away from Her or you will suffer the consequences."

"Who talks like that? Really? What do you want from Her?" I retorted.

"You don't need to know. But stay away from Her."

"Or what? Do you understand that I love this girl? Yes She's my client and I have no right to feel this way, but She's not going to be my client forever now is She?"

"I said stay away from Her. That means cutting all ties with Her. If you don't, I will be forced to have Her killed and sent here for eternity!"

"Right, and I don't even know if this place exists beyond my dreams." I challenged.

"If proof is what you need then proof I shall give you. Thor, hand him the emulate."

Before I could ask what an emulate was this heavy, gold meddle like object on a chain was placed over my head and hung around my neck.

"This is your proof. When you wake up you will remember."

"So, you're telling me that if I don't stay away from Sam, you will kill Her?"

"That is correct."

"OK, if I'm willing to do this there are conditions." I said bravely.

"You dare deal with your God and Father?"

"Yeah. Do you have a choice? I mean if I disobey you, you can't use Her for whatever you want Her for and you will loose a son...again. If I obey you, what's in it for me? Sounds like a loosing situation for me either way!"

"Alright. What is it you want?"

"I want you to promise me that you'll stay away from me if I stay away from Her. None of your guards or ghouls or whatever you send to other dimensions to watch over people. And this is to be done on my own merits. I don't want any of that mind bending Vulcan crap that makes people do things that they don't usually do. And I still want to know what's in it for me."

"OK, so if I promise to stay away from you and not use any supernatural abilities as you call them you will do this for me?" He questioned.

"What Son wouldn't?" I said with a smile. "And what about what I get?"

"I will guarantee you another suitor. Samantha will be replaced for you with something a little sweeter to the eyes."

"OK, deal."

- 20 -

"You're up"

"What?" Asked Samantha.

Jason pointed to the stage.

"You're up. It's your turn."

"Ah shit, I'm not drunk enough for this."

"Go for it Babe, you'll be fine."

Samantha got up and sauntered towards the stage of the Karaoke club. The music started as Samantha stared at the screen. The room was filled with the intro to the classic 'Black Velvet' and Samantha's shaky voice began. There was clapping and whistling – the crowd approved. Samantha smiled as She realized that Her voice hadn't failed Her. She looked over to Jason who has been Her rock. She thought about all the good things that they have been through then She thought about the lies that She has put him through. He has stayed there for Her through thick and thin and He wouldn't leave Her side. Maybe He was the guy that She was supposed to be with. He was the one that treated Her like a queen and She dumped him for a type of misunderstood life that She now leads. And He is still there. The thoughts of how good it was came bubbling to the surface and cracked Her voice a bit. She stumbled off the words and managed to compose herself a little more and the crowd let it go. He was wonderful, but somehow She didn't think that She was worth it. All Her life She has been waiting for the right guy to come around and when He finally does She doesn't think that She deserves him. She's not good enough for him, so She felt guilty. She felt so guilty and She couldn't give him what She was getting and had no idea that He didn't care about that stuff. She couldn't allow herself this wonderful experience of a good life, so She blamed herself. She blamed the fact that She was a terrible person and went back to someone else; someone else that treated Her like a rag doll. Treated Her like She thought She was meant to be treated - like shit. She knew what She had lost. With the drugs and alcohol in Her body and the emotions rampaging through Her mind She dropped the microphone and took off outside with Jason in hot pursuit while the crowd went silent and the music stopped. Outside moments later Jason found Samantha sitting on the stairs crying into Her hands. He sat down next to Her and put His arm around Her.

"Look, I'm sorry about Lorraine, but there was nothing you could do."

"You don't understand. This is nothing to do with Lorraine." Cried Samantha.

"Then what is it?"

"Nothing."

"Fine." Said Jason and got up to hail a taxi. "I wish I knew what your problem is, so I could help." He said looking down at Her as a taxi pulled up to the curb.

"I told you, it's nothing." She whimpered.

"So, why are you crying then?"

"It's nothing that you need to worry about."

"You know I worry about you." Replied Jason as He grabbed Her under the arms. "Come on, we'll get you home."

"OK. Are you going to stay with me?" Asked Samantha.

"Just try and stop me. I'll take the couch." He replied as they got in the taxi and headed back to Samantha's flat.

Once they were there Jason helped Her into Her room and sat Her down on the bed. Samantha realized just how much She had been drinking and tried to shake the drunkenness off.

"Could you get me some water or something? I'm feeling a little woozy." She said staring at the floor.

Jason nodded and went to the bathroom to get a glass of water. When He got back to Samantha's bedroom She was slumped over with Her head on the pillow and Her legs hanging over the bed. She wasn't asleep, but She could barely keep Her eyes open. She managed a smile when Jason put the water down on the bedside table and crouched down to take Her shoes off and get Her in a more comfortable position, so She could sleep it off.

"What are you doing?" She slurred.

"Taking your shoes off."

"OK." She whispered.

Jason chuckled and managed to get Her shoes off. He grabbed both of Her legs and swung them round, so She was lying comfortably on the bed, but now the problem was that She was on top of the covers, so He went to the cupboard to get a blanket for Her.

When He got back into the room He saw She had managed to slip off Her skirt and was undoing Her blouse ready to get under the covers.

"Well, hello sailor." She said looking at him with a smile.

"Ah…err…sorry, Sam. I thought you were pretty much asleep."

"Don't be silly, Baby. It's nothing you haven't seen before." She purred.

"Yes, but we were going out then, remember?" He said as He realized just how dickey it sounded.

"Ah yes, the old mahogany man; never wanting to sleep with a woman for just a night." She slurred smiling with that sexy lopsided smile of hers.

"Monogamy. And that's not the point." He answered in a short tone.

"Well I swear I won't touch you. Come on, come here and sit with me 'till I'm asleep. I don't want to be alone."

"OK, but I want you to get under the blankets and I'll turn off the lights."

"Wow, are you trying to seduce me Mrs. Robinson?" She smiled slipping Her knickers off and reaching around for Her bra clasps.

"I really wish you wouldn't do that Sam. You're making me uncomfortable. You know I love you and you doing that is not fair. I don't care how drunk you are."

"Well come to bed then."

Jason turned the lights off and headed to the other side of the bed and quietly lay down next to Samantha. As soon as His head hit the pillow Samantha snuggled up next to him and He could feel Her hard nipples through His T-shirt. It just wasn't fair and He was getting uncomfortable.

"What are you doing?"

"I'm Lonely, Jase. I just want to hold on to you."

"You're making this very hard on me."

"Well do something about it."

"What, like get up and sleep in the lounge? I think I should." He joked.

"No," She said holding on tighter, "I don't want you doing that. What I mean is that you've been the most wonderful person in the world to me."

"And you're saying?"

"I love you." She whispered.

"You're drunk. You do know this don't you."

"I'm not that drunk and I'm feeling much better with you here. I just want to let you know how grateful I am for having you in my life."

"Well, a 'thank you' will suffice."

"That's what I mean." She said and moved Her hand over His chest like a cat on the prowl.

Jason could feel the stirring in His body the feeling that He ached for from Her; but He knew it wasn't right. She was drunk and they weren't together. But then what would it hurt? No, He told himself, this wasn't right. Besides before long She would be asleep and nothing would happen. He wanted nothing more than to snuggle up next to Her and sleep. That's what He always wanted, but the thought of the feeling

She gave him when they had sex was hard to ignore. She was very good in the sack, but He shouldn't even be thinking that.

"I don't think this is right." He spoke His mind.

"Don't think then."

Her hand went lower and started to massage the lump that had formed in His jeans. He shot up and looked at Her.

"What are you doing?" He hissed.

His eyes had adjusted to the darkness and He could see Her beautiful smile right there in front of him. This was all He wanted in life, but He knew that if He went through with this He would want more and She wasn't going to hang around to play happy families. It would hurt too much.

"Sam, I can't do this with you."

"Are you going to deny me tonight?" She replied slowly pulling the blankets away to reveal Her perfect breasts.

Jason just looked at Her for a while remembering the times that they had been together. He was so happy, but He was also hurting constantly because She was such a free spirit. He was always jealous about what She might be doing when She went out with Her friends without him. He was insecure about Her looks because She was a catch in any man's language. But He still wanted to be in Her life. He wanted Her so badly, but wasn't going to be burnt again. He could see Her changing into somewhat of a more mature person looking for a way to settle down, but She was all mixed up. He knew He shouldn't go there again, but man He wanted to. As He was thinking this She reached over and kissed him gently on the lips and He fell into Her. There was nothing that He wanted more right now and He couldn't resist the passion that had been building up inside of him over the months. Their tongues twisted and turned around each other as His hand played over Her body. Samantha rolled him over and slid His T-shirt off as She straddled him. Her movements were fluid and with the moonlight catching Her beautiful body Jason just closed His eyes and let it all happen. Within a few minutes He was lying there naked with Samantha pressing Her warm body against His. He flipped them over, so He was on top and slowly kissed Her neck to the sounds of whispered moans from Samantha's mouth. He moved down as the memories flooded back of the first time they had been together like this and He was about to taste Her again. It was a stormy night and they had both been stoned from one of the designer drugs that Samantha had scored. The lightning randomly cast its light through the curtains and danced around the room exciting the pair of them and brought intensity to the writhing with each clap of thunder. His mouth reached Her erect nipple and with slow seduction He teased Her with His tongue before moving down to Her navel. She arched Her back as the softness of His mouth and the scratchy stubble on His face played on Her clitoris sending waves of pleasure through Her body. Moments later as She reached Her first climax Jason kissed His way back up Her body to Her mouth where they shared Her flavours. She was in ecstasy and He couldn't hold on any longer. He slowly entered Her and welcomed Her warmness. Samantha let out a long sigh as the tears ran down Her face while Jason slowly, sensually made love to Her. Samantha started to sob which stopped Jason in His erotic movements.

"Are you alright?" He said. "Did I hurt you?"

She pushed him off Her and cupped Her hands over Her face. Jason propped himself up and put a hand gently on Her stomach.

"What's wrong?"

"I can't do this any more." She whimpered.

Jason sighed and looked up to the ceiling in frustration.

"It's PJ isn't it?" He asked.

Samantha nodded and started to cry harder. He hugged Her one more time.

"It's just not right, you know that."

He got up and dressed leaving Samantha in bed, naked and crying. Twenty minutes later Jason had left in a taxi.

- 21 -

"Nurse, He moved!"

"OK, relax. Let's just see if He can hear us. Robert? Robert?"

I don't know who it was, but the sound was sweet. I don't know where I was and what happened and I couldn't remember a thing. All I know is that these two angelic voices where trying to talk to me. The light was shining through my eyelids painting an orange glow that hurt me eyes.

"He's responding." Said one of the voices.

"What's He trying to say?"

"I think it's the light, it may be hurting His eyes. Could you pull the curtains please."

The glow disappeared and my eyes were relieved. Painfully I tried to open my eyes so I could see who was in the room with me. I must have had one of my drunken nights because I couldn't remember a thing from the night before.

"He's opening His eyes!"

"Yes, thank you Miss, I can see that."

"Well you don't need to be like that." Snapped one of the voices.

"Girls, could you stop that? I have a headache like someone has put a bullet through my brain." I said.

I could barely hear my own voice, but it was there.

"Oh may God, King, you're OK." I recognized this voice after hearing it a little more.

"Is that you Sam?" I asked hopefully.

"Yes. Thank God you're OK. I couldn't bare loosing someone else."

"What are you talking about?" I asked. "Who have you lost."

"Um, She'll tell you about it later, but right now you need you're rest. Do you know where you are?" Said the other voice.

My eyes hadn't fully adjusted to the light, but the room did not look familiar. Oh god, not again. I have woken up in someone else's room in someone else's bed. I've got to lay off that Scotch.

"I have no idea where I am and I have no idea who you are. Wherever I am and who ever you are, I'm sorry. This won't happen again."

"What's He talking about?" Asked Sam.

"Um, I think He thinks He's got a hangover, not too sure though. Robert, I am Nurse Swanson and you're at the hospital."

"Was I that bad?"

"No." She chuckled. "You've had an accident."

"Oh, one thing though, could you call me King? I don't like that other name." I said.

"Sure. Do you understand you have been in a car accident? You were almost killed. If it hadn't been for Samantha here you would probably be dead right now."

"So, I wouldn't have to put up with this headache. Gee, thanks Sam." I replied sarcastically.

"This isn't a joke King." Said Sam. "The Nurse is serious."

"You have been in a coma for eight days now King." Said the nurse.

What could I say? I wasn't expecting any of this, but I guess that's why they call it an accident.

***

My head was pounding and I guess that's what woke me up. I slowly opened my eyes and suddenly remembered where I was and what had happened.

"King, you're awake again." Said the beautiful voice of Sam.

"Yeah, I guess. What happened?"

"Well you weren't really in the most lucid state yesterday and you tried to get up. You had been in a coma for about eight days and I guess you passed out again when you exerted yourself too much."

"Right, my bad. So, how did I get here then?"

"Well, you had an accident. A bad accident. You're alright now and there is nothing wrong with you except for your head which will be fine in a couple of days." She said.

She reached over to the side cabinet where a pitcher was standing and poured a glass of water for me. I guess She read my mind because I was parched.

"You see you hit the steering wheel with your head and it wiped you out." She continued. "If it wasn't for the fact that I was there at the time…well, the doctor said that you didn't have very much time and you could've died." She said handing me the water.

"Thanks. I just have one question for you." I said.

"What's that?"

"What were you doing there in the first place?" I asked.

She went quiet for a while.

"Sam?" I urged.

"The car that you hit was mine."

"Oh my God Sam, are you alright?" I said sitting up. "I'm so sorry. I had no idea!"

"Yeah, I'm alright, there's nothing wrong with me, but…"

"But what Sam? Tell me, what happened?"

"It's Lorraine."

"What? What's wrong with Lorraine?" I asked.

I kind of already knew the answer though.

"She was in the car with me. She ah...She wasn't wearing a seat belt and She went through the windscreen."

"Holly shit. Is She…" My fears seemed to have been right on the money.

Again, She went silent and bowed Her head. I could hear Her start to cry softly and then I realized what had happened.

"Oh, man. Oh Fuck. I, I don't know what to say. Sam, I'm so sorry."

She cried louder and fell into my arms.

"It wasn't your fault. Had She been wearing Her seat belt She'd be here now. I killed Her King. She's dead because of me!"

We just sat there silently. I held Her tight as She cried. I felt so bad for Her, but there was nothing I could do. I felt useless.

"There is something else. Something that I need to tell you because I can't go on living a lie." She started.

"What is it?"

"It's you and me."

"What about you and me, what about us? I don't like the sound of this."

"I can't let it continue." She said waiting for my reaction.

"I don't like to say it, but I have to agree with you." I replied.

I have no idea where that came from, but it was something that for some reason I had to say.

"I can't even help you out with your life. We can't see each other again." I said with a cold look.

"What? Why?" She sat up and looked at me with Her hand on my chest. "What's this?" She said looking at Her hand.

"What?"

I didn't know what She meant or where She was going with this, but it was starting to confuse the hell out of me not to mention piss me off.

"This…" She said pulling down my hospital gown to reveal a golden emulate hanging around my neck.

"Oh my God, now I remember." I said looking at the ceiling. "The bastard, that fucking bastard! It's all true! Now I get it."

"Get what? What the hell are you talking about?" She said getting flustered.

"This is the proof. It exists and this is why I can't see you any more."

"I'm not following. What exists?" She said shaking Her head.

"Thor gave this to me." I just looked at Her with fear.

"What? You met Thor? What about Odin and all those…" She shrilled forgetting about the fact that we were breaking up.

"Yes." I interrupted. "I had to make a deal with him. I have to let you go otherwise He's going to kill you. I didn't believe it and I thought I was dreaming. This is way too much for me to handle right now. What the fuck is going on?" I said.

This was just not computing for me.

"I need to tell you something, King." She said solemnly.

"What?" I snapped.

"I have, I mean for a long time, I have been having…I um. I don't know how to tell you."

"Well, I don't know where this is going, but I think it's just as well I'm lying down."

She seemed to have remembered what She was talking about in the first place.

"Yes." She said blankly catching me off guard. "You see, for the last five years I have been seeing this guy. I still am and I was when you and I were together." She stopped, waiting for my reaction.

"You mean… fucking hell! This day just keeps getting better and better. I guess this makes it easier for me to tell you to fuck off then doesn't it! I really don't want to see you again. What were you thinking? Oh man! Oh man! I thought…" I said looking at Her with part hurt and part disgust.

"King," She interrupted, "I still need you. I still need your help."

"Forget it! You used me." I said angrily. "I want my money now, right now. Hand it over and fuck off."

"I didn't think you would react like this." She said with a tear on Her cheek.

"What did you expect? 'Oh, Sam, that's all right. I don't mind you FUCKING SOMEONE ELSE!!'" I yelled. "What do you take me for? I was in love with you!"

"That's why I had to tell you." She said trying to reason.

"You know, I don't get women any more. Not that I want to know, but what's this guys name?"

"PJ"

"PJ? You're sleeping with this guy who's named after pyjamas? That's wonderful that is. You bitch! You complete bitch!" I could only look at the window.

"Look," She said in a shorter tone, "I wasn't going to tell you at all, but I thought you deserved the truth. Why would I tell you this if it wasn't important. I still need you to work this case for me…"

"Well you can find someone other schmuck for that I'm afraid." I said indignantly.

"…and I needed to tell you this, so that it didn't ruin our professional relationship."

"Great. Well thanks for that." I said sarcastically. "Don't let the door hit you on the way out – go on, go back to you PJs and have a wonderful time. I guess you were thinking of him while you were playing hide the sausage with me were you?"

"You're disgusting. I did love you, but it's more complicated than that."

"Oh, there's more is there? What could make my day any worse than it already is?"

"He's my step Brother!"

- 22 -

I felt like shit. It was like She had ripped out my heart and fed it to the dogs. I wanted to cry, but I couldn't let myself, not here. So, how was She feeling? Did I care? Not at all. Well that's what I told myself as I absently traced the amulet with my finger. I found myself hoping that She was just as cut up about the whole thing as I was; if not more. That wouldn't really make me feel any better though. I guess I should be glad in a way because I didn't have to tell Her I made the deal with Odin. In a way I did, but I don't think She really heard me or even believed me. If it was me I wouldn't have believed me. I felt so sick I went to the bathroom to wash my face. I think I was about to throw up. An overwhelming feeling, that awful aching feeling in the gut that you get when someone stamps all over your heart. This was ten times worse though because She was actually with someone else when She was with me. Granted, She never actually said that She had cheated on me, but I could read between the lines. Man I was pissed off. I ran the tap to fill the basin and looked in the mirror. My face was red and my eyes were puffy from the crying I'd been holding back. Why did this girl cause me so much grief? I have never been this torn up before about a break up and I've been through some pretty heavy break-ups before. What made it worse is that this Angel probably couldn't understand why I was so cut up about it and why I took it so personally. I couldn't work that one out myself.

She was so affectionate when we were together like there was only the two of us in the world and when we were apart, well, we always spoke over the phone and emailed each other. There was contact there every day even if it was only to say 'hi'. Come to think about it I don't think I ever loved Her, but my feelings ran deep. She had hurt me so much. I'll give Her one thing though, She ripped my heart out in front of me instead of a 'Dear John' letter or worse. I don't even know what could be worse, but it made me feel better to know that Her last ditch effort to bring me down gently was done to my face. I didn't react well though. In fact in retrospect I reacted really badly! I should have seen it coming as I've never had a decent relationship in my life, but She was fantastic! She was not only one of the most spectacular looking women I have ever met She was also intelligent and free as a bird. I guess I wanted to tame Her and make Her mine. But then that would never have happened because She always had this so-called PJ on Her mind. She was probably thinking of him when She fucked me. Ouch, that hurt. She was good, really good and that made me nervous because I never thought I would ever bed a beauty like Her. Looking back I guess that made me not so great under the covers and another reason why She dumped me.

I felt like reaching and was almost physically sick. I knew this was one of those phases, but that couldn't stop the anger, frustration and paranoia that rushed around my body. I turned the tap off and splashed some cool water on my face to wash away the grief. Man it felt so good to be with Her. I don't think I will ever find another Sam, but if I do I'll definitely do things differently; but I really don't know how. She was so young and She probably thought She had the world in Her hand not realising how She was hurting people. Stories of Jason filled my mind. He was enough to make me jealous, I guess it was because they were so close and although I was on intimate levels with Sam I would never be as close as they were. In fact chances are that I would never be that close to anyone in my lifetime. The tears started to well up again. I just couldn't believe it. My mind was bombarded by thoughts of the way things should be, could have been. How could I get myself out of feeling like this? How could I possibly feel good? I had been dumped by this girl for Her Brother - albeit Her Step Brother – it made me feel sick again.

I had been with a girl that had been doing something that I just couldn't agree with. But She was dong it and wasn't going to stop. I was devastated. I needed an exorcist to rid me of what I was feeling. The memories of when we were together filled my mind and I collapsed to the floor and cried myself to sleep.

***

"Hello, King Investigations." I said in my usual manner of answering the phone.

"Hi." It was Sam.

"Um, hi." I replied.

I wasn't being very enthusiastic about this call. I was a little surprised and it was no less than a day after I had got out of hospital. My head was still sore.

"He stood me up."

"Sorry?"

"PJ, He stood me up. We were supposed to go away this weekend, but He got a call from one of His mates who invited him out for Saturday night. Apparently He would prefer to spend time with His mates more than He wanted to be with me."

"I'm sorry to hear that, but why are you telling me this?"

Actually, I wasn't sorry to hear this. Vindictive I know, but all I wanted was Her. Now PJ may be out of the way. I couldn't believe I was thinking like this.

"I needed to tell someone, I needed someone to talk to." She said shakily.

"What about Jason?"

"He's taken off. Long story, but He said He needed some time away from me."

"I see. So, you've come to me, the guy whose heart you just ripped out." I said.

Maybe I was a little malicious, but it was true and She needed to hear it. The fact that I had promised my so-called Father that I wasn't going to see Her any more was beside the point.

"King, I want to explain something to you." She pleaded.

“Whatever it is I don’t want to hear it. You know how much you’ve hurt me?” I asked with a tremor in my voice.

“I know and that’s why I feel I owe you the truth.”

“The truth? To say that you’ve been in a five year relationship with someone else and that it’s you Brother…”

“Step Brother.” She corrected.

“…your Step Brother isn’t truth enough!” I was almost shouting down the phone. “So, you mean there’s more? Are you going to tell me you used to be a guy or something?”

“No, I just wanted you to know how it all came about, so you knew that I was never meant to hurt you.”

“Fuck me! I guess you should tell me then because, man, I’m hurting like a Mother fucker right now!”

There was a pause on the phone. I was getting worked up and I guess it wasn’t helping my situation at all. I knew that I wanted Her back, but things could never be as they were. Not with PJ in the picture. Suddenly I had visions of him being hit by a car or something.

“Look, I’m sorry, I’m not really in that good of a mood right now.” I said calmly.

“I understand how you’re feeling.”

“Oh, don’t even go there. You have no idea how I’m feeling. I guess you’re gonna say something like ‘It’s not you it’s me’. Well save it Sam. I have heard every line in the book and unless you’re going to tell me that you have recently had your heart ripped out and stamped on I don’t think that you have the first clue as to what I’m going through.”

“OK, maybe you’re right.” She started. “It was a stupid thing to say, but I couldn’t think of anything else. You’re not making it very easy. I just wanted to tell you the story.”

I was silent for a while trying to decide if this was going to make me feel better or worse than what I was already feeling.

"OK, spit it out." I said finally.

"When I was twenty I met this guy called PJ, well that's what everybody called him back then and it just stuck. He was the most wonderful guy that I had ever met and I fell in love almost instantly. We just clicked right away. It wasn't long after that we were going out and we tried to be together as much as possible. He came around to my place, I was still living with my folks at the time and He was always around for dinner. Now my parents were kind of old fashioned, OK, very old fashioned. They were full on catholic and didn't approve of premarital sex or anything even close to it. I was no virgin, not by a long shot, but they never knew about it. They thought I was pure and innocent, but I guess I was just a rebellious little bitch. They never knew about half the stuff that I got up to. I had even fallen pregnant once. It never came to anything because all the drugs I was taking at the time caused a miscarriage, which was just as well.

"Anyway, PJ and I were having a full on relationship and it was very sexual. You probably don't want to hear this, but He was the best. Now being that my parents couldn't know about it we hid the relationship from them, but not just them, the whole world. To this day there are only two people that know about us. You are the second."

"Jason knows right?"

"Yes. He knows all to well. But He's not going to say anything. He only found out because He caught us at it once. So, we had to keep it a secret all this time."

"I can hear the violins. I thought you said He was your Step Brother? I'm not following here." I interrupted.

"PJ was an only child. It was him and His Mother, that's about all He knew as His Father took off on His Mother when He found out that She was pregnant to PJ."

“So?”

“Let me continue. As PJ and I became closer and He was around at our place a lot my folks decided to invite His Mother around for diner one night. Anyway, one thing lead to another and both families became very close and best friends and all that. Worse luck for PJ and I. Now when I was twenty-three my Mother got cancer and died very quickly. Dad and I were so cut up about the whole thing and I used PJ for my support and Dad used PJ’s Mother as His support. It wouldn’t have been six months later that those two were married. Now PJ’s Mum is my Step Mother and PJ is my Step Brother.”

“I see now.” I said after a moments silence.

“And you can also see why we can’t go public.”

“Surely there is nothing wrong with that?”

“Listen, our family is screwed up enough with out some sort of semi-incestuous relationship happening.”

“Yeah, well, it hasn’t exactly made me feel any better.”

“It wasn’t supposed to. But I needed to explain what was going on.”

“OK, well I’m going to bed now I suggest you do the same thing.” I said and then hung up.

- 23 -

"I have some information for you about what you have been asking."

This was from my online contact. I had met this mystery person when I was searching for answers about what I was experiencing through this spiritualism thing.

"I need you to go into whisper mode as this is sensitive stuff."

"OK." I typed and clicked into whisper mode.

The sight I found was a chat site that catered for people who are interested in UFOs, ghosts and the likes.

"So, what is it you have for me?"

"Are you alone?" The name was Phoenix.

"No, I have six naked cheer leaders here dancing to the song 'You Sexy Thing'."

"Good, I don't want anyone else knowing about this."

"I think you're safe there." I responded.

"So, what do you know so far?"

"I'm not too sure," I said shuffling in my seat, "I kind of get the feeling that there is more to life than what we see."

"Yeah, that's right."

"OK, lets start there."

"Sure. What is your question?"

"Um, I don't get it at all. I really don't understand that." I typed.

"You're asking a very common question. It has been raised and speculated about in many debates, books and movies and everybody has a different opinion. Usually the question is more of a statement though. Kind of 'there must be more to life than this'."

"Yeah, sounds about right." I responded.

"Yours is different though. You know that what you see is not what you get and it haunts your dreams."

"You have no idea."

"OK. Think about a rock. You look at it and see a rock."

"With you so far." I typed.

This could take a very long time.

"Everything that you know about the rock tells you that it's actually made of particles and each particle is made up of many atoms."

"Yeah, school boy stuff."

"Well, do you see these atoms?" Asked Phoenix.

"I'm not Superman."

"But you know that they are there."

"Yes."

"Now you can look at the rock and see something different. The rock is not real." Explained Phoenix.

"Carry on, I think I'm getting the picture."

"That's just it. It's only a picture. What you see is not what you get. Life is a perception, it's not real. It's all in your mind."

Just then there was a knock at the door that made me jump and set my heart racing and my legs shaking.

"GTG!" I typed and switched the monitor off.

I got up and headed for the door. This strange feeling surrounded me. It was like something had happened, something was wrong. I opened the door and there standing in the hall was Sam. She was looking very dishevelled and tears stained Her face.

"What happened, what are you doing here?" I surprised myself.

"Jason's dead." She said and burst into tears.

I was stunned. I didn't know what to think! I stood looking at Her for a moment and then at the risk of the worst happening I took Her by the shoulder and lead Her in checking the hallway out of paranoia before shutting the door.

"What?" I said confused.

"Jason. The police just called and told me He had been in an accident. He's dead." She whimpered and fell to Her knees.

I actually felt terrible. I had wished this, but I wasn't seriously hoping He would die. Had I done this? No, it was just a coincidence.

"Are you alright?" I asked.

I was nervously remembering the warning not only from Odin, but also from that guy I met on the street. This was all too much to be just a coincidence. First Lorraine gets killed and She was very close to Sam. Now it's Jason. What was going on here?

"No. I can't believe it. It's only been a month since Lorraine died and now Jason is dead." She cried.

"None of this is your fault." I offered, but even I felt like it might just be. "It's just a terrible coincidence."

That word hung in the air like a dense fog.

"Odin told me that they were bad people. He said He was going to protect me against the evil in the world if I do His bidding. Does that mean they were evil?"

"What a load of shit. They were good people. I mean I never met them, but from what you told me they are - were - good people."

"You know that Odin is a good god." She said with sudden gusto.

"I'm not so sure that I know what you're talking about." I said trying to figure out where that had come from.

"Odin. Odin and Thor, they are good. They just want the world to know that they're back and they want to help out." She whimpered.

"I don't know who you're trying to convince here, but from what I have seen there's no good there." I said and was met with a sharp slap on the face.

I reeled back and looked at Her in stunned silence.

"How could you say that? You can't have seen them then. They are angels! Odin is a provider and protector then you say He's evil. Who the hell are you?" She shouted at me hysterically.

She was definitely out to lunch this time.

"What's gotten into you?" I said nursing my face with the palm of my hand.

"The truth. Don't you understand that people like you have just thrown all knowledge of Asgard into the ancient stories and passed them up as fables? Just some sort of hick theory of how the world might have been like for those poor sods hundreds of years ago."

She was so mad that She was crying again. This was starting to scare me and I moved away a bit.

"They are good gods!" She said looking me square in the eye.

Her body looked as though it had changed somewhat. I couldn't place it, maybe it was just the way She was standing, I don't know, but when I looked Her in the eye I suddenly saw a red glow in each pupil and I jumped. It was just a glimmer, but it was there. Fuck me, what's going on? The glow disappeared and, so did Her mood. She suddenly relaxed.

"So, if that's all I'll be going now." She said composing herself once more before She turned towards the door.

"Wait." I reacted and held onto Her arm.

"What? I need to go." She said pulling away.

"Well just let me check the hallway first. If you are seen leaving this place it could be very dangerous for the both of us."

"What do you mean?"

"I made a deal." I said looking at Her empathetically.

She looked at me strangely and shook Her head slightly as if to say that She didn't follow. The night had all of a sudden closed in and the room somehow got darker. The bulb in the lamp that sat on my desk suddenly exploded sending shards of glass splintering to the floor making the both of us jump and She gave a little shriek.

"What's going on here?" She asked apprehensively.

She was looking at me through the corner of Her eye while at the same time trying to see what had just happened.

"I'm not sure, but you being here isn't safe. I have been to Asgard and I know some thing's going down. Odin made a deal with me."

As soon as I had said that, my Private Investigators practising certificate somehow fell of its hook and smashed to the floor. Sam let out a louder shriek.

"That's it. I'm getting out of here." She shouted.

"Wait. I have to explain." I urged.

The floor started to vibrate a little and the glasses in the liquor cabinet where clinking together.

"But apparently not here." I added.

I grabbed my coat and jacket and headed for the door dragging Sam by the hand all the way. As I went to open the door the whiskey decanter exploded like a tan coloured grenade. At precisely that time there was a knock on the door, which scared the shit out of both of us. My heart took a ten-kilometre hike and when it came back everything went quiet. I caught Sam going to say something, so I cupped a hand over Her mouth and put a finger to my mouth.

"Shhhhh. You're not supposed to be here." I whispered. "Um, quick, hide."

I pushed Her into the bedroom as fast as I could and She slid under the bed. I rushed out of the bedroom and closed the door. My heart was racing and my hands were sweaty. I calmed myself down enough to answer the door.

"Who is it?"

"Bob, can I come in?" Came the voice from the other side.

It was a kid's voice. My god, could it be that girl that I almost bowled over. After securing the chain I carefully opened the door to peek out.

"Hi Bob. You're not busy are you?"

It was the kid. What the hell was going on here? How did She find me? Did I smoke something strange to make me paranoid? I was totally confused. I may be loosing it.

"What do you want kid?"

"To come in. I've got something for you." She said.

"How do you know my name?" I said in a shaky voice.

Everything seemed to be happening at once and none of it looked good.

"Lucky guess?"

"WHAT?"

This kid was having me on. There was something about Her that I didn't like. I mean apart from the fact that She knew me by a name that only my parents called me.

"It's a long story. Can I come in?"

This kid couldn't have been more than eight or nine maybe younger and She was talking like She was three times Her age. I didn't trust Her, I couldn't trust Her because one thing is for sure; things like this don't just happen. She was shifting Her weight from foot to foot and starting to get impatient. OK, now She was acting Her age. I unhooked the chain and let Her in.

"So, what have you got for me?" I asked sceptically.

"This." She said and produced my wallet. "You dropped it when you bumped into me a while back."

"Oh, OK. Thanks kid." I said.

I was a little dazed and more than a bit relieved.

"Why are you so nervous around me? And my name is Billy."

"Ah huh, you mean like Billy the kid? Nice one."

Sarcasm just happens to be something that I am very good at when I don't know what else to do.

"What?" She just stared at me.

"Nothing. Thanks kid, I mean Billy. There are not many honest people around any more."

"No problem. Sorry, do you have someone here?" She said craning Her head to try and see past me.

"What do you mean?" I frowned.

"Well, it smells like perfume. Have I come at a bad time?" She said looking at me curiously.

"Yes, I mean no. I mean, no I don't have anyone here and yes it's a bad time. I haven't had the best of days." That was true.

"OK, I'll just go then."

She finished then turned and walked out the door. I swear nothing like this has ever happened to me before. I was more than a little freaked and I didn't have the first clue how to deal with it. I needed a drink. Damn! That idea went out the window when it exploded. And what the fuck is with that? An exploding whiskey decanter? Sam, shit! I ran to my room and flung open the door and stopped just as abruptly as I saw Sam floating about three inches above the bed.

"What? Is this the fucking Twilight Zone?" I said under my breath. "SAM!!!" I shouted.

I rushed over to Her and as soon as I touched Her She fell to the bed and woke up.

"What the hell is going on?" I demanded. "I have exploding bulbs and whiskey decanters, I have you with the glowing eyes and this little girl that knows my name and now it's you again, but this time hovering above the bed! What the fucks going on?"

"I really don't know King, but you're starting to scare me." She said innocently.

"Look I think you're bad news. I don't know what's gotten into you and what the hell has turned my office into the house on haunted hill, but you've got to get out of here until I can figure out how to get us out of this mess!"

"You're kicking me out?" She said and started to cry again. "You're kicking me out again?"

"I have no choice. You're in danger and I think my office is trying to eat me." I reasoned.

"I need you King. I can't be on my own. Not tonight, please." She sobbed.

"As much as I hate to say this why don't you go and shack up with PJ tonight while I try to get some answers here. You'll be alright. Go be with your um…family!"

I can't believe I just said that.

"OK, if you insist. Call me tomorrow." She said sorrowfully and left.

This was just not my night. I closed the door and slid down onto the floor as the last bulb popped.

"Fucking great!" I whispered in the dark.

- 24 -

It was chaos in my head and I was loosing control, loosing focus. Odin must be behind all of this. I can't be sure of that because it seems like everything is just a figment of my imagination. I was sitting at my desk with a glass of cheap bourbon that I found under the kitchen sink in one hand and a cigarette in the other. I guess at some thing's I'm just not a quitter. The room was clouded with the tobacco, it was a smell I was familiar with and that's what I needed at the moment. Everything was just so up in the air. Every time I think about something that has happened, my thoughts always come back to Sam; the accident, Lorraine's death, Jason's death and that scary little girl, Billy. Not to mention the dreams I had been having about Asgard. This is just not sanity! That girl though, where does She fit in to any of this? It all seemed perfectly reasonable and explainable, She was just dropping off my wallet. I mean, granted it has been almost a month since the accident and She could have come around earlier to drop it off. Then a thought occurred to me. I took a drag from my cigarette and tried to piece something together because something didn't add up. I reached around and brought the keyboard across and switched on the monitor, maybe I could find something that I haven't been looking for. Something that I've been missing all this time. As the monitor was lit up I drained my glass and began to refill it when I realized that after I had left the hospital I went and bought a paper.

I bought a bloody paper!

How could I have bought a paper if I didn't have my wallet? I got down to work mapping out a who's who and a time line of all the events that had happened since I met Sam. First of course, there was Sam. She was twenty five, but an mature twenty five. I don't even know what I meant by that, but I typed it in. There was PJ, Her Step Brother who She is having an affair with that nobody knows about. OK, so those circumstances are not as bad as they sounded when I first heard them, but still.

There is the girl, Billy. How did She have my wallet? Hang on; too far, I've skipped a bit here. There has to be some other connections. I never met Ray and Rena before and I may never meet them, but Sam talked about them all the time, so I typed that in. There were still a few parts missing here and there and I needed to find them. I knew what they were, I had to. I was only out of it for a few days seemingly in a coma. That dream I had, maybe it wasn't my imagination. After what Sam had told me about Her time there, brief as it may be, and the way She described it – I must be going mad, but I wrote that into the time line. It was after this point that some very strange things started to happen. There were Sam's glowing eyes and what the hell was that all about? And Her voice! Before the accident there was that voice that came from Her. I remember now, how could I have forgotten that? What was it She said? Something about 'I am He that you shall call Odin'. It can't be that simple. Is a god somehow making things happen around Her? Alright, I'll admit that if Odin is a god then He can obviously make things happen, but why all of a sudden? I needed a bit more help on how these things work. Where would I go? Who would I talk to? I'm the one who is supposed to have all the answers here. I got up and moved around trying to get some blood flow to the brain. I stretched and yawned. I needed some breakfast as it was about ten AM and I was starving.

***

By the time I got to the coffee shop it was eleven thirty and almost time for lunch so that's what I decided on. There were so many things on my mind as I sat down to a hearty serving of eggs, toast, bacon and hash browns. I couldn't get it out of my mind that Lorraine and Jason were dead because of Sam. I hadn't met either of them, but Sam spoke of them a lot. Were they getting too close to what was going on? Was it some sort of conspiracy? If I was to believe my dream about Asgard then I would have to say yes. But what could Lorraine and Jason do to Sam that could stop Odin doing whatever it was that He was up to? Then there was the guy who stopped me in the street telling me that Sam was bad news and to stay away from Her. He was warning me about something, but what did He know? I was almost killed by crashing into Lorraine and Sam, Lorraine *was* killed. Was I getting too close to Sam, was I in danger of my life? It all started to make a little bit of sense. So, why did Sam come to see me? She hired me to do a job and this wasn't in the brochure. I know that at times Sam just hadn't been herself and in fact at times I was quite scared of Her. I've heard of possession, but this was a little far fetched wasn't it? Was it? It was like She was on a war path right up to Odin's back door.

"Excuse me sir." Said a young lady and I almost spat my egg over the table.

"Err, yes?" I replied.

"Next week there is a meeting on for a new church. Read this and I hope to see you there." She handed over a pamphlet, smiled and left.

Not the most unusual thing to happen to me in the last twenty four hours, but it rated right up there. I flipped through the pamphlet while chewing on a piece of bacon. Evidently there was a new church formed called the COO. That's really all it said and they were to have their first meeting in a weeks time outside the old library at the DTOAS. Usually this would have been of no interest and I would have chucked it then and there, but this time, however, after all the goings on around here it may just have been what I was looking for. You never know. So, I pocketed it and concentrated on finishing my lunch.

There was one other thing that was getting at me. Ray and Rena. Sam never did say what had happened to them. Did they get killed too? No, She would have said something. I don't know, maybe I was still cut up about Sam dumping me and I was trying to come up with some lame ass reason for it all. At the end of the day it did sound like I was being paranoid. I knew the reason, it was PJ. Plain and simple. She loved him, always had, and that's who She wanted to be with. The better and younger man won. And that's another thing, He was Her age and I could have been Her Father. Yeah I got hurt big time. I kind of figure sometimes that I'm only in this life to get hurt and walked over. I always thought that I must have done something really bad when I was younger or in a previous life. Someone once told me that these things happen for a reason; I'd really like to know what that reason is. They said that the stuff that is happening to me now is making me stronger for what is coming, something fantastic, but I'm not ready for it yet. It's like if I won a billion dollars; unless I knew what to do with it I would probably waste it and I'd end up worse off than I am now. It's like I would be ready for it once I have learnt how to handle money. I never did like that guy!

- 25 -

"See, that's the thing. I don't know where I got it from." I said naively.

The guy behind the counter eyed me suspiciously.

"Did you find it at a flea market or something?" He questioned.

The shop was dark and quiet and I had to watch what I said; I guess He dealt with dodgy types all the time.

"It was a long time ago. It may have been a present or something." I lied.

He wasn't buying it.

"I drink a lot and things are a bit hazy you see." I added.

I don't think He believed me, but there were no more questions and He refocused His attention on the amulet.

"This is really something." He nodded.

There was a long silence before He went on.

"I can't be sure, but I think I know…" He trailed off and turned to consult His shelf full of books.

I could feel the tension building or was that just me? He found the book He was looking for and opened it on the counter with a thump. Flicking through the pages He muttered a few exited words before stopping at the page He wanted and slapping His finger on a picture.

"That's it!" He smiled.

I looked up at him waiting for more information.

"If this is real," He continued, "and I have a feeling it is," He paused taking a closer look at the amulet, "then its centuries old."

That's what I was afraid of. This was getting way too creepy for my liking.

"In fact according to this," He said referring back to the book, "it's the Optic Woden!"

“Huh?” I grunted.

“The Eye of Odin. This is the artefact, *the* artefact – the amulet the Nordics created as an offering to the Father of the gods himself. Where the hell did you get it?” He asked again.

I was speechless. All I could do was shake my head.

“I will have to get my people to look at this, but I think this is it. The only one in existence and it’s priceless. I’ve got to make a phone call.” He said turning to the phone.

“No, wait. Um, I’ll get back to you on that one.” I said grabbing it back off him. “Thanks though.” I said heading for the door leaving the owner looking rather dumbfounded.

***

So, it was all true. I guess I believed it, but I had my doubts until now. It’s not the first time in this adventure where everything that I’ve known has been turned upside down by new information. But now it looks like I have the proof in the form of a priceless amulet given to me by the Norse Father of the gods himself who also claims to be my Father. Though I couldn’t stop asking myself what it meant to be half-immortal? What does this mean about Sam and what looks like possession? I had to step things up a bit and get to the bottom of it all.

- 26 -

There was a knock on the door. Who could that be at this hour? It was about eleven PM and I'd had a few drinks. I wasn't really in the mood for visitors especially if it was Sam. I got up and walked towards the door when whoever it was knocked again.

"I'm coming, I'm coming." I hissed.

I opened the door and to my surprise it was the guy I had run into on the street a couple of days ago.

"Hi." He said.

"What the fuck do you want?"

"Um, can I come in? I have something for you." He said.

"Who are you?"

"My name is Paul, that's all you need right now."

"How do you know me?" I asked.

"Let me in and I'll explain." He said pushing His way past me.

"Do you have any idea what time it is?" I said looking at my naked wrist.

"Yeah. It's been a rough day do you mind if I grab a drink?" Inquired Paul.

"Be my guest, that's what it's there for." I answered as He wondered over to the liquor cabinet.

All I had was the cheap bourbon, but He didn't seem to mind.

"Can I pour you one also?" He said looking at me.

"Please." I smiled dryly.

He was right, it had been a rough day. With one thing and another I was feeling tired, weary and I was looking forward to slipping myself into another relaxing drink. In fact I was waiting for him to leave, so I could make my way over to the desk with the bottle in one hand and a glass in the other. Paul prepared two glasses with ice and poured a good serving into each glass. Putting the bottle down and picking up the two glasses He padded across to me and proffered me the first and raised the second one in a toast.

“Cheers.” He said.

“Cheers.” I reciprocated.

“I do like this office. It could do with some brightening up though.’

“Why are you here?”

“I have some information for you. Something that you might find quite interesting. It’s a about Odin.”

“How the hell did you…” I jumped in.

“All in good time, yours is not to wonder why just use me while you have me.” He said with a wry smile.

I wasn’t too sure that I liked His smoothness, but one must go with the flow I guess. I had a sip of my drink and felt it making it’s way down my throat. It felt good.

“So, who are you anyway?” I asked.

“That really doesn’t matter.”

“So, how do I know to trust you?”

“Do you trust anyone?”

“Not really.” I admitted

“Well it wouldn’t matter how I answered that now would it.”

“I suppose not. So, what do you know?” I said taking another sip of my drink, cueing him to carry on.

“I know that Odin has an Achilles heel.” He said with a raised brow.

“Like what?” I took another sip and I started to feel the alcohol working.

My body relaxed a little and I could feel the pressure of the day slip away and found myself getting more curious about this man in front of me that claimed He knew about Odin.

“Let’s just say that one of His many is a real rat bag.” He said cryptically.

"Are you saying that it's something from the other world?" I asked.

"Your words, not mine. Remember that all worlds are connected and nothing that you know about is real. There is another dimension, well lots of other dimensions and all that you see is a figment of your imagination." He said taking a large draw from His own glass and draining.

"I'm not following."

"You want another?" He said tipping His glass.

"Sure." I drained the last of my drink and handed him the glass.

"You see," He continued as He walked over to the bottle, "we consider this world to be real. It's how we forget about the confusion and the things we don't understand. But just because we forget about it doesn't mean it's not there."

He poured two more larger drinks and came back over to me.

"That should put some hair on your chest." He said as He handed me the glass.

"Why would we want to forget about some other world. All that we could learn could be right at our fingertips. All the knowledge, all the answers; why would we pass that up."

"Some of us don't, my friend. Some of us don't." He said provocatively, trying to urge the conversation on. "You see we are all in this world to try to learn about who we really are. Some try to control that. Some, like our friends in Asgard, are a bit sore that we have forgotten and would like to take their revenge on this imaginary world."

"So?"

"So, they try to poison our minds by making us believe that we have no choice about this world and we are merely following our destiny, our fate. The thing is we do have a choice in what happens to us. We can change the course of our lives because that combined consciousness has given us free will and the power to go where and when we please while at the same time everything happens for a reason."

"That all sounds very confusing."

"That's why we want to forget about it all and pretend that what we see is real and living our lives is nothing to do with us. So, we leave our fate to the gods."

What He was saying did sound kind of familiar. I downed my second drink in one and felt the increased effect as my body relaxed more and my mind started to wonder. I felt very much at peace as though nothing really mattered right now.

"So, how do the gods do that? I've met them and they are nothing, but brutes."

"That's one way to put it I guess. Let me try to illustrate. How's your drink by the way?"

"I could use another one." I said almost automatically.

"You see. The alcohol is taking away inhibitions, taking away your minds control over the situation and allowing your subconscious to come to the fore and make your decisions for you. That is like what the gods do with their powerful, almost hypnotic forces."

"No matter how drunk I get there are some things that I just wouldn't do though."

"You say that now. But I think I could change that."

With that He took the glass and placed it on the table next to His. Paul straitened up and looked me right in the eyes.

"When the subconscious mind takes over it has the power to do two things. First, it takes you where you really want and need to go hence your subconscious becomes your conscious and you follow. It also offers you the pleasures and the happiness of freedom and the excitement of life that in any normal situation seems dull and boring. This is how we were meant to live."

"I'm not following."

"Your conscious is now being controlled by your subconscious. Now that the rooms in your mind are open they are susceptible to suggestions of pleasure."

"Like what?"

He took a step closer and opened His eyes wider. He had the most incredible green eyes, almost hypnotic. As I stared into them He inched forward, so that I could start to feel the heat of His face on mine. This was starting to worry me. I hope He was just playing around. My heart started to beat faster and I could feel my body shaking. I smelt the bourbon on His breath and the Old Spice on His skin, I closed my eyes. Just then as if I was almost willing it to happen He kissed me on the lips. My eyes shot open and I took a sharp breath in and stumbled backwards a little.

"What are you doing?!" I exclaimed.

He just smiled at me and came closer still, giving me a long kiss on the lips. This wasn't supposed to be happening. My body was taking this in. Like a forbidden pleasure. I couldn't do anything and His lips were on mine and for some reason I wasn't able to pull back. I swallowed heavily and before I knew it, somehow, my mouth opened and before I had time to think His tongue was playing inside. I couldn't understand this. My body went into autopilot and I found myself kissing him back. I was playing with His tongue and starting to enjoy it. At this point I had no choice and I let myself fall under His spell. I have never had any thoughts about this type of encounter before and the mere mention of it used to make me feel sick. But here I was kissing this man as He started to embrace me. I was shaking like a leaf and there was nothing that I could do, or wanted to do, to stop it. Somehow He had moved me over to a near by wall and pinned me to it. The feeling of excitement and exhilaration filled me and I could feel a stirring in my pants. This was so wrong, but it felt so right. His hands were all over me like a rash. I felt them here and I felt them there. He broke away and started to kiss my neck, so I threw my head back and took a long breath in as He started to undo the buttons on my shirt. Lower and lower His hands moved as He came back up to my mouth and kissed me deeper. With grace and precision He had my belt undone then He reached for my fly and button of my pants. Suddenly His warm fingers were around my member and the feeling shot threw me like a thunderbolt. This was definitely something new and for the life of me I didn't want it to stop. My pants fell to the floor and as He pulled away again He started to kiss my neck once more. My dick was as hard as a rock and the way He was stroking me I felt like I was in heaven. His kisses started to creep lower. An unbelievable pleasure rocked my body as I felt His tongue play on my nipple. How could this be happening? With one long lick He lowered himself to His knees and started to massage my penis in long, slow strokes with both of His hands. I just looked at him and when He looked up I saw the passion in His eyes. The anticipation was killing me, so I flicked my head back and closed my eyes as I felt His warm breath on me. Then it struck home. His mouth was on me. I was in His mouth and the feeling was indescribable! He did things with His tongue that I have never had from any woman. Some thing He was doing drove me wild. My god this was incredible. Never have I felt like this before and I thought I was going to cum right then and there. He then took long, slow draws of my member each time taking it in further and further until I could feel the uneven ridges of His throat. Then the sensation of a vacuum as He sucked hard and deep. I felt a ball of pressure building up and I knew I couldn't hold on much longer, then I asked my self why. Why was I holding on? Paul said this was a life of happiness and we should use it to our advantage. Man I was on the edge, so I let go of myself and went with it. The pressure inside me built to a crescendo and I exploded in His mouth. A shudder of pure ecstasy thudded threw me. An utter feeling of calmness fell on me as I released something in me that I never knew I had. While Paul drank me down I slowly regained my composure and I felt myself go limp in His mouth. He raised slowly with a smile on His face and I opened my eyes to look at him. He looked very sexy right now, but that could have been the alcohol and the moment. The alcohol!

"What did you put in my drink?!"

"Just a little something to help you relax. Did you enjoy that?"

"Like you wouldn't believe." I replied with a big, happy smile.

With that He kissed me again and I could taste myself on His tongue. The sweet salty taste of pleasure and passion. It dripped into my mouth and down my throat. I swallowed hard as my heart started to thump again.

"You don't have to you know." He whispered in my ear.

"I want to." I didn't know where that came from, but it was true.

This was something that I couldn't understand. It filled every pour in my body. I wanted to do this with all my soul. But why? With that thought He went to the bottle yet again and left me there with my shirt unbuttoned and my pants around my ankles. I really was in a world of my own just then lapping at the wonderful feeling of peace. All I could do is watch him as He poured my drink. This time it was quite clear what He was doing. He produced this small bag of what appeared to be some sort of white powder. Delicately He tapped on the bag until a small amount of it dropped into my drink, and then His. He smiled at me and brought it over. I downed it in one and He did the same. Discarding the glasses onto the small table He lightly took my hand and led me into the bedroom where we both fell onto the bed.

"So, what was that you put into our drinks?"

"2C-B."

"Wow! Where did you get that from. Didn't think anybody made that any more!"

"I have my ways."

"You certainly do." I laughed.

"Good, so how do you feel now?"

"Like I want to fuck you." I said right out of the blue.

I had no idea where that came from, but I'm glad I said it.

"That would be nice, but I'm not that easy." He said with a smile.

"What do you mean?"

"I think you owe me a little bit of that tongue action."

I was stunned, I really was. Am I really going to do this? Am I really going to give this guy a blow job? I couldn't believe it. This was not me at all, but I liked it.

"You only live once I guess." I said with resignation.

With that I slowly moved on top of him and gave him a long, slow kiss. This was amazing, never in my dreams had I thought I would ever be doing this. As I was thinking this I found myself moving slowly down His neck then I pulled His T-shirt off to expose His chest. Not a hair on it and His muscle definition was startling. I didn't know what He did for a living, but it made him look good. I couldn't help myself, I had to taste His chest. I licked up the middle and onto His neck then down again to His nipple. I felt His body move and I circled the nodule of flesh on His well-developed peck. It was salty, like playing with a woman's breast, but harder. I could feel him breath deeply as I moved down slowly to His navel. Just the thinnest hint of downy hair tickled my tongue. At this point I was straddling His legs then I sat up and moved myself down a bit, so I had access to His belt and zipper. This was just not happening. What was I doing? Even as I was thinking this I had His belt undone and I was slowly opening His fly. He wore these baby blue silk boxers that did something funny to me. I put all my weight on my legs and raised myself a little to hook my fingers into His pants and with one smooth motion I stripped both His pants and boxers off His body. There I was face to face with His dick, which was stiff as a board just looking at me. I could smell the hormones and the excitement and a shiny drop of pre-cum found it's way to the tip of His member. He was clean shaved and I don't know what it was, but it brought up some very unnatural feelings inside of me. I tentatively placed my fingers around it. What a weird sensation this was. To feel another man's penis. I heard him moan, so I knew I must have been doing something right. I brought the foreskin up and over the top of the head and down again, slowly repeating this until I found my rhythm. I pictured giving myself pleasure and used that to try and please Paul. It seemed to be working because I could feel His dick pulsating in my hand. This was it. If I was going to do it I had to do it now. I lowered my head just a little and I could smell the musty sent of His member. My heart raced and I could feel my own dick get harder. I opened my mouth and licked the droplet off the tip of His head and swallowed. It tasted good. For some reason I had always thought that it would be too salty and horrible to even contemplate. But now I found myself wanting more. I opened wide and took His entire member into my mouth to feel the warm, meaty flesh. I closed my lips around the shaft and started to massage His penis with my tongue. The noise He was making turned me on and the want in me grew to a hunger as I greedily sucked. I was enjoying it all and I don't know if it was five minutes or an hour, but all of a sudden I felt Paul arch His body. With a sudden, enormous throbbing He released into my mouth the sweetest tasting warm liquid that I hungrily swallowed down. Wave after wave of His semen flowed over my tongue and down my throat giving me a high that I have never felt before. My head went swimmy and my body collapsed next to His.

***

The next thing I knew it was three AM and I woke up naked in my bed. The smell of sex filled the room. I rolled over to see Paul had gone. What a night, but now what?

- 27 -

"Are you ready for some more?" Asked Phoenix.

It was about ten AM and I decided I needed some more answers, so I was sitting at my computer once more.

"Yes." I typed.

"Now you're not going to run off again are you?" He joked.

"I promise."

"Good enough for an electronic geek like me. Now what you have to remember is that nothing is real OK."

"I still don't fully understand that, but keep going." I urged.

I could hear the rain start outside and felt something change in the atmosphere.

"Where should we start?"

"How about 'in the beginning…'?" I said trying to lighten the mood.

"That would be great if it were like that, but from what you already know, how could it be. That is just man's arrogant view of man." He typed.

I was lost again. Every time I heard a different side of things it seemed to contradict what had already been said.

"I don't understand. In the bible it says that God created man. I don't get arrogance from that, I get humble from that."

"Simple. Man has not always been intelligent. There has been a very large space of time where man was nothing more than a dumb ape. Doesn't really make God look very good if man was made from His image now does it?" He typed.

"Seems to me that there is a huge chasm between what we know of creation and what we know of evolution. Looks like it's not so much a case of believing in both any more." I typed.

"Don't go there. You would be making the mistake of those that were around when the first fossils were found. What you have to remember is that the bible was put together by man and at that stage man was dominant. The only way to keep it that way is to write God as a man and make man God's choice. The Patriarchal society would forever continue."

He was definitely making some sense now.

"So, how did it start? Why did they write Genesis the way it is?" I asked, baiting the hook for my theological unravelling.

"As it says in the bible, you just have to see it from a different point of view."

"Like how?"

"OK, in the beginning God created Man."

"Yep, that's how it goes and that's what we have just disproved."

"No we haven't. We have just proved that there is another way to look at it. So, in the beginning Humans discovered God. To say that God created man is saying that man is apart from God. This is just not true. Everything is part of everything else and therefore man came from god as part of god to discover the world that was of god also. What they are trying to show us in Genesis is the first time that man shrugged off the blanket of ignorance and became aware of who and what He was." He typed.

I was totally overwhelmed. All this time I felt that the bible had to be right, but then all the evidence to prove the contrary was dug up. All through time people have been trying to disprove the Bible when all they have been doing is proving it. How many people are there out in the big wide world of ours that have seen what I have just seen?

"Do you mind if we finish for today?" I said as my head spun.

I took a large sip from my coffee reminding myself that it was time to replace the broken decanter.

"Sure. Are you OK?"

"Yes, I just don't think I can take everything in at once."

"Wise call. I'll talk to you next time then." He said and signed off.

I reached over to turned the monitor off and just sat there in the blackness listening to the rain and thinking about all that Phoenix had said. Every time He tells me something it's like I already knew it I had just somehow forgotten it. And then it's like all of a sudden I remember. I'd kick myself for forgetting, but I don't think that I have ever forgotten. It's so hard to explain the way I feel.

- 28 -

"Excuse me, Mr Kingly."

I was walking down Q2 Street on my way to the library when I heard this. I wasn't paying much attention to those surrounding me until I heard my name. It was a busy street and for the most part people kept to themselves not wanting to make any trouble with anyone else. I turned around and saw this man standing right behind me.

"Shit!" I said with a fright.

He was tall with grey hair and I had never seen him before in my life. 'Not again' I was thinking, what does this guy want?

"Who's asking?" I said.

"Detective Simon Rous."

"What's this about Detective?"

"Are you in fact Robert Kingly?"

"I am."

"Are you working a case involving a Miss Samantha Samson?"

"And I ask again, what's this all about?" Client confidentiality has always been a big thing with me.

"Could you accompany me down to central Mr Kingly?" He said.

"If you stop calling me Kingly."

As I said this an unmarked car pulled up to the curb.

"OK, Sir, what shall I call you?"

"King."

"That's a bit arrogant isn't it?" He said with a raised eyebrow.

"You don't know me very well then do you. That's what everybody calls me and until now it hasn't been an issue."

"I guess it remains to be seen then."

"So, what is this all about Detective, or shall I just call you Dick?"

"Detective will be fine." He said in a short tone.

He grabbed me by the arm rather forcefully and escorting me into the car. It must have been more serious than I first thought because the car squealed away from the curb and into the busy street with the siren on and the grill lights flashing. We had a short trip into central and until we had all been seated in the interview room, not a word had been spoken.

"Do you know Samantha Samson?" He questioned again.

There were two uniformed police standing guard by the door playing witness. I knew the drill all too well. Their homework had obviously been done as they were playing this one by the book. A small neon sign above the door with 'RECORDING' printed on it was glowing and the three cameras that were dotted around the room were pointed at me.

"Where are you from Detective?" I asked nonchalant.

"Why do you ask?"

"Because this is my old station and I've never seen you before."

"That's right King, or should I call you Sergeant?"

"That was a while ago now Detective. So?" I prompted.

"So, I was transferred up from Wellington after the shoot out on Second Fort Street." He said as He stared at me blankly.

About five years ago there was a brown out Downtown where a couple of the underground cables had exploded. This lead to a few small riots, but nothing too serious. One of the riots resulted in a shoot out between the police and four armed rioters. Ten cops were killed before the offenders were eventually taken out. I looked him in the eye waiting for His next move.

"Do you know Her or not?" He said, His patients starting to wear thin.

"And what about these two goof balls?" I said pointing at the two cops by the door. "Who are these guys?"

"New recruits." He said.

He knew what I was up to and I knew what He was up to. I had done this before a number of times. The only thing He could do was ask the questions and answer mine.

"Do they have permission from their mothers to be here?"

The two cops looked at each other and then back at me like they wanted to kill me then and there. They shifted their weight from side to side and became a little uncomfortable as I smiled back at them.

"Do you mind King? Just answer the question."

He stood up and wondered around the room trying to stretch His legs and calm himself down. It wasn't a big room, just big enough for a table and two chairs. It was bland and lifeless to make anybody who was unlucky enough to be interrogated feel nervous.

"Why? What do you want from Her?"

"She is the prime suspect in a murder."

"Impossible!" I said in a slightly raised voice.

No way could She be into anything the police would want Her for.

"So, you do know Her?"

"I wouldn't be here if you thought otherwise now would I?" I was starting to get a little annoyed now.

"For the record, King, do you know Samantha Samson or not."

"She's my client for fuck sake! Yes I know Her!" I was shouting now.

No matter how bad I was feeling about what She had put me through I still had a soft spot for Her.

"And I know She hasn't done anything wrong." I added

"We think otherwise." He said flatly

"Like what? What do you think you know?" I asked.

"We can't give out information like that."

"Don't give me that shit. You know you can. You know that if I can expand your theories in any way then the information you have can be disclosed."

The Detective gave a long sigh.

"OK. Jason Parsons was killed." He said sitting down.

"Yeah, in a car accident." I said watching him.

"No, King, He was dead before the car left the road."

"What are you saying?"

"He was poisoned." Said the Detective in less than an empathetic voice.

He pulled out a pack of cigarettes from His top pocket and offered me one silently. I shook my head and He shrugged taking one out for himself and put the pack on the table.

"And you think Sam did that? The only exercise you guys get is jumping to conclusions isn't it. What makes you think that She has anything to do with this?"

"Jason Parsons was one of Her best friends, and so was Lorraine Pierce." He said lighting His cigarette.

"So?"

"Lorraine was poisoned also."

"Her neck was broken!" I spat.

"In the accident, yes. But She was dead before that."

"I don't believe I'm hearing this. I don't believe you." I shook my head.

"We have the Pathology report if you want to see it for yourself." He turned and started to ask one of the cops to get it.

"That's OK, I believe you. What I don't get is why you think that it's Sam that poisoned either of them."

It was my turn to stand up and walk around a little. I was lost. I didn't know what to think.

"Lorraine was dead before the accident. Samantha was obviously aware of this as She was in the same car."

"I was told that Lorraine was driving."

"By whom?" He said.

"By Sam. Shit, I guess that doesn't really mean anything does it. Maybe She found Her in that state and was just trying to rush Her to hospital to try and save Her life. Have you ever thought of that?" I protested.

I finished my pacing and leaned over with my hands on the table and looked him right in the eye.

"Have you?"

"Is that what She told you?"

"No, She said that Lorraine had died in the accident. But She did have a nasty bump on the head and She could have forgotten about what actually happened!"

"Do you believe that, King?"

"I'm trying to." I said pathetically.

I stood up tall and wondered the room again trying to get through this.

"The hospital is on the other side of town, She was heading in the wrong direction. Whatever you say as a defence for Her isn't going to stand up in a court. Lorraine was dead before the accident and Sam knew it. Not only did She know it, but we believe that She was trying to dispose of the body because She was heading in the direction of Old Auckland."

"To do what?"

"Well, we can't be sure of course, but we have a strong feeling that She was going to dump the body over the dykes and into the sludge."

I stood there for a time just thinking. How could this be? Sam wasn't like that. Sure She had a few unexplainable things happen to Her and a couple of those I was part of or witnessed. But murder? Why, what would She have to gain? I took my seat again.

"Do you have a motive?" I asked.

"Not yet, well, none that we can rely on." He said a little uncomfortably.

"What do you mean? You have a theory don't you, you must have something."

"Yes, but it sounds ridiculous and I don't want to use it."

"Detective, you and I both know that the more bazaar the motive, the more likely it is to be true."

"You really want to hear it?"

"I wouldn't have asked now would I? What you keep forgetting is that She is my client and She is in danger of Her life. She doesn't even know it yet. She came to me for protection and to help Her solve a few issues. Now if there is anything that you have that could make my job a little easier no matter how fucked up it is I want to hear it."

"We have some insider information." He sighed resigning to the fact that He couldn't get out of telling me. "She is planning some sort of rebellion or something in this city. It could be nothing, but if She is planning what we think She is planning then She needed to get rid of anybody who knows Her too well. I'm afraid to say that one of those people could be you."

"The fact that my life is in danger because of this woman is no news to me, but taking over the city? That's a new one." I allowed a smirk.

"Maybe, but do you have any light that you could shed on the situation at all? Anything that could help us? I know that it's not what usually happens around these parts, but if you could help us with our work we will help you out with yours." He said with a grin.

I had no idea about what He was getting at. All that Sam needed was a little bit of protection and they want Her behind bars.

"So, if I can find out where She is you will take Her into custody and She would be safe until the trial."

"At least until the trial. By that time, with your help, we may have got to the bottom of all this and all our worries will fade away into the distance."

"OK. I don't have any info at the moment, but I will keep in touch."

"King, you were a good cop and I dare say that you are a great PI. I'm sure we can work this thing out quickly. I look forward to working with you. The stories of your Father impressed me. Hope you're made of the same stuff. For now though, you can go. Just keep in contact." He smiled.

With that He got up with the two police guards in toe leaving me there to think.

***

I got a lift to the library by one of my old police buddies I happened to bump into outside the station. We had a bit of a chat and promised to meet up for coffee one day and catch up. I was really in a rush to find out all I could about what was going on, so I couldn't spend a long time with him. I went into the library and was hit by that musty smell of old books that I could never get used to. I didn't know where to start and I stood in the middle of the library for about two minutes just thinking about what I had heard. There has to be more to this than what they lead me to believe. I couldn't believe that someone like Sam was a killer, but then I guess you never really know what a killer is like until they start to kill. But not Sam. Though this could be me trying to hide away from the denial because of our relationship. The library was empty apart from a lone staff member at the counter flipping through some returns and a couple of kids quietly giggling as they were thumbing through the pages of a

National Geographic magazine. I slowly moved my way down the first isle I came to trying to figure out were I might start when I noticed that there was another person sitting in one of the three couches provided for readers. She looked up and smiled at me with one of the warmest smiles I've seen for a long time. She was short, very short and although She was sitting down I could tell that She was only about 5"2' or there about. She had long, dark, wavy hair with dark red streaks and a girl-next-door type face. Not the most beautiful girl, but She was sweet looking and attractive. Let's just say She was the type of girl who looked like She could be a lot of fun. I looked around a bit and saw a sign advertising the section for religions, so I strolled over to it and began my search.

"Hi." Came a voice from behind me.

I was startled, but managed to keep my composure. I turned around to see who my stalker was. It was the girl who was just smiling at me.

"You gave me a fright. Hi." I said weakly.

"Sorry about that. I noticed that you were looking in the religious section. Not many people go directly there it seems that God is dead these days right."

"Yeah, I guess you're right. Do you get into all of this stuff?"

"You could say that. I would say I like to keep an eye on the world. In case you haven't noticed there are a lot of very strange things that have happened lately."

"No shit." I said. "Ah, sorry. I didn't mean to offend or anything."

"That's alright." She said smiling. "I like people that can speak their mind."

"You have no idea."

"The name's Sophia." She said offering Her hand.

"Hi Sophia," reaching out and shaking Her hand, "you can call me King."

"King, that's an unusual name."

"I've been getting that a lot lately." I responded and realised that I was still shaking Her hand. "Sorry." I let go and looked away "So, strange things you say."

"Yeah. I have a theory on it."

"I'd like to hear it." Was I flirting?

"Come, sit down and I'll tell you." She said with another fantastic smile.

Was She flirting? She wouldn't have been any more that about twenty five and She walked with grace. I followed Her to the couch and sat down next to Her.

"So, what's this theory of yours then?"

"Have you heard of the Norse gods?" She said striking a cord.

"I have become more familiar with them over the last couple of weeks, yes."

"That's the basis of all our beliefs. A very long time ago when man was first discovering himself everything was so unknown to him. There were a few things that became very important like fire, water, air and earth. These are the four elements; it's what makes us and what keeps us alive. Without all four of those we just couldn't exist, so they needed protecting."

"OK, I'm following so far."

"You and I both know that you can't protect something like air or fire or the other two, but what we can do is make something that can look after it for us. Thus the gods were born. Early man was much more intelligent than what we give them credit for. You see there is something out there, something that runs the whole show if you know what I mean. Some call it the spirit, some call it God. I call it the ethereal being. The thing that is everything and nothing."

"OK, slow down. How can something be everything and nothing? That doesn't make sense." I said shuffling in my seat, so I could face Her.

"It's the ultimate paradox. You see if something is everything, then it must be nothing as well. Now this ethereal being is everything. The clouds, the ground, the sea and the fire. It's part of us and we are part of it. Early man had this feeling about the ethereal being and the fact that it provided everything for them. Now what they did was divide it up, I guess you could say, so that man had a better understanding of himself; hence the gods. You have the god of water and the god of thunder and the god of this and that. All these gods were brought about by man to protect what man most treasures – life itself."

"OK, that makes sense in a round about way. But what is your theory?"

"Well when I say man, I actually meant woman. History tells us that we have lived and now live in a patriarchal society where men are in charge. This was not always the case. The gods that ruled over everything where basically of service to the women of the world. The men had very little say in anything. Now as time went on the males became aware of just how powerful they were and decided that enough was enough, so invented the Father of all the gods. Women naturally took the role of the superior because they were mothers. You know they didn't understand how it was done they just knew that they could create life."

"Right. I see. The Father of the gods was Odin right?"

"Not then it wasn't. That was later on in the game, for now it was up to man to show the women that they were stronger than them. This isn't hard because as you know generally men are stronger than women, so when it came to be that the Father of the gods spoke to one of the tribesmen the women naturally got scared and the Matriarchal society was over thrown and men were on top. Very little has changed."

"Thanks for the history lesson, but you haven't told me about your theory yet."

"It's coming, but until you know where everything fits in you won't have a clue as to what I'm talking about."

"OK, carry on."

"So, on through time we go till we get to civilization, well, a form of it anyway. This was in a place called Germania, which was pretty much all of Europe. One particular area was what we now call Norway. The Nordics were the people who defined the gods, gave them names and from there it spread around the world. Even the early Church had many different gods all adopted from the Nordics. The Nordics had a god for just about everything and when they were in battle they called on these gods to protect them. If a warrior died they say He went to Asgard, the place of the gods which is in another realm, another reality. They met at a place called Valhalla, which means great hall; the meeting place of the gods and fallen warriors. Asgard is where Odin lived. These gods, as I said, were adopted by many different religions around the globe. What is curious is some of the cultures who had never been exposed to the Norse gods had their own very similar gods. When all is said and done we as a race became more intelligent and had less and less need for all these gods and slowly whittled them down to just a few. Then the Church got hold of those last remaining few and scared them away with Jehovah, the one true god, and killed any who disbelieved that there was only one god."

"I can see that. From everything that I have been told about it sounds like it's the truth."

"It is, but it gets more complicated than that. You see man is not as intelligent as what He believes and by employing only one god He has in fact taken away our understanding of god. Our minds are so small that we cannot comprehend who or what god is and we make all these outrageous claims about him and we kill in His name and have made him a him. God maybe an entity, but god is not a sex."

"That much I can agree with."

The more I listened the more I started to see how the past that shaped the way we have become is like propaganda.

"Now there is a universal law that says whatever the mind can conceive is achieved. In other words, we invented gods that we have just thrown aside and now they are pissed. Have you ever felt unneeded?"

"Yeah, just recently. It was a family matter you could say." I said with a little despondence. "So, what you're saying is that we as humans brought gods into being and then just decided we didn't want them any more; but they are still there?"

"You got it."

"Some theory."

I couldn't help, but try and make light of it, after all I had first hand experience with what She was saying and knew it was more than just a theory; it was fact. I just didn't want to admit it.

"There is more to it." She continued. "All these things that are happening are a direct result of the gods wanting to take their revenge."

"And what about the one true God? Can't He or She or whatever do something about it?"

"This is the part which is hard to explain. You see God is an amalgamation of all the ideas from all the races and beliefs around the world therefore god is everything and nothing. God is the combined consciousness and the creator, but doesn't have what we would call a personality. God has many personalities and no personalities all rolled into one. God is not an entity, not an intelligence and therefore has no will. It is the smaller parts of god that have will and freedom of choice, not the greater God."

"I'm starting to see where you're going with that, it's a bit confusing though. What you are saying is because no one on earth is able to agree with what or who god is then God is nothing. But because we are all here and exist, God is everything. Put them both together and it just is. Am I close here?"

"Spot on. Most people blow a fuse when they try to work that out hence the wars." She said with sadness in Her eyes.

"So, what do you mean by revenge?"

"Well Odin is the Father of the gods and has been, shall we say, smite by man. Now He wants our world as His own, but He can't do that. He cannot twist the will of man as we all have freedom of choice. What He can do however is prey on the weak and use them to do what needs to be done. Have you heard of the Church Of Odin?"

"No."

“Otherwise known as the COO.”

“Yes. Is that what it means? I think I kind of knew that in the back of my mind.”

“That is another thing that we can talk about, but not now. Look I’ve got to go, but here’s my card.” She said as She stood up “Give me a call and we can get together over coffee or something and discuss this further. That should be enough to get the old grey matter working overtime for you. I can see that you are a searcher – I can tell by your aura.”

“My aura? Are you one of those new age freaks?”

“With everything that has been going on around here would that really bother you?”

“I guess not.” And with that, She was gone.

But I had Her card. I looked at it carefully “Sophia Jones” it read with a mobile phone number under the name. That’s all there was on it. I would definitely have to give Her a call. After just five minutes with Her I was armed with more understanding of what was going on than any other time since I had started this investigation. She had also given me a clue as to what I was looking for in the library. I checked out a book of the Norse gods, one on early man and made my way back to the office.

- 29 -

Sophia blew me away with what She told me. It has totally unravelled everything that I have come to believe in and maybe that was the point. I guess in today's society we have this thought that if it has been this way for thousands of years then it must be true. Perhaps what we've forgotten is that thing's change; ideas change. It seemed more true to me the way Sophia had told the tale than anything I had learnt about in church. It almost feels like someone has been pulling the wool over our eyes all this time. We have been taught to look back on our history and see where we have come from, so we can learn from our mistakes, something that we as humans have a hard time doing. The picture I got about us as humans is one of stupidity to put it mildly. Everyday we learn small things, but it's the big things that we never learn from. It's so simple and it makes us look worse off now than we did when we first started as a race. When we look back to the time that we discovered fire we have used it as our best friend and worst enemy, another illustration of the all and nothing I guess. We would put our hand in the fire, get burnt, pull it out and nurse our wound, but know never to do it again. These days it's not so simple. We put our hand in the fire and we get burnt, we pull it out and sooth the burn with cold water and eventually the pain goes away and we kind of forget about it. We go back to the fire and put our hand in again thinking that it will be different, but it's the same result. We do this time and time again and never learn from it as if never happened before. When we look back into the history of man most of us only look back a couple of thousand years to learn about why we are 'saved' today. We're not saved; far from it. We are out in the water with our hands in the air waiting for a lifeguard to see us and come to our rescue, but what we don't see is the shark in the water we are showing ourselves to. We have not been put on earth to make our own decisions, which is a fact that I'm still not completely able to accept because the church tells us differently. They say that God has given us free will and therefore should worship and exalt him. But what Sophia has said puts a new slant on things. God is nothing without us and we are nothing without God, but what is it we are all doing here anyway and what does it all matter at the end of the day? Are we here to suffer? Are we here to make God feel good about His or Her self? What is the meaning to it all if there is a meaning? What happens when we die? Some say that we go to heaven, but what is heaven and what is hell? Of all the times that I have heard Christians preach and gone to church and all the rest of that holy stuff I have never been given a straight answer. I have been told to seek my answers in the good book, but it's not as easy as that because every time that I get an answer the bible seems to say something different several chapters further in. If God really is who the Christians say He is then what about all the other religions of the world? Are they just fooling themselves? From my very recent experiences I would have to say that none of us can be sure.

Everything that I have been through over the last month or so has lead me to the fact there is so much more out there than we choose to accept. Perhaps the reason for this is we are such creatures of habit and if anything goes against what we have already formulated in our mind as fact then it must be false. But then if we look back on those times when the church renounced all other gods for the one true God surely that tells us that we can change. It's obvious to me by just looking around the world that the ideas given to us years ago just don't work and possibly never have. Have we been so blinded by fear that we either become so paranoid about where we will go when we die or we become those who choose to ignore what has been taught and become atheists believing that there is noting out there. I believe that life has to be better than that, better than all the dogma we have suffered, better than the prejudice that has fallen on us and better than the judgements that those of the cloth have burdened us with. It has to be. This is not a new thought to me and I dare say that it's not a new thought to a lot of people even those that are set in their ways in the church or any other religion for that matter. So, what does this spiritualism have that none of the other religions do? Answers. It is not an organised religion nor is it something that shoves law and order down your through; it's simply a way to look at the world in another light, a light in which I was trying to see. I had more questions than answers, but after talking to Sophia I had the feeling that those questions and many more would soon be answered and everything that's happened in my life up until now will make complete sense. I hope so. But for now I just need to get my head around some of what She said.

Another thing that raised questions is the fact She appeared right when I needed Her. Why has nothing like this ever come to me before? Was it because I wasn't ready for it? There is an old saying that goes along the lines of 'When the student is ready, the master will appear'. Does this mean that I am ready to be taught? And what was it She said? She told me that I'm a searcher. Isn't everybody a searcher or is it just me that wants to know what it's all about? Am I alone in this world? Surely not, not if there are people in this world like Sophia. I guess now I have to wait and see what unfolds in the coming days and weeks, but one thing is for certain, I haven't had my fill yet and I can see why so many people get drawn into this type of thing.

- 30 -

Perhaps things were going my way for once, I don't know. I wanted them to. All I have come across lately is one brick wall after another. Just as I seem to have the answer to something another question takes its place. However, every time I ask a question the right person seems to come along and help me out with it. I don't know what it is, but I've learned more about life in the last couple of months than I have for the other forty-five years. Is it because I've been asking the right questions or is it because I have been looking in the right places? The answers, or the people that have the answers, come to me. Maybe it's just my time. I stood staring out the window trying not to think too much. I had already gone through every emotion and I felt drained. I padded over to get another drink from the cheep bottle then back to the desk to have a smoke. Looks like I was going back to the old habit once more. Was there nothing I could do to kick this? I lit the cigarette and inhaled deeply then noticed something from the corner of my eye. It was sitting on top of other files in my 'in' tray. I picked it up while having another sip of my drink. It was the flyer advertising that new church thing that lady had given me. I hadn't paid it much attention, but when I thought about it I realised it was only me She gave it to. Out of all the people in that café it was only me She approached. Why is that? My gut instinct took over as I sat myself down flicking the mouse to remove the screen saver. The computer read 5:36 PM, just enough time for me to get ready and go down town to check it all out. I switched the monitor off and went to the shower to start getting ready for what I was hopping would be some more answers.

***

This was obviously not to every ones taste. I walked down Q2 Street on my way to this new church looking here and looking there for the masses that would throng to see what it was that could save us all. But the streets where normal, no signs of anything happening what so ever. Maybe I had the time wrong. Maybe the day. I looked at the pamphlet again to double check myself, but there it was in black and white 'Tuesday 7pm at the Down Town Open Air Stage'. Perhaps people thought it would rain. I don't know, but I kept going. As I turned the slight curve that lead out onto the DTOAS I did see a small congregation massing next to the stage. The Open Air Stage was huge, it could hold about 500,000 people at once. There were no seats unless needed and there was a storage facility tucked in behind the stage were tour organisers could get at anything they needed for what ever function or concert was going on. In this case a rudimentary shelter had been set up with the use of scaffolding and tarpaulins just in case the weather did turn sour, but on a night like this it was quite unnecessary. There wasn't a cloud in the sky and one could just make out the moon and stars through the dense smog. On either side of the stage was a massive loud speaker, this was designed to get the message across, sometimes right across town. The small amount of people probably added up to about two or three thousand. I didn't see anyone I knew and that kind of relieved me as this is not the type of thing that someone like me would attend, but I was there for some reason. The lights on the stage came up and the speakers crackled. Soft, wafting music filtered through the loud speakers as the spotlights hit the stand-up mic, which was in the centre of the stage. Moments later a man came onto the stage and stood behind the mic. From the distance I was I couldn't make out any facial features, so I fished around in my pockets for my glasses. By the time I found them He started to speak.

"Ladies and Gentlemen, welcome to the Auckland Down Town Open Air Stage." He paused.

There was silence. My eyes adjusted and I could just make him out. He was a man in His early thirties I suppose with dark hair and a small moustache.

"My name is Andrew McKinley, but you can all call me Andy." He said with a smile.

The Audience was still and quiet.

"I would like to thank you all for coming to what I can assure you will be a night to remember." He continued. "From all over the country you have come. Everybody that we have invited is here which thrills me to the bone. So, without further ado I would like to introduce you to the speaker for tonight. She has been doing so much to get the new Church up and going over the last week and a half that it is an absolute pleasure to welcome to the stage Miss Samantha Samson! Ladies and gentleman, a big hand please." As a quite round of claps filled the courtyard, my mouth dropped open.

Sam? I couldn't believe it! I was stunned. What was She doing on the stage in front of all these people going on about a new church? Obviously Her connection with Odin is much more than I thought it was. I was dumbfounded.

"Ladies and Gentleman," She started "thank you all for coming. There are so many of you here that I can't thank you individually, but you all know who you are. I would like to take this opportunity to tell you a little bit about what we are doing here at the Church Of Odin." She paused and the music increased in intensity, but not in volume.

It was rhythmic and pleasant to hear.

"Let me assure you that this new outlook on life has been coming for a very long time. Before there were Christians, before there were Muslims or the Catholic Church. Before there was anything there was Odin. Through out our history we have raised gods and have plundered their world and raided their power and then left them to die. What have we done people? We have forgotten where we came from. Odin, the great and powerful god that brought us life has been forsaken for one of the under gods. We have cheered and exalted a god that had no more say in the creation of this or any other world than all of us. Yet we set Odin aside in the mists of time and forgot about him. We have tried to forget that Odin ever existed apart from those stories that we tell our children. Why? Because Odin was a loving God, the Father of all the living gods and one who gave us everything. He let us get away with so much and then we let him fade away until one day one of the under gods arose and showed us His wrath. He showed anger and fear and since that day we have not been free." Again She paused.

At this cue I started to move closer to the stage trying to weave through the crowd and get Her attention. I knew this was not going to work simply because She had the lights in Her eyes. But I had to try.

"King." I heard someone shouting at me from close by.

I turned around to see who it was. From out of nowhere a figure appeared.

"Paul." I said surprised. "What are you doing here?"

"I came to see what it was all about. I got a special invite like everybody else here." He looked around with a big smile on His face.

"Paul, I've been meaning to tell you something."

"Isn't She wonderful?" He said as if He hadn't heard me.

"Paul. About the other night."

"Don't sweat it man; it was just one night. Unless you want to make it a second night."

He turned to give me a smug smile, raised His eyebrow and turned His attention back to the stage.

"It is time to take up the opportunity that this world has now given us," Continued Sam "and take back the throne of the lost God Odin."

The crowd didn't seem to be responding that well.

"People, let me tell you one thing. When we first stood on two feet we knew who we were, we knew who our creator was and we knew where our loyalties lay. Now we have taken that away from our maker and all hell has broken loose. Take a look around you, what do we have? The folly of man as He has bitten the hand that fed him. It's time to go back to our God and resurrect a peaceful and respectful civilisation."

This time there was a clap from somewhere at the front of the throng and gradually more people started to join in and before long the entire crowd was cheering and whistling.

"She's real good. I love this girl." Said Paul.

He disappeared on me again, but not before telling me that He was going to come and see me very shortly. This got me wondering, but not for very long as I saw Sam exit stage left. I tried to make my way through the crowd, but it was too thick. There was no time at all as I saw a car pull out from behind the stage and take off up Q2 Street and down Shortland The Second Street. She was gone, so I waited for the crowd to thin out and I wondered home.

- 31 -

After everything I went through the one thing that was on my mind was still Sam. I could not or would not abandon the thoughts of Her. I'd fallen in love with Her and no matter what Odin said and no matter what Sam had told me I knew I had to be with Her. All this new knowledge about the way gods were and where they all came from was starting to make a lot of sense, but what the Detective said was also foremost on my mind. There is a way that I can protect Her as well as find out what the hell is going on. I still can't see Her as being the murderer, so what I needed to do was find Her before anything else started to happen or anyone else got murdered.

I was sitting at my desk furiously typing everything I could remember about what Sophia had told me knowing that She expected me to call Her. She had, in a way, opened my eyes just wide enough to see that there was another side to life that most of us just choose to ignore. I tried to fill in as many details about the chronology that I could remember from the beginning of this case, but there were a few blank spots. Not because I couldn't remember, but because there were some big jumps that had happened. This whole murder thing, if it was as the Detective said, is almost as if Sam was two people. Maybe that's it. Sam was two people. This is impossible, but at least it's an answer, which was more than I was getting right now. It was so simple and that's why I couldn't believe it. I slowly typed the words into the bottom of the page, so I didn't forget and I could ponder about it later when it hit me. One of the first freaky things that had happened with Sam is that strange and frightening voice that came from Her. I knew that couldn't be Sam though after that night I chose to believe I had imagined it all, but it was starting to come together. Then there was the meeting with Odin that She had told me about, again, I thought She was nutty, so chose to ignore it even after I had been through the same thing. Then of course there was the time that She was floating above my bed. There was no way to explain that.

All this time there seems to have been a block in my brain about these things. Something was telling me to forget about them and pass them off as nothing. Was this just the normal human response or was I being influenced. That's possible isn't it? Some sort of possession? I don't know, but what Sophia had said made me take a closer look at the possibility. My fingers where going crazy, it was almost as if they had a mind of their own. I'm not the best typist in the world, but it seemed that as soon as I had a thought, there it was on screen. There were no spelling mistakes and I never had to go back and correct what I had written. I was on fire with everything that was coming out of my head. It was almost autopilot! Then I remembered what somebody had said to me a long time ago; sometimes the first things that come into your head are right. That's how you follow your instincts, by listening to your gut instead of your head, or something like that. By this time I wasn't even looking at the keyboard the way I usually do I was looking directly at the monitor and the words were just gliding on. I couldn't feel my hands after a while and my mind was almost blank. More and more words where coming up on screen. It was as if I was reading the words before I had a chance to think them. Then four words appeared on screen 'don't forget about Sam'. I stopped cold. Had I just written that? Had I just thought those four words? Whatever the case maybe it made me stop and remember what I was supposed to be doing. I would carry this on another time.

I stood up and stretched. It seemed like I had been sitting at that computer for a good three hours and I needed a break before I could do anything more. I walked over to the liquor cabinet to get some more of that cheap bourbon while I tried to think of my next move. How was I to find Sam? Obviously, I thought as I poured myself a double, I would call Her flat first, but what if She wasn't there? I had no way of finding Her. I didn't know any of Her friends and the only ones She spoke about were dead.

This whole thing was starting to look like a big mess when from the corner of my eye I saw a flash of white. It was nothing really, just a glimmer, a hint of something moving. I looked around to see where it came from, but there was nothing. I sat there staring in the direction I thought I had seen whatever it was, but nothing happened. I downed my drink and went to get another one. I was starting to freak myself out I think. I picked up the bottle and there it was again, out form the corner of my eye was the same flash of white that I had seen before. I almost dropped my bottle. Placing it back on the cabinet I looked towards where I thought I saw it. I remained completely still. I didn't even breath and the silence was deafening. The only noise that I could hear was the whir of the computer. My heart was racing and I was starting to sweat a little. Once was an acceptable perception error, but twice was something less random and there had to be something there otherwise I was going mad and I don't think I was going mad. I was staring into my bedroom through the open door. The light was off, so all I could see was the shaft of light from the office that traced the outline of my bed. I took a step forward and jumped as I saw it flash past the doorway in my room. My god it scared the hell out of me and I dropped my glass, which landed in tact on the carpet. I crouched down to pick it up when it happened again and for the briefest of moments I caught a good look at what had scared the living crap out of me. It appeared to be the little girl, Billy. What the fuck was She doing here? My heart was racing faster and I was shaking like a leaf. Was this a ghost I had seen? I was frozen to the spot. It was just a girl, but what was She doing here. Was it the ghost of the girl? I've read about this type of thing, ghosts of living people being spotted just before that person dies. I began to back away from the door and I bumped into my desk. Suddenly I heard Her laugh behind me and I span around in time to see my swivel chair spin to a slow stop. There was nothing there and I thought I was about to shit myself. What the fuck was going on. There was a strange noise and I realised that it was coming form me. I was beside myself with fear and I grabbed the first thing that I could find which was heavy enough to be used as a weapon. Ironically it was a trophy I had been given for bravery in the line of duty. I was petrified and I needed one of my pills. This had gone way too far and I was beginning to loose it. Her face appeared from around the door frame in my room and I yelped again as She disappeared back into the darkness. I was poised with the trophy in my hand ready to throw it as soon as She showed Her freaky little face again. I drew closer to the door frame and tried to adjust my eyes to the darkness inside, but it was no use I had to turn the light on. I inched further forward and when I was close enough to the door to reach my hand around feeling for the light switch. In my fear I couldn't find it. I knew it was there, but I was scrabbling around for it and all of a sudden something spiked my hand and a shaft of pain shot through my body and by reflex I jolted my arm back. The pain was so intense and looking back at my hand I could see why; there was a ballpoint pen sticking halfway through my hand, there was at least five centre metres poking out through the other side. Even though I was acting on adrenaline I knew to leave it in to stop the bleeding. I was dazed and confused and that seemed to push me on into the bedroom like a bull and turn the light on with the trophy and ready myself for anything. The room was quiet. There was nothing here, but my stuff and my bed. I turned to see the light switch, which was covered in my blood and a little bit of flesh that used to make up part of my hand. I was feeling a little woozy from the shock my body had gone into, but I had to at least look under the bed before I could get to the hospital. I crept as silently as I could to the left side of the bed. All I heard was the dripping of blood on the carpet. Crouching down I slowly put the trophy on the bed. I got into a kneeling position and carefully grabbed the sheet corner and readied myself. It was now or never, so I counted in my head one, two, three and I pulled as hard and as quickly as I could.

There was nothing there.

Nothing.

This couldn't be right. I know that I wasn't imagining things. For sure I wasn't and I had the pen through my hand to prove it. I know what I saw and there is no way that She could have got out of here with out me seeing. I jumped up and rushed to the door narrowly avoiding the glass that was still on the floor and looked around the office.

Nothing.

I went back into my bedroom and looked back under the bed. Still nothing, but from there I noticed something else. There was something on the floor under the bed, so I reached for it and pulled it out. It was a match book. Now how did a match book get under the bed? It was only a month ago I was looking for a match or a lighter and I searched everywhere for something that would light my bloody cigarette. I must have crawled under this bed a dozen times looking and this was never here. I flipped it over to see where it might have come from. It had a logo from one of the nearby hotels. It must have been Sam's. Why would She be hanging out at a hotel room? What was She doing with matches? She didn't smoke. I didn't really have a whole lot of time to think about this because I was starting to bleed a lot. I locked up the office and went down to call a taxi and go, for the second time this week, to the hospital.

- 32 -

"God damn that hurt!"

"Oh don't be such a wimp." Said the nurse who was more than a little rough with the needle. "You know you need it. We have to make sure that it doesn't get infected and we also need to irrigate the wound and throw in a few stitches."

"Could you throw them in from over by the curtain because you're not tickling me!" I retorted.

"You're not the worlds best patient you know."

"I never claimed – ouch, man – to be."

"There, all done." She said and started to take the rubber gloves off.

"Um, thanks, I think."

"You're welcome. Don't forget to tip the waiter now will you." She smiled putting the gloves in the rubbish bin and heading out of the cubical.

"Oh, you're a riot you are."

"Thanks," She said form the other side of the curtain, "I'll be here all week."

I got up and just stood there for a couple of moments trying to get it all right in my head yet again. This was getting to be way over the top and I was getting a headache just thinking about it, though it could well have been the morphine the nurse gave me. Either way I felt like I was going to be sick, so I sat back down. I've never been one to take pain, especially the pain that hospitals administer. I have to admit it though She did make me smile in between the torturous pain and humiliation of having the pen slowly removed from my hand. I think She kind of enjoyed it. The local She gave me didn't do the job or wasn't strong enough, but by the time I found that out it was too late and She just kept going. The doctors had a good laugh when they saw what had happened. I couldn't even explain how I came to have a pen through my hand and the best I could come up with was that I was walking through my office with the pen in my hand when I tripped over the rug. Lame I know, but what else was I going to tell them? A ghost did it? I don't think so.

When I got outside it was very cold. It must have been about eleven or twelve PM and the streets were steaming. There were people here and there all hunched over against the cold. I slipped my good hand into my pocket for warmth and found the match book again. It must have been Sam's. Then I remembered what She told me about PJ and the fact that they could never be seen as an item. That must be it. They must be doing the wild thing in a hotel room. OK, that thought made me cringe with jealousy, so I tried to get the picture out of my head while I made the decision to find the hotel and try to get some information about where She might be. It was worth a shot. It was only five minutes down the road and the walk may do me good. The fresh air around here wasn't very fresh, but it was the exercise that I needed, so that balanced things out. When I got to the hotel I went right up to the front desk to speak to the guy behind the counter. He was about twenty-five, neat and tidy and He greeted me with a smile.

"Can I help you sir?"

"Yes, well I hope so. A friend of mine told me to meet Her here yesterday. Thing is I can't remember which hotel She said, I'm only guessing it was this one. She was booked in not long ago. I don't know if She still is, but if you could just check to see if you have Her rccords on the computer, so I know if I'm at the right place?"

"Certainly Sir, what was your friends name?'

"Ah Sam, Samantha." I wasn't even sure that She would have booked in under Her own name. "Samantha Samson"

"Just a moment, Sir. Yes, here She is. She is currently booked in. Would you like me to check to see if She is in?"

"That would be great thanks, just let Her know that I'm down here."

"No problem, Sir. And whom shall I say you are."

"Um, tell Her that it's PJ."

Stupid, stupid. I'm sure that PJ would know where She was and go right up. But it was all I could think of at the time.

"She is on Her way, Sir. Is there anything else I can do for you?"

"No, thank you. That's fine I'll wait here for Her." I said.

I walked over to one of the comfortable looking couches and sat down to wait. The place was quiet apart from a few staff walking around doing whatever they were being paid to do. There were one or two guests sitting about in chairs reading, but that was about it. Then the elevator chimed and seconds later the door opened. There She was. She never failed to make my heart pound that little bit harder. My angel. She looked around expectantly and completely failed to see me. I stood up and started to walk towards Her.

"King. My God, what are you doing here?" She said in a load, harsh whisper. "How did you find me?"

I produced the matchbox.

"Ah, fuck. I was supposed to be hiding out. Why did you use the name PJ? I wasn't even expecting him and I was all excited."

"Yeah, thanks for that." I said and just gave Her a dirty look.

"You know what I mean. It's not that I'm not happy to see you it's just that I thought you were angry at me and I didn't want to go through any more shit than I've already been through you know. I fucked up and now I just want to leave it." She said.

This was totally not what I wanted to hear, but I guess that if half the stuff She was going through was true then it's at least partially understandable.

"Look, we need to talk. You are in danger and so am I. The cops are after you and there are a whole lot of very nasty things waiting to happen. I don't want to talk about this here. Could we go up to your room? There is something that I need to explain to you." I said with a mortal sense of emergency in my voice.

"It's eleven thirty at night. I'm tired and I really don't think we've anything to talk about." She said.

I just looked at Her and She looked at me and saw that I was serious and flicked Her head for me to follow me. We rode up to the fifth floor and walked to Her room as quickly and with out fuss as possible trying to look inconspicuous. The room was warm and inviting. There was a queen bed and a small coffee table with a scattering of magazines. In the corner next to the door was the mini bar and I made a B line towards it not asking if I could pilfer from it. I grabbed the first thing that my hand found and a glass that was sitting on top of the fridge. I had another look around as Sam pulled the covers of the bed up over the pillows in an effort to make the place look neater for all the difference it made to me. There was a desk with a phone on it and the place was decked out in white carpet with soothing lights.

"So, this is the place that you and PJ come to - ah…"

"That's really not what you came to talk about and more to the point it's none of your business." She said sitting herself down on the bed.

I walked over to the desk and pulled the chair out and sat myself down so that I could lean forward against the back of the chair. Sam was not the only one who was tired.

"OK, I'll level with you. There is a whole lot of really freaky shit that is going down and my life is in danger." I said.

"I thought you said *my* life was in danger."

"Would I be here now if it wasn't?" I asked while pouring what appeared to be gin into my glass.

"No and I should kick you out right now for lying to me."

"Lying? My god Angel, who's just called the pot black?"

“Point taken. What is it that you feel threatened by.”

“Not to put too finer point on it. You.”

“Me. Do you think I’m out to kill you?” She said almost yelling.

“I never said that. I just said I'm threatened by you. Don’t take it personally…”

“How can I not take it personally? You told me that you are threatened by me.”

“…the cops are after you.”

“What? Why?”

“They have you pinned for the murder of Lorraine and Jason.”

“Are you out of your mind? They weren’t murdered. And they were definitely not murdered by me!!” She exclaimed almost in tears.

“Hey, don’t get your knickers in a twist. It’s the cops that are after you, not me.”

“OK, you know what happened to Lorraine and not even I really know what happened to Jason.”

“In your own words tell me what happened to Lorraine.”

“You know what happened why do I have to go over all that again?’ She was in tears.

“Because the cops don’t know where you are and I do. I want to get everything sorted out and try to get you off the hook. I can’t picture you as a killer, but I can’t use that as an alibi now can I. I am here to help you and you need it, so just relax and tell me as much as you can about the day when Lorraine died.” I told Her calmly.

“I need a drink.” She said.

“Sure, what do you want?”

“Whatever there is I’ll have it.” She said with a sigh.

I got up and went to the fridge to get Her a drink and thought that I would help myself to another while I was there. I poured Her a rum and myself a bourbon then took it over to Her before sitting down again.

“Thanks. Well, as you know I don’t remember much. I was at my flat with Lorraine and I was upset. I knew that things were just going from bad to worse with the relationship between you and I, and me and PJ. Something had to give. My life was going down hill and I couldn’t decide whether to tell you what was going on or just to leave it as it was. I was just so lost and alone and, well, I just wanted everything and I knew that I had to choose.”

She paused to take a sip of Her drink and catch Her tears with a tissue that I had handed to Her.

“He has hurt me so bad over the last couple of years,” She continued “and I kept going back to him. It seems that one moment we are so much in love, and then the next minute it’s as if He doesn’t care for me at all. I can’t stand it, but I can’t break it off with him.”

“You can’t or you don’t want to?”

“Both I guess. He’s been one of the only stable things in my life for the past five years and I can’t just let that go. I know I should because every time He hurts me I just want to die.”

She started to cry again, so I got up and sat down beside Her and put my arm around Her waist.

“That’s what I feel like now and I have no one to turn to. Jason is dead and Lorraine is dead. I feel like I am loosing everything!”

“Lets talk about Lorraine for a bit. What do you remember about the day of the accident?”

“We were just talking and I was an emotional wreck because of something PJ did. It’s always PJ that gets me upset. I don’t know why I… anyway, I just told Her I was thinking that I will never find true happiness because of him and then, as I told Her, you came along and brightened up my world.”

“Me. You’re telling me that you did have those feelings for me?”

“Yes. King, I loved you. I still do. But while PJ is in my life there is nothing that I can do about it. I love you and I miss you. I can’t put you through that and I’m sure you don’t want to have anything to do with me. When PJ and I are happy we are the happiest people in the world. That’s what makes me keep going back to him.”

“OK, lets get away from that. What happened next?”

“Well. I went to have myself a drink when Lorraine went to the toilet. I sat down and had my drink and the last thing I remember was dragging you out of the car and trying to find Lorraine. She had gone through the windscreen because She wasn’t wearing Her seatbelt as you know. You were unconscious. I remember waving to a driver who stopped and called the ambulance. After that, well, you know the story.”

“Yes, but there seems to be a whole lot missing from your story. Are you sure you don’t remember any more than that?”

“I swear. Lorraine wasn’t murdered. She broke Her neck when She landed on the road.”

“The pathology report tells a different story. They say that She was dead before Her neck was broken. They say that She was poisoned.”

“Poisoned?!” She echoed.

“That’s right. Until we can find some evidence to the contrary or that takes you out of the picture. Since you can’t remember any of this you don’t have a leg to stand on. You are it Sam. What about Jason, tell me what you know about how He died.”

“He and I were at a bar and I had a bit too much to drink. He took me home and put me to bed and as far as I know He left in a taxi. From what I was told, when He got home He got into His car and smashed himself into a tree. I knew He was angry because of PJ, but I didn’t think He was going to do something stupid like that.”

“So, you think it was suicide?”

“More like Russian roulette. You see He was very drunk and knew He couldn’t drive. I guess He just took the wheel and decided to see how far He would get. If He killed himself, well all the better. I just didn’t realise how bad it was for him.”

“You think He loved you?”

“I know He loved me. He told me all the time how much He loved me and wanted me back. All I could ever think of was PJ and it never crossed my mind when I talked about him that Jason was totally jealous.”

“And that’s all you know?”

“Yes. I swear. Unless somebody took my body when I wasn’t looking and used it to kill them. No, I was not the murderer of my two best friends.” She said.

She looked me right in the eye. I believed Her.

“Why are you looking at me like that?” She asked.

“Because of what you just said.”

“You mean about somebody taking my body. Don’t be ridiculous.”

I just looked at Her for a moment and She started to freak out a little.

“Do you mean to tell me that you think somebody took my body? How is that even possible? It can’t be. I was only joking!” She said emphatically.

“I can’t explain it, but there seems to be a few things that you are missing from your stories and I believe you when you say that you don’t remember. Have you ever heard of possession?”

“Yeah, it’s nine tenths of the law. Are you nuts? Here I was thinking that I was going crazy and here you are talking about demons and things.”

“I never said anything about demons.”

“Well, you mentioned possession and unless you think that angels go around killing people then you must be talking about demons!” She hissed sarcastically.

“I was actually thinking more like gods. Well, *a* god.”

“What?”

“Look it’s a long story. But right now I have to get you safe.”

“Me? You just finished telling me that you were the one whose life was in danger.’

“It is, that’s why I want you safe. When I know that you are completely safe from yourself and others then I can relax and try to sort a few things out. I can do what you’re paying me to do, which just by the way got more expensive for you!”

“So, what are you going to do?”

“Watch you fall asleep.”

“What do you mean? If you think I’m going to fall asleep after what you have told me you have another thing coming. I was tired before, but right now I have never felt so awake! And after everything I have told you don’t you think it’s safer for you when I’m awake than asleep?”

“Yes, but if you’re asleep then it makes it easier for the cops to arrest you and lock you up.” I said with a grin.

“I am not going to let you call the cops. What are you on King?” She said standing up and pacing the bedroom. “What the fuck do you think you are doing to me. If I go to jail there is nothing that will stop them from throwing away the key. No way am I going to let you call the cops!”

“I know.” I said calmly.

She started to sway and made Her way to the bed. She began to blink rapidly.

“That’s why I spiked your drink with a sedative, a very powerful sedative at that.”

“You bastard, you complete…” She tried to say, but before She could finish Her head hit the pillow and She was out to it.

I picked up the phone and called the Detective.

“King here, I’ve got Her. Just come to the Centurion Hotel, room 511. Yeah, see you then.” I replaced the receiver and sat waiting.

- 33 -

Did I feel guilty? About betrayal, yes. I felt like I had taken someone's trust and smashed it into tiny little pieces. I felt like shit to be honest, not even the thought that She had not only defied my trust, but also PJ's did anything to relieve the retched feeling inside. Do I feel guilty about saving Her life? No and I would do it again in a heartbeat. Sam was now safe in a lock up at least until the trial. Now it was up to me to find someway of proving Her innocence. The problem was from everything that She has told me about what happened I get the feeling that She is not so innocent as She makes out. There is no alibi and the only defence She has is that She doesn't remember. I have to take sides with the law on this one; if I was the prosecutor I know which way I would tell it. She will need one hell of a good lawyer for this one, but I don't know if She could afford it. I know I can't.

Sam had been processed in the morning when She woke up. She looked at me with those eyes and I knew that She just couldn't understand what I had done for Her. All the love and trust had melted away from Her face leaving a big question mark in Her eyes asking 'why'. What could I say? I told Her why I had done it, but She just cried and told me that She never wanted to see me again. It was heartbreaking, but maybe one day when it all comes out in the wash She'll see it in Her heart to forgive me. As for now I had to find proof. Anything to show that Sam had nothing to do with it. It wasn't easy when both of Her best friends are now dead and I knew none of Her other friends. I decided to go down to the station and try to find out all I could about what they had on the case already and try to piece the story together myself. I could only hope that there were blood tests done after the accident for alcohol, maybe that could shed some light on the situation. I had this gut feeling that something wasn't quite right inside Her and, grasping at straws, Her blood might fill in some of the blanks. Well that was my way of trying to deny that possession by a god was the answer. I didn't know which of the answers I was looking for sounded more naïve. There was no escaping the fact that I had attained the amulet, but that's not going to make a scrap of difference in a court and if I tried I'd be the one being locked up. My computer just sat there staring at me. The glow was starting to hurt my eyes and the letters on the screen were dancing around. I had to get out. It would have been about one PM and the sun barely shone through the dirty glass of the office. Of all the information that I had compiled it all seemed to come back to Sam. Was She a murderer? That's what it looked like, but why? Why did She want to get rid of Her two best friends? I had been over the same old ground before and there was nothing new. As far as I could tell those two, like me, were in the way.

I thought about the way we were together and the things She had said to me. For all intense and purpose She was a bright young lady that could, with a lot of help, become somebody. All She had right now was two bodies. As I was thinking this a little envelope came up on my screen. I clicked it twice and opened the email. It was from Phoenix. How the hell did this person get my email address? I never gave it out. I hadn't advertised it in the telephone book because I didn't want to get all the Spam and strange emails from people that I had put away or caught out! But there it was, as clear as day.

"You haven't been online for some time, so I thought I would see if you needed any help. I don't know what kind of trouble you may be getting yourself into, but I hope you know what you are doing. I have some more information that I thought I would share with you. By now you will be quite familiar with the concept of Asgard and Valhalla and all the gods. Well maybe it's time that you and I talked about what it is exactly that you are up against."

I was about to reply to the email without reading all of it asking where He or She got my email. I wanted to know where this person came from and all the questions that naturally spring into your mind when someone obviously knows you better than you know them, but I thought better of it and continued to read.

"Asgard is a place that was conjured up from the darkness of the human spirit. It was something to be believed in when times were gloomy and it seemed that there was no reason to live. This you already know, but what you may not understand, due to your recent experiences, these gods are not evil. Far from it actually. They have just been forgotten. What you don't know is that it is in the same realm as what we call heaven. There is no hell and even if there was Asgard would not be it. There is also the idea of heaven you need to understand. It is not something that is 'up there' with God. It is all around, it is every where and it is within us. We are in heaven all the time, but we wonder around in a hell. Hell is that feeling that we get when we ask the question 'why are we here'. That feeling that we don't belong anywhere and can't figure out our reasons. Once we understand, once we know, once we remember who we are and where we came from everything becomes clear to us. At that exact point we know heaven because everything makes sense. Unfortunately most of us are still in hell. You are looking for the door to heaven because you have a little understanding of what else is out there. The problem is that because you are already in heaven there is no door; there is just knowledge."

That's where it ended. I was stunned; I just didn't know what to think. It made so much sense and I could feel the emotions welling up from inside. A lifetime of pain and suffering for nothing. All the angst, anger, desire and the question 'why'. I thought that was just a human condition, I thought we all felt like that. Well maybe we do, but we don't need to. I closed the email window, shut the monitor down and made my way over to the liquor cabinet to sort out some of my thoughts. I was blank. Once more it felt like my whole life had been turned upside down and inside out leaving me feeling numb. I poured myself a drink and made a mental note to myself that I had to get some real bourbon and I still hadn't replaced that decanter. I downed the drink and grabbed my keys off the table and out I went shutting and locking the door behind me. Perhaps the fresh air would do me some good and get some perspective back in my life. No sooner had I stepped outside to make my way to the police station than I almost tripped on that kid again. I managed to steady myself by grabbing hold of the rails that protruded from the stairs.

"Christ kid! Where do you keep popping out from?"

"It's alright Bob, there's nothing wrong with me." Said Billy.

"What are you talking about? Are you OK?"

"I just answered that. Are you OK Bob?" She said with a smile.

"Yeah, all apart from you scaring the sh… scaring me." I said almost slipping with the profanity.

I don't know why I was holding my tongue for Her.

"I'm sorry I scared you I didn't mean to."

"So, how do you know my name, Kid?" I asked, not really wanting the answer.

"You have also asked me that before. Do you ever listen to yourself and others?" She said innocently.

"Look all I want to know is what you're doing here." I said a little bit angrily.

"Why didn't you ask that in the first place instead of the other questions?" She started, "I'm here to help you."

"You? Here to help me? Why would I need help from a kid like you? By the way, were you in my bedroom last night?" I asked with a raised eyebrow.

My neck was hurting from the constant looking down, so I crouched next to Her.

"Was that you Billy?"

Black clouds covered the sun at that point making the surroundings suddenly colder and darker as if to add drama to the already mystifying horror that was beginning to unfold.

"You're a funny man, Bob. I know your office, but I don't know where you live."

"But you know my name." I said.

I Didn't let on that my office and home are one in the same.

"Is your name Robert?"

"Yes, yes it is. How did you know that?" I asked.

There was no reply, but the kid reached into Her back pocket and produced a small newspaper clipping. The headline read 'King Cop Kills Crim'. Fuck, just what I needed. That happened over ten years ago before this kid was even born! What was She doing with that? It was unfair, it really was. How we could just be doing our job and all of a sudden be involved in a homicide. It took me so long to get over that. I was told many times that it wasn't my fault, but how do you argue with your conscience?

We were standing around the station when we got the call. It was an armed offenders call and our special force was at a shoot out, so it was down to my partner and I to sort the situation out. It was a normal run-of-the-mill call out as guns and burglary went together like rum and coke. I used to be scared of this type of thing, but after many years in the force it became routine. The first time was the hardest because all I could think of was my Father, but that passed. I had drawn my weapon at least once a day if not more and I had fired only twice and killed just one person. An innocent bystander. All She was doing was trying to get home and She was totally oblivious to what was going on around Her. She came out from nowhere at the exact point I got a clear shot at the perp.

Bang.

I still get nightmares to this day about that. The trials lasted for months, but telling the family was the hardest. That was my punishment. It was about eight PM as I drew up to the family home while my heart did somersaults in my chest. This would be the hardest next of kin that I will ever do because I knew the person who shot their daughter dead. The house was old and wooden, one of the last left in the city. I climbed the darkened stairs to the door and knocked. A small tabby scooted in front of me and off into the bushes. I grew weary and weak. Tears stung my eyes as I heard the footsteps of one of the occupants of the house approach the door. I had no idea what I was going to say. I had seen the reaction thousands of times and every time was like the first time. I had been thumped in the chest and cried on, I have even had the door slammed in my face, but it was always the fault of someone else. Until now. The door opened and standing there was a man in His early fifties.

"Mr Lawson?" I asked.

"That's right. Do I know you?"

"No, Sir." I showed him my badge. "Mr Lawson, are you the Father of Kathy Lawson?"

I could see it starting, the hatred in the man's eyes swelled.

"Yes I am. What has She done?"

"Sir, I'm afraid it's more than that. I have some bad news." I said looking down.

There was silence. I looked up and the anger had formed into sadness. A pain welling up inside the poor man. He started to breathe heavily and I could see His hands starting to shake.

"Who is it, Hun?" I heard from another room.

The man remained silent and seconds later I saw Her face. The face of the Mother of the young lady that I had shot and killed. I couldn't help it, a tear welled up in my eye and a lump formed in my throat.

"Who is it Chris?" She asked.

"This is Sergeant Robert Kingly." He said taking a deep breath. "He has come to give us some bad news about Kathy." He said in a shaky voice.

He reached out His arm and She found Her place next to him as He held on tightly to Her. I looked at the both of them.

"Mr Lawson, Mrs Lawson. I never know quite how to handle these situations, so I'll be as direct as possible. You daughter has been involved in an accident. Two youths were holding up a liquor shop when we were called out. There were guns involved and all hell broke loose. Your daughter was riding by…" I stopped, I took a deep breath and sighed a sigh for the dead, "…She was shot."

"Oh my God." Shouted Mrs Lawson as She took refuge in Her husband's arms.

Tears were streaming from Her face.

"Is She dead?" Said Mr Lawson in a frighteningly calm voice.

I hung my head.

"I'm so sorry."

I was staring at this kid. Billy was too young to remember this yet She had the article. Was I on a different planet? What was going on here?

"Where did you get that?"

"I found it." She said as if She wanted to play games.

I took a deep breath.

"Where?"

"My mummy gave it to me to remind me that it's not safe to wonder on the streets without a grown up."

"She's got a point." I said looking around. "How did you find me?" I asked going way off track to what I was thinking of.

"I was playing on the Internet doing a project for school when I found you.'

"What project?"

"It was about the old English Monarchy. I was trying to find out what it was like when they ruled, you know, before Camilla." She said.

I remembered those days.

"I don't understand."

"I was looking through a search engine under kings and queens when you web site popped up. Do you know that you don't have your email address advertised on that page, just your phone number?" She said innocently.

"I'm aware of that, thanks. So, you recognized me from that did you?"

"Yes."

"So, why did you come and find me?" I asked.

"Because you were one of the good cops. That's what mummy said anyway. I just thought that if you were that good you could help find my daddy." She said.

And then She just walked away down the road and out of my sight. I stayed there crouching for a while watching Her wander off. I didn't know what to do. I had a feeling She would be back though.

- 34 -

I don't know what it is about my phone, but nobody seems to use it; there was a knock on the door. I shook my head and sat up on the bed enjoying an afternoon nap trying to get some much needed shut eye. I rubbed my eyes and brought my room into focus before I stood up and walked over to the door.

"Who is it this time?" I said under my breath.

"What if I was a new client? No wonder you haven't got much business." It was the voice of Paul.

I'm not sure if I was pleased about this or not. I opened the door and there He was. I can't deny that He was very good looking and I liked what we did the other night. Something deep inside me wanted more, but I also knew that it wasn't right and it wasn't me. I honestly didn't know what to think about the whole situation.

"Are you going to ask me in?"

"Sorry man, come on in." I said.

I hung my head to clear some of the fog and stepped aside for Paul to come in.

"So, how you doing King? Met any spunky young men lately?" He said with a smile.

"That's not even funny. What do you want?"

"Just to talk. I think you and I have a few things that we can help each other with."

"Like what?" I inquired.

He wondered over to the liquor cabinet while I closed the door.

"Like what the hell was that Church Of Odin thing all about?"

"I have no idea." I lied.

"Come on man. You think you're the only one with information about this Odin guy? After all I have told you about don't you think that I might have at least a clue as to what you may or may not know."

“I still don’t know what you are on about.” I said trying to fish something from him.

“That girl that you have taken for a client.” He said taking the hook I had baited.

“You mean Samantha?”

“Yeah. She’s bad news, man.”

“OK, you want to be helpful? What do you know about spoon bending?”

“It’s all energy. You want one of these?” He said pouring a neat rum.

“Not if you’re going to put some of that funky stuff in it.”

“Don’t worry,” laughed Paul, “I don’t think I could get away with that again. Besides, that was just to prove a point. But I could show you something.”

“I’ve seen it.” I said sarcastically.

“Not that. I mean something this girl may not have shown you.” He said, then cocked His head, “Where is She anyway?”

“Jail.”

“What? What did She do?” He said surprised.

“Don’t worry it’s nothing. It’s more for Her protection until I get something to work on. It’s nothing really.” I lied for the second time.

“Her protection? Or yours?” He said looking me strait in the eye.

I didn’t say anything; I just gave him a dirty look.

“What do you know? What did you want to show me?” I urged as He proffered me a drink.

I took it and made my way over to the window. I pulled the blinds, so none of the fading light could get in.

“Well, it’s an energy thing.”

“You said that already give me something that I can work on here.” I said a little impatiently.

“Like I said, it’s all an energy thing. We all have it within us. It’s something that we can get from the ground, the air, the tress, even our own bodies. The way we look at people and the way we treat them and get treated. The way the sun shines through the clouds and the way our brains tell our muscles to do something. This energy comes from our chakra where it can be turned into anything. It's there, but it's not there. When we learn how to harness this energy we can do anything with it."

"Like bending spoons."

"Yeah, like bending spoons. It's all mind control. Some people have it and some people don't. It can be learned or it can just come to you after a jolt or a shock."

"You say it can be taught?" I asked.

He had peaked my curiosity.

"That's right."

"Can you teach me?"

"Not the spoon bending thing, but I do know a few tricks." He said.

He was walking over to one of the two chairs on the opposite side of my desk. I wondered over in silence to sit down in my chair and just looked at him.

"Like what?" I urged.

"Like controlling the electricity in my body."

"OK, show me."

"Dim the light." He said.

I stood up and turned the desk lamp on facing it towards the desk, so it was only a glow and then went over to the light switch to turn the main lights off before going back to my desk and sitting down.

What happened next was incredible. Paul stood up and shook His hands a bit as if to loosen His muscles. He took three deep breaths and just stood there for a moment or two before raising His hands. With His two index fingers pointed towards each other He brought them slowly together until they were only about two centre metres apart and then opened His eyes. There was a bright blue spark that jumped from one finger to the other and back again. I jumped and blinked my eyes a bit.

"What the fuck was that?" I exclaimed.

"That was nothing, keep watching."

He stood there for a moment more. Again there was the spark and again I jumped. Then again the spark, and again. Time after time, faster and faster the sparks jumped. They were now jumping so fast that I couldn't even tell if they were still jumping. All I could see was a bright blue line between His fingers like the electricity in one of those electric balls that you put your hands on. I just stared. The line was jumping around like a live wire in water and the glow was getting brighter. All of a sudden a huge spark leapt across to my hand and I yelped in pain as I saw the scorch mark.

"What the fuck. Shit man!"

"Sorry about that I didn't mean it."

"Turn that bloody thing off before you give me a heart attack!"

As I said that a big bolt of electricity stretched the length between His hand and the desk lamp blowing the bulb and turning everything dark.

"Not again." I said digging in my pocket for my lighter.

I flicked the flint and the flame danced in the dark to lead me to the light switch once more. On went the lights and I just looked at Paul.

"Happy now?" He said.

"That you blew a bulb?" I questioned.

He smiled at me.

"Something like that. Do you want to see something else?"

"Not if it means my office will go up in flames no."

"No, it's perfectly safe this time." He laughed.

He stood up and walked over to me. I had a strange suspicion that I knew what He was up to.

"Just relax." He said.

"Relax? After all that? Are you fucking mad? I just lost another light bulb after seeing you glow in the dark like some refugee from Muraroa and you're asking me to relax. I don't think so kid – I half expect to see oxygen masks fall from the ceiling!"

"Have another drink if it will calm you down." He suggested.

This I was more than willing to do. I walked over to the cabinet and poured myself a triple.

"And one for me."

I did as He bid and handed him the glass.

"Lets sit somewhere more comfortable and I'll show you what else this energy can do." He said with a smile.

I eyed him suspiciously, but went along with it any way. I walked into my room and sat on the bed. I was more than a little nervous about what He was going to do. He followed me in and sat next to me.

"Now close your eyes and trust me." He said.

I took a deep breath and closed my eyes. I jumped slightly when I felt His finger touch my forehead just between the eyes, but that's all it was and I was kind of looking forward to whatever it was He was going to show me. The light show was scary, and painful, but it was enjoyable too.

"Now, just let your mind wonder and your thoughts disappear. I'm going to count from five to one and when I snap my fingers you will be nicely relaxed. Are you ready?" He asked.

I nodded.

"5…4…3…2…1" and He snapped His fingers.

And right then my mind went blank and all I could feel was complete relaxation.

"Can you hear me?" This was His voice.

But it wasn't from the outside it was from inside my head.

"Um, yes. Can you hear me?" I thought.

"Of course. This is something new that I found out about. Do you like it?" I heard him think.

"It's amazing and really quite frightening."

He then took His finger off my head and I immediately opened my eyes.

"Cool aye?" He said with a smile.

I just looked at him and my body was totally relaxed. I could feel His body heat next to mine and He looked me right in the eyes.

"Um, yeah. Look…errr…I got to, um." I stumbled.

"Got to what?"

Whatever He was doing caught me like a deer in a set of headlights and I couldn't move. Nor did I want to. At that moment He leaned over and kissed me lightly on the lips. I snapped out of it.

"What are you doing Paul?" I said as I pulled away.

"Nothing that you don't want me to do." He said as He put a hand on my lap.

I looked down at it as it rested there and I felt that familiar movement in my loins.

"Look I…"

"Don't think about it." He said.

He leaned over again and kissed me gently on the cheek. This time I didn't pull away and for the life of me I don't know why. I felt His hand move up my leg and draw close to my crotch. I actually wanted this. I could feel something welling up inside of me ready to explode. He kissed my lips, and then again. I closed my eyes and just let it happen. My mouth fell open as I felt His lips press against mine once more and then His tongue playing with mine.

"What the fuck is going on here?"

This was a new voice and it jolted me out of the place I was at. My heart raced and I felt my face go bright red as I realized that I had been caught doing something that I shouldn't have been doing. Paul's hand snapped back from my crouch and I turned to see who had just invaded my space.

"King?"

"Sam! My God!!!"

All I could do was stare at Her.

"Sam? What?" Said Paul and turned around to see Her standing there.

"PJ! What the?" Shouted Sam.

"PJ? What? Paul? OH GOD NO!" As I realized what was going on.

"Fuck me!" Said Paul.

He headed for the door followed closely by Sam.

"Wait, Sam! What the hell have I just missed?" I said as I saw the both of them scurry out the office and the door slammed behind them.

The full weight of the situation hit me like a tone of bricks. This can't be happening! I fell back on the bed and let out a load, frustrated moan.

- 35 -

I really didn't know what to think. This couldn't be happening, not to me. What had I done to deserve all this? I felt sick and not just because of my indiscretions with another man, but because that other man just happened to be the man with whom the woman I was in love with was in love with. Even just the thought of it confused the hell out of me and I never thought I would be involved in anything even closely resembling this.

What the hell was I doing?

I consoled myself by saying that I had no idea that it would turn out like this. But then, there it was. A secret shared between Paul and myself had now been breached by another. I don't even know if I could look at Her again and not think of what was going on inside Her head now. Not only was Sam having an affair with Her Step-Brother, but that same Step-Brother had an affair with me. Could this be any more sordid? This whole turn of events had turned to shit and I couldn't see a way out of it. I had no idea what I would say to Sam or what She would say to me. I felt panicked and frustrated and a mix of other emotions that I couldn't understand. Midnight had been and gone. My hand was still throbbing and now I might just have lost all hope of ever being with Sam again. I had to do something to take my mind off things, so I wondered over to my desk and sat down at the computer.

"I have discovered the link between Paul and Samantha."

What the hell was I writing here?

"Paul is PJ, the man that Samantha has been talking about these last few days. On reflection of the past murders I now understand that Paul's life may also be in danger."

I suddenly realized that Sam was no longer in the protective custody of the police. What happened there?

“Further to this it appears that the plan I had put into place for Samantha has failed. She is now in just as much danger as Paul and Myself.”

I thought for a while and picked up the receiver.

“Hi, detective. This is King.”

“Ah King. We’ve been trying to get hold of you for a while. Your phone hasn’t been working, so we’ve sent an officer around to see you.”

“I’m using my phone, so don’t give me that shit.” I said.

“I’m not telling you stories, King. I’m too busy for those games.” He said.

That would explain a few things I thought. There was a knock on the door.

“Um, there’s someone at the door, but I just want to know about Sam.”

“That will be my man. He’s a plain-clothes cop and He’ll answer all your questions. I’ve got to go King. I’m sorry this didn’t work out for you.” He said and the line went dead.

There was a second knock on the door, so I put the receiver back on its cradle and went to answer the door.

“Who is it?” I questioned.

“Robert Kingly?” The man said.

I chained the door and opened it enough to see who it was. There was a young man standing there looking through the gap back at me.

“That’s me.” I answered.

The man nodded and showed me His badge. He was young as I said, but I think a little too young to be a cop. I guess with stretched resources the department needed all the people they could get.

“I’m Officer Baker.” He said.

I unchained the door and I stood aside to let the Officer in.

“Take a seat.” I said motioning him to one of the two seats as I took my place in my own. “How can I help you Baker?”

"The department just wanted to let you know that Samantha Samson used Her phone call to contact Her lawyer. I must say She's not very happy with you."

"Go figure. I drugged Her and got Her arrested."

"Still, I don't know how you are still alive. She swore death onto you my friend." He continued. "Her lawyer said that as we had no hard evidence to go on that we had to release Her."

"How about probable cause?"

"That only washes with chicken shit lawyers. I don't know where this guy came from, but He smelled of money. She must have something of a rich family." He said a little insensitively.

"I'm just starting to question that myself. So, She's out and about again is She?"

"Yes sir, and from what She said She was intent on doing you some serious harm. She was headed over this way when the Detective tried to call you. He sent me over because He couldn't get you on the phone. To be honest with you, Kingly," He said with a sigh, "I didn't expect you to be alive when I knocked."

"Thanks for the vote of support."

"I'm serious. She was hell bent. None of us could've stopped Her. She was like this totally different person." He said.

"I get the point. Well Baker, thank you for dropping by. As you could imagine I have a lot to think about, so if you don't mind I will see you out now." I said as politely as I could.

"Don't mind at all sir, just happy that I found you alive."

"I guess that makes two of us." I said as I showed him to the door and locked it behind him.

I walked over to my desk and reached for the cigarette packet and my lighter. I paused to think about what the officer said. I pursed the cigarette between my lips and lit the end. I inhaled the first plume of smoke and released waiting for that buzz to hit me.

So, inadvertently Paul had saved my life. I have been told time and time again that nothing happens with out a reason. Was this really the reason that Paul and I had that intimate moment? Surely not, but it made sense. Did I want to admit to it? That's a different question and not one that I was ready to face. I mean, what am I? I'm not gay; I love women too damn much. I don't even fancy men in that way, but with Paul it was different. My first and only time I'd say, well, almost second. The thing that really gets me is that I enjoyed it and kind of wanted it to happen again. It was hard enough to grasp the fact that I had oral sex with a man who is, for all intense and purpose, a stranger. Now I had to face the fact that it was meant to happen to protect me. But who was in control? That's the biggest question I'm faced with, who was pulling the puppet strings?

***

"Hi Sophia, this is King." I said to the receiver.

"Hi, King. I thought I'd never hear back from you again."

"Was that what you could see in the future?" I said jokingly.

"No, a personal thing." She said.

I let myself smile.

"I need your help, Sophia."

"I know, that's why we met." She replied.

"Look I'm still not too sure about all this universe stuff and reasons and why we meet people. All I want to know is what I am faced with here."

"King, let me tell you something about all that 'stuff'. You have the answers, all of them. Their locked in your memory and you just have to unlock them somehow and figure this whole thing out."

I realised, a bit ashamedly, that every time we talk we only seem to talk about the universe and stuff and I'm asking all the questions. What ever happened to small talk and 'how's your family these days?' I thoroughly enjoyed talking to people about this type of thing I must admit; it gives me a slight tingle up and down my spine when suddenly I'm hit with something that makes so much sense.

"You mean everything that has happened so far will lead me to what is going on? The killer?" I said sceptically.

I got up from my desk and grabbed the bottle of rum or what was left of it and brought them over while pushing the speaker phone button.

"What killer? No, never mind I don't think I want to know. As to the your question, actually if you're talking chronologically no. But if you're talking reality then yes. Everything that is about to happen has already happened. Every moment happens at the same time therefore those feelings you get when you know something is going to happen, that gut feeling; it's the memory. Do you see what I mean? Everything that has happened, is happening and ever will happen is happening right now. Our minds can't handle this concept, so we 'see' only the chronological path." She explained.

"I'm no closer to understanding what you just said than before you started."

"If every moment has happened already then you already know what's going to happen. You just have to listen to yourself."

"OK, I don't really get it, but I'll go along with it. What you're saying is this," I started as I poured myself a drink, "the gut feelings that I have are like premonitions? Are you saying that the situation can't be changed?"

"Sort of. The actual outcome will remain the same, but the path to get there may vary."

“So, there is nothing that I can do? It’s already happened, so I may as well sit back and watch.”

“No. The mere fact that you are involved tells me that whatever your input is it will make a difference. Everyone has a part to play whether you are successful or not depends on what the universe has planed.”

“OK, so whatever happens I’m involved no matter what.”

“Yes your input makes the world of difference.”

“What if I decide to sit back and watch?”

“Then that’s what was meant to happen.”

“Oh Christ. See, you *are* telling me that I have no choice? Whatever I decide to do is part of the plan?”

“You got it. So, the best thing to do if you don’t want any hardship or anything is to listen to yourself. Your mind and heart will tell you what you need to do.”

“Could we meet again?”

***

I hadn’t seen Her since the first time we met and there was something different about Her. She looked smarter, wiser. I don’t know maybe it’s just because of everything She had taught me. She saw me and waved me over. It was a beautiful Auckland day as far as Auckland days go, on the rooftop of Her apartment. One could see between the taller buildings for miles if it wasn’t for all the smog and pollution in the air. She lived on the outskirts of town in a twenty story high rise. The roof sported a couple of small gardens and the elevator shaft motor that was hidden away in a shack-like box in one corner of the roof. Apart from a few scattered chairs there was nothing else. The entire city was visible and you could even make out the waterfront, but anything past the city limits was kind of obscured by the dense fog. I wondered over to where Sophia was and sat down next to Her.

"Beautiful isn't it." She said.

"Honestly?"

"Oh go on, admit it. It's a spectacular site. The only reason you think it looks disgusting is because you know what it's all about and why it looks like that."

"That is what makes it look disgusting, yes."

"Try looking at it from a non-purist point of view. I know what it used to look like, but just try to imagine that everything that you see is natural. When you look at it from that point of view it really is beautiful. The refracted light trying to fight it's way through the cloud. The buildings jutting up from the ground in a forest of steel and glass. The array of colours of the people moving around way down there and the sound floating up from the street. I know this is a different generation, but could you imagine if you were about fifteen or twenty right now? This is what you would be used to if it's what you are born into. If you don't know any better then you assume this is the way it is. Then it's beautiful."

"I see what you mean. It actually is amazing." I said.

Maybe it was the first time that I had looked at the city that way or any way for that matter. I guess I just never took the time out to smell the roses as it were.

"The colours." She said.

"What's that?"

"The colours. When the sun peeks out from behind the clouds the city sparkles with a million different colours. Do you want a drink?" She said directing my attention inside with a flick of Her head.

"I'd love one. I mean I shouldn't really, but I don't think it will kill me to have just one."

I took up Her offer and followed the lovely woman inside and into Her apartment. It was amazing what She had done with the place. It was so small, but She was able to take advantage of every little inch She had. There were shelves filled with books and little bottles of different coloured liquids. There were pieces of art from all over the world hanging on the walls which added to the rich, fullness of the place. One drink turned into three drinks, three drinks turned into six and pretty soon we were both rather drunk and just enjoying each other's company. Sophia was the one who started down the track that I wasn't too sure I wanted to go down.

"Have you ever done regressive hypnosis?" She asked.

"Depends," I said, "what is it?"

"It's a away that we can take our selves back to a time in our lives or one of our lives to find important moments that have shaped our destinies. We can look back and see where we have come from and make a clear picture of where we are going."

"Sounds very…um…silly."

"Yes it does, doesn't it." She smiled. "Psychologists have been using this technique for decades. Would you like to try it? I swear to you that it is perfectly harmless. Although it is guided hypnosis you will only do what your subconscious will let you do. You can't do anything that you don't want to do."

"So, you won't turn me into a chicken or anything like that? I won't suddenly start barking if I hear a whistle?" I asked sceptically.

"No." She laughed. "Nothing like that. That's for entertainment, stage stuff, fun and magic. What I'm talking about is therapeutic."

She said it with a smile that I couldn't resist, so I didn't. Before long She had me sitting in a comfortable position on the very relaxing couch listening to my breathing. With a few words in Her lovely, melodic voice I felt myself drift away into a world that was so totally different to anything I had ever experienced. Not even the meditation that I went through with Sam was anything like this. Relaxation was the word and that was me completely. I've never felt so at peace, not like this anyway. I could think clearer, but there were no thoughts. Everything around me was so alive. And then I heard Sophia speak again.

"Where are you King?"

This question caught me off guard because I didn't think that I was 'anywhere' other than in Her apartment. It was when I thought about it I realised that my mind had put me in a different setting and the image started to swirl into a type of realness.

"In a bright place. Not too sure where it is or even if it is a place." I found myself saying. "It's just bright and cheery. This is great. I feel so good, so ready for – for anything."

"You are going between what we call alpha and beta states. This is the wakeful sleep of the mind where the conscious talks to the subconscious. In other words, you are hypnotised."

"Get out of here!" I said.

"OK, try to open your eyes." She challenged.

I tried it. For the life of me I couldn't open them. They were shut tight!

"I can't."

"That's right. You are in a suggestive state which means that you can now be guided. Your eyes are your escape pod now. If things get to a point that you can't handle at any time in this session just open your eyes and you will come right out of this state and feel refreshed and alive. You will remember everything that we have done here." She said.

By just giving me the option to stop this thing at any time made me make a promise to myself that I was going to be strong and nothing could make me want to stop it. Reverse psychology works well on me.

"Are you ready?" She asked.

"Lets rock!" I said with a slight slur.

***

I don't know how long I had been sitting there for, but I was cold, very cold. The dampness made its way through all my clothing to make me shiver with the frigid wind. The mud was thick and smelly, but it was something that you got used to at least that's what you tell yourself anyway. But the worst bit was the waiting. There was nothing else to do. It was so quiet and it seemed as though everything was asleep out there. Nothing stirred. I had seen it when things were happening here though, boy have I. People everywhere, shouts and cries, pain and anger from all times of the day and night as if it would never stop. But it stops. Yes, it stops. When it stops it's very quiet, too quiet. The quiet does help though. It helps to hear if anyone is coming. Right now though there was nothing. Just the cold and the mud and the stillness of the night. Everything was uncomfortable and I hated the waiting. I couldn't see anything as it was all so dark.

Was there any point me being here? I could just as easily kill someone that I wasn't supposed to kill and then I would get in trouble. Then again there shouldn't be anyone that I know wondering around at this time of night, so I guess the chances of that happening were quite small. Still I was cold and shivering, damp and unhappy.

What was that noisc?

I grabbed my spear and got down low and let the light of the moon guide my eyes.

Nothing.

Suddenly there is a whizzing sound and a thud. Then the pain hit me and I realize that I have been hit with an arrow. This can't be happening! I didn't see anyone out there. Who did this? The pain is unbearable. I got up to see where it came from and try to raise the alarm when I hear another whiz and thud. This time I have been hit in the shoulder. I'm bleeding heavily and my sight is growing darker and everything is getting very cold. My energy has been sapped and when I try to yell nothing comes out. I slump back down and everything goes black. Now the pain is gone and all I can see is a wonderful white light.

***

She was right. I felt refreshed and alive, awake and invigorated. The memories of what I had just been through were still fresh in my mind.

"What was that?" I asked Sophia.

"That was a memory from one of your past lives." She replied.

I'm still rather sceptical when it comes to past lives. I don't know how long I'm going to hold on to the imagination that everything is as it seems and that nothing has changed. It's as if I can't seem to get away from the fact that everyone I meet up with is a fruitcake.

"OK, you're going to have to explain this to me." I urged.

"About what? The past lives?"

"Yeah. Is that something to do with reincarnation due to our merits here on earth or what?" I asked.

She laughed softly and rearranged herself on the couch next to me.

"This is how it works, so try to follow."

"I'll try." I said smiling.

She was so calm, so under control and I felt like I was borrowing Her energy or something. It was weird, but I felt very comfortable around Her.

"There are new souls and there are old souls; I'll explain about that later. We have many lives as different people and each life we lead teaches us something new. There is a lesson to learn."

"So, what is my lesson?"

“Only you know that.” She said.

Apparently She didn’t know either.

“I can’t tell you anything about your journey because that is part of your lesson. But there are a few things that I can tell you just by looking at you.”

“Like what.” I smiled.

She closed Her eyes and sat there silently for while. All I could do was look at Her. She was beautiful and I felt a few urges well up from inside of me. Suddenly it was as if I was talking to someone different. I don't know what it was, but She had changed. The only thing that went through my mind then was 'not again'.

With Her eyes shut She started to speak.

“I come to you as oneness. I am your desire; I have learnt. Please allow me the honour to demonstrate my power and your need.” She paused and my mind went swimmy again.

Why is it that everybody I come in contact with speaks like this at some point? She looked to be in a trance of some sort. Was She communicating with the spirits or something?

“You see the touch of a man. The feeling you get is rough and full of sexual vitality.” She continued.

Oh God, how does She know? This was getting crazy! She couldn’t know about that it’s impossible. My face went red as She touched on this most private side of me. Maybe it wasn’t spirits She was contacting, but my deepest thoughts. Did I say something while under hypnosis?

“It is a feeling that will leave you hollow and wanting more. A feeling that will come and go.”

I readjusted myself uncomfortably in the couch as Her face grew closer to me. It was like She was speaking from someone else. A vague familiarity swept over me.

“The touch of a woman, however, is soft and gentle. A felling that screams love and passion, hot and sensual. A feeling that leaves you full and peaceful. That feeling will last forever.

“The words of a man are powerful and deep leaving you breathless and weak. ‘I feel what you feel, I want what you want. I taste and smell what you do. I long for your body and passion to fill my soul and to make me a man.’ Fulfilling, but temporary. The words from a woman will make you fell whole and wanted.”

She seemed to be summing up everything that I was thinking about my recent experiences. It was like She was in character; but what character? Was She a medium? Could She read my mind? Was I that transparent? Whatever the case I was transfixed on what She was saying.

“A woman will make you feel alive and wanted. ‘You are the sun, you are the moon and the stars are the gifts you gave. Your moonbeam is my stairway to heaven. I offer you my mind, heart and soul. For the nights are brighter and the days linger. The rose blooms redder and the angels whisper your name.’ Longer lasting and warm.”

So, what was She trying to tell me? That I can have both? Or is She saying that one is better than the other? I closed my eyes and focussed my thoughts on what She had just said. She was amazing. I could see Her in my mind as if I still had my eyes open.

“I am here as oneness for I can give you both. I am borne to man, but raised by woman. I can give you the world in what you want. Just let me show you.”

And with that I felt Her lips on mine and I fell into the most wonderful, soft kiss and I just let myself drift away on Her sensual tongue. The room started to spin for me and I couldn’t help myself. I took hold of Her shoulders and kissed Her deeply as the emotions came to the surface. She was an incredible woman and I felt like I was floating on air as Her breathing became heavier. Then the words of Odin filtered through my mind 'There will be a replacement' and I couldn't go on. I just stopped. Gone were the lustful thoughts of a second ago. Gone was the longing to pick Sophia up and carry Her to Her bed and connect with Her on another level. I tensed up and pushed Her away making some space between the two of us.

"This isn't right. I can't do this?" I said huskily as a bead of sweat rolled off my forehead.

"What are you talking about? Of course it's right! What could be so wrong? Don't you like me or something?" She replied wide-eyed.

"No it's nothing like that. You wouldn't understand."

I couldn't tell Her that I felt like this was a set up and I felt like I was cheating on Sam.

"I just can't do this now. I can't explain it."

"You *don't* like me do you?" She said standing up looking like She had just made the biggest fool of herself.

"I do, it's just that…it's just that I have something very important that I have to do and this isn't helping." I stood up with Her and touched Her lightly on the forearm. "There is something that I am working on. Some place I should be. This was never meant to happen and I'm sorry."

"I wanted this. You wanted this." She said as a tear rolled down Her cheek.

"No, I didn't," I lied, "it just happened. I got caught up in the moment. Look I've got to go. I'm sorry."

I looked Her in the eye to show that I was actually sorry. I did feel all those things and I did want it and…well it was just that I am in love with Sam. There I said it. I am in love with Sam and no matter what anybody else does and no matter what the situation is with Her and Her Brother I was in love with Her and I had to find out what was going on with Her.

I had to find Her.

I excused myself from the house leaving Sophia crying which made me feel even worse. I looked back at Her before shutting the door.

"I really am sorry." I hung my head and closed the door.

- 36 -

I was far too drunk to drive, so I decided the walk would do me good. The air was warm and a light wind shifted the smog a bit, so breathing was a little easier. So many things were going through my head and I couldn't understand any of them. What had gone so wrong? Why were all these people dying on me and what the fuck is the deal with Odin and Asgard?

Nothing made any sense or it was making too much sense and began to get frightening. I tried to piece it together and work it out almost trying to disprove it all, but the only person that could shed any light on it was Sam and She was…wait, I had a thought. There was something about the walk that cleared my mind enough to figure that whatever it was that I was looking for was in Sam's flat. No it didn't make sense to me, but it was a gut feeling and I was told to listen to these feelings. It was about seven PM and rush hour was almost over; it was still hard to move, but at least you could move. There were a couple of taxis waiting on the other side of the road, so I wondered over and got into the first one.

"Hey, first of the night. Where to man?" Said the driver.

I gave him the address to Sam's flat and we were off.

"Going to a girlfriends place aye?" He said trying to make conversation.

I was not in the mood, so I just answered with a grunt.

"Wow, had a fall out did you?" He pressed.

"I guess you could say that?"

"What is it? Someone else involved? A third wheel huh? God I hate that. Women can be such bitches can't they?!"

"Actually we both dipped our feet into the temptation pool."

"Ah, you stud you!" He said with a wry smile. "A bit of stiff competition was it?"

"You have no idea!"

I couldn't help smile at the irony of it all. Who would have guessed that both Her and I would have been having an affair with the same person? Nothing I'm proud of, but it would have been a great subject for a chat show. Something told me, however, that it was going to get a whole lot more complicated.

"So, your woman, is She mad at you? Do you think She has the right? Well, you know women!"

"No actually, I don't. I don't think I will ever know them."

"Amen to that my friend. Here you go, that'll be…err…$150. Look seems like you're gonna be needing to buy something special to make up for what has happened, just make it $100 OK."

"Thank you very much, but what makes you think that I was in the wrong when we both screwed up?"

"My friend you have to learn that you are a man and men are always wrong even when they are right!"

"Amen to that!" I echoed and got out of the taxi.

I looked at the flat and the memories came flooding back. This was going to hurt. The taxi took off with a toot and I wondered down the steps. There was a light on inside and for the briefest moment I started to get my hopes up. I walked down the stairs and knocked on the door. The air had grown a little cooler and the crickets were in full swing giving the air a feeling of loneliness to the night. I waited for about a minute and knocked again. Still nothing. I walked around to the side of the small flat to see if there were any other lights around, but there was only the reflection of the next-door neighbours outside light and I realised with plummeting spirits that this was the light I saw from the front. She must have left in a hurry because all the curtains were left open. I spotted a box crate and moved it over to the wall, so I could use it as a standing stool and take a peek inside. As I lifted myself I had a brief hope that I was going to see Her asleep on the couch or something, but when I looked in all I could see was Her furniture and the shadows that played on the wall from the light outside. The place was deserted.

"Oi!" Cried a voice from next door.

It scared the crap out of me I almost lost it and fell off. I regained my composure and stepped back on the ground. There was a torchlight that circled around my feet and then up to my face blinding me to all else.

"What the hell are you doing here?" It was a female voice, barely.

"Ah…err…do you know Samantha that lives here?" I asked with a cough.

"Who wants to know?"

"The name is Robert Kingly. I'm a private investigator and I want to talk to Her."

"What the hell are you private investigating at eight o'clock at night?"

The light had completely faded into night and the torch was trained on my eyes.

"I'm sorry, but client confidentiality prevents me from discussing this with anybody else other that Samantha." What the hell was I saying?

"Well, you won't find Her here. She's been gone for a while now. Couple of days. Get lost!" She said and the torch was switched off.

The silhouetted figure withdrew into the house. I walked around to the front of the house to see if there was any other way in. Along the front was just one window and it looked to be locked from the inside, so I wondered down to the corner. There were shrubs and trees that made the few steps difficult to navigate in the dark and it seemed that my legs and face were fair game for the rouge branches. I got to the corner and tentatively peered down the other side of the house and saw a window that was slightly ajar. Bingo. I slowly, quietly made my way down the side of the house trying to be as inconspicuous as I could to the open window. Reaching up I pulled it open even more and realized I had come to another problem. How do I hoist myself up? I jumped up to grab hold of the sill and lift myself in, but my hands and arms were shaking and I couldn't help thinking that I must have put on a few extra kg, I just couldn't lift myself up. I hung there for a moment or two before I finally gave up, let go and fell the few inches back to the ground. My next option was to get something to give me the lift I needed, but there was nothing around that I could use. I walked to the back of the house to see if there were any other windows or at least something I could use to get into this one. I couldn't see Samantha as the gardening type, but there lined up against the wall were some potted plants a couple of garden tools and a few cobblestones stacked up. I grabbed a few of the cobblestones and piled them against the wall under the window, so I could get a boost up and in. This being done I promptly fell into the house knocking over a hopefully inexpensive vase, which smashed on the floor, but I was in.

I was about to search for the light when I decided that it was best if I didn't turn them on in case the mad woman next door got too suspicious and decided to call the cops; that would be awkward. So, I just prayed that there wasn't anything lying around that I could trip up on or gouge my shins against. Though, as I remembered, Sam was always a very neat and tidy person, but it seemed like She had left in a hurry. The place was very dark and I barely made anything out. I moved slowly and stealthily into the lounge where I saw a blinking light, which on closer inspection turned out to be Sam's answer phone.

Apparently She had a message.

I was about to press the button to see who it was when all of a sudden the phone sprang into life and almost gave me a coronary! I jumped about a metre and had to calm my self as it rang again. The noise it made in this quiet flat was deafening. It rang again and I waited patiently for the answer machine to kick in. Yet again it rang and it seemed like it was taking forever to answer. The fifth ring was interrupted with the beeping of the machine and whirring of machinery as Sam's voice floated through the air.

"Hi, this is Sam." The message started, "Sorry you can't reach me. I'm either not in, in the shower, in the toilet or having a shag. In any case you can't talk to me just yet, so you can leave a message and I'll get back to you."

The message ended and there were another couple of beeps before it started to record.

"Hi Sam, it's me." Said a very familiar voice. "I know you're not going to get this for a couple of days until you get back, but I was hoping you would check the machine remotely while you are away."

That voice, who was it?

"Look about the other night, I'm really sorry. I don't know what happened."

It was Paul. My God! I lurched to pick up the phone.

"Paul!" I said.

"Huh, who is this?"

"Paul, its King."

"King, what the fuck are you doing there? Is Sam back?" He asked in surprise.

"Err, don't ask difficult questions. Do you know where Sam is?"

"Yeah, but what are you doing there – oh, and about the other night."

"Forget about it. Where are you?" I asked anxiously.

"At home licking my wounds, why?" He asked.

I could understand; if I had time I would be doing the same thing right now.

"Like I said don't ask any questions right now. Do you have a key?"

"For Sam's place?"

"No, for Buckingham fucking Palace!"

"Hey now there's no need to take…"

"Do you have a key?" I asked again almost shouting down the phone.

My voice sounded horse as I tried to sound load, but was constantly worried that I could be heard from next door.

"Yes."

"Come around now. I need your help."

With that I hung up the phone and heard the machine click a couple of times and then go silent. I sat on the couch and just waited. I felt quite sober now.

- 37 -

The fact that I liked smoking was just an excuse not to quit. I know I hated the feeling of not being able to breathe in the mornings and having to take a puff of Salbutamol from a blue inhaler that sat on my bedside table. On top of everything else I didn't feel like this was the greatest of all times to give up. What was I doing? Ever since that day almost a month ago when I folded and had that last cigarette that was sitting, teasingly in that lonely packet. I had purposefully left just one smoke in the pack. I found it was always harder to try to give up when you didn't have any smokes than it was if you actually had some. It must have been some kind of psychological thing knowing that if you really wanted one you could have one, but you could tell yourself that you didn't need it. Well that was the plan anyway and it backfired very badly because when times are tough all a smoker feels like doing was having a smoke. I hadn't exactly been a heavy smoker since that day, but right now I had no cigarettes and a lot of alcohol in my system. It had been at least forty-eight hours since my last drag and I was starting to feel it again. My mind was wondering and I started to think of nothing else, but breathing deeply on that disgusting, acrid smoke. It was the in thing now, not to smoke that is, but that didn't really make things any better for me. A long time, full on smoker for the last thirty years takes a lot out of you and like a reformed alcoholic you know that you will always be a smoker no matter how long it's been since your last cig. I was definitely feeling it now and the more that I thought about it the worse it became. My nerves were frayed and there was not a thing I could do about it right now. I kept thinking about the way it felt as the smoke from a deeply inhaled cigarette clawed its way down my throat. Then there was the hit of nicotine as my blood was furnished with the poison and rushed it to my head giving my whole body the feeling of being very heavy. All at once you just don't care any more as the stresses of the world evaporated and the thought that you got what you craved for. The drug of choice for generations was enough to make a smoker smile with euphoria every time He or She lit up. Right now that's what I needed to feel. Again the complete lack of any cigarettes on my person was enough to make me crave more and the fact that I wasn't able to smoke in Sam's flat made it worse. This was all too hard on me and my whole body was going into hyper-drive. My hands were shaking and my throat was dry. My knee was nervously pumping up and down on the ball of my foot giving me the image of one who is strung out of heroin – just looking for that next taste. I could kill for a cigarette right now sitting here in the dark just waiting, just wincing and moping and getting more and more aggravated by the second until I heard that unmistakable sound of a set of keys playing into the lock on the door. No sooner had I jumped up ready for action to hound whoever it was that invaded my territory than I realized that it was more than likely Paul and I had told him to come over.

"I still don't know what you are doing here man." He said as He saw me jiggling on the couch.

"Shut up, sit down and give me a cigarette!" I said tersely.

"Hey, fuck you! Show a little respect! You don't live here and I don't live here. We're not here legally and you're telling me what to do! Get a life and get out of here." He said with a power I didn't think He had.

I was getting more and more upset and uptight. Strung out on a habit that I couldn't get a fix on.

"SIT!" I shouted at him. "YOU LISTEN HERE YOU WORM." I realized that I was shouting and I had to calm down. "Look, you have some nerve. I am so pissed off with you right now and not only because you hurt Sam, but you hurt me also. I have never been put in a position where I have doubted myself and you made me do just that. I could literally garrotte you right now! Why did you do it?" I asked trying to get my mind off Sam.

“I never meant to hurt anyone.” He answered a little nervously.

I must have been intimidating him which was my goal because He hadn’t moved since I first started to yell at him.

“To be honest with you, I didn’t think anybody would find out. I thought I would get away with it.”

“Give me a cigarette!” I snapped.

“King, I don’t smoke.” He said, almost apologetically.

“Well, that’s no excuse. Well, it is, but it isn’t. What do you know? Where has Sam taken off to and what was the last thing that She said to you? And for Christ sake don’t just stand there! Turn a light on and come sit down you’re making the place look untidy and making me feel uncomfortable.” I may have been a little over the top.

To be honest His sad little lost boy look would have been softening me up right about now if it wasn’t for the fact that I could have quite happily and literally put my mouth over a chimney and taken a deep breath.

“Well She told me” He started fumbling around for the light switch, “to fuck off – AHH!”

The last was in response to the light as it came on and stung His eyes.

“Not the most romantic thing to say, but granted in light of the situation wouldn’t you say.” He said with a ‘what-you-gonna-do-about-it’ smile. “She said She was going to visit relatives down in Wellington for a while until all this stuff is sorted out. Can’t say I blame Her.” He said as He sat down.

“So, what exactly did She say?” I asked, looking right at him and slightly under my eyebrows.

I had no idea why, but I was hoping it didn’t look like I was flirting. Although, maybe that would actually help the situation.

"Like I said, She has family down there. She said something about having to get down there before the next full moon or something. Personally I think any mention of a full moon when She is already stir crazy is kind of scary." He said with the giggle of irony.

"That's not funny." I said defensively.

"You love Her don't you? I mean, you're *in* love with Her aren't you?"

"Not that it's any of your business, but yes I am." I replied. "But, apparently the better man won the affections of Samantha, albeit Her Brother."

This caused a look of shock on His face that could have been a winner on the world's funniest home videos.

"Step Brother! She told you about that?" Was His high pitched answer.

He wasn't sure what to do or say as His face went bright red.

"Nobody was supposed to find out about that. Only Her and I know." He said flustered with a shake of His head and an accusatory pointing of His finger.

"Sorry to disappoint you and not that it makes any difference, but Jason knew also." I said.

There was the sound not unlike the mating call of a tomcat coming from Paul as He cupped His hands around His face is despair.

"This can't be happening." He said with a hollow sob.

"No use worrying about it now. As horrible as it is it's out now even if it is to only two people and even if one of those is dead anyway."

"Do you think it's horrible? What am I saying? Of course it's fucking horrible! I feel like I should be in a circus or something. I'm a freak!" He said melodramatically.

"Hey hey, don't go overboard it's not as bad as it seems and certainly not illegal. Now pull yourself together. Do you know these relatives of hers?" And as I said it I realized that I had just put my foot in it big time and the look He gave me confirmed my suspicions.

"Oh man, I'm sorry. I really wasn't thinking. Forget I said anything. Let's just go down and get Her. Something about that whole full moon thing gives me the creeps. We only have two days to figure out if there is anything we should worry about. God knows there have been stranger things going on. Anything to do with the moon is bound to be one of the least bizarre." I said.

With that we both got up and headed for the door. Paul switched the lights off and stopped right in front of me when all was dark. I could feel the heat of His face on mine. I could feel one of those moments, but swore that there was no time for any of this shit; now or ever again. Yet, I felt His hand brush up to mine.

"I'm really sorry. Honestly. I never meant for any of this to happen." He said in a hushed voice.

I just stood there with emotions streaming through my body again.

"Lets go." I said

I pushed passed him and out the door. I heard the door close and lock and Paul's footsteps follow me as I headed for His car.

- 38 -

"How could you? How the fuck could you do it? I'm still at a total loss as to how you could do something so stupid." I announced breaking the two-hour silence.

From the time that we got into Paul's car, to my office to pick up my wallet and throw a few clothes in a suitcase, to stop at a shop to buy some smokes, to Paul's place, so He could grab some clothes, then to the airport; nothing had been said. Paul had talked to the lady at the ticket counter at the domestic terminal and said 'thank you' to the guy at the boarding platform, but apart from that not a word was said until I opened my mouth when we were taking off and made Paul jump.

"Um, what?" He said, not having the faintest idea what I was talking about.

"You cheating on Samantha like that and with me no less! It's disgusting. It's horrible and She doesn't deserve that."

"And you? I suppose you are a saint in that department." He said with a raised eyebrow.

I was kind of stuck for anything to say to that. Surely I hadn't been as bad as He was. I thoughtfully sucked my upper lip. I couldn't have been such a bastard? I don't do that type of thing. I started to get a bit flustered when suddenly a thought occurred to me.

"You drugged me the first time remember."

"Ah yes, well I can explain that." He defended.

"So, can I. You wanted to shag my brains out…"

"King!" He said in a harsh whisper, "People can hear you in case you had forgotten."

My face went red.

"You wanted to shag my brains out, so you bloody well drugged me." I whispered. "How else do you explain it?"

"OK." He whispered looking around to see if there was anyone listening in, "But I only did it because I thought you wanted it."

"Bullshit! You wanted to get off!" I whispered hoarsely, trying to sound as angry as I could without anyone over hearing me.

I could just imagine what anybody would be thinking had they been able to listen in, 'Look at that dear. That couple over there, their having a right old fit of an argument aren't they. I reckon it's the age thing'. No, I couldn't handle that on top of everything else that had been happening.

"And the second time? There were no drugs involved then. You were right into that weren't you? Yeah, I could tell." He said with a raised eyebrow. "If Sam hadn't have walked in just them…"

"Hey, hey." I interrupted before He said anything that would make me throw up, "Sam and I were over then, OK. She chose you over me! Of course I had no Idea that Paul and PJ were one in the same person! But you, you knew who I was and still you went for it!"

"What can I say? You're a very attractive man."

"Don't give me that shit." I slumped back into the seat and let out a long sigh.

Paul relaxed as well, though there was still an enormous amount of tension in the air.

"Hey, I have an idea." He said.

"I'm afraid to ask."

"Lets join the mile high club!"

"PAUL!!" I said struck with horror.

He looked right at me and let out the most sincere, joyous laugh.

"You should see…" He said between fits of laughter, "…your face." And then burst out laughing again.

I looked at him and couldn't help but feel some humour welling up in me that made me smile. I couldn't suppress the chuckle that made my stomach lurch a few times and then turned into a laugh out loud fit as the full hilarity hit me. Tears started streaming down Paul's face and I followed suit. I was so close to wetting myself as the flight attendant pulled us back to reality.

"Would you like a light meal?" She said politely.

We both welcomed the food and dug in to the bread roll and small salad that had been presented to each of us on a small plastic tray. Everything was so small on planes almost as if they were designed to make you uncomfortable.

"I think we met on purpose." He said, catapulting a piece of lettuce onto my tray narrowly avoiding my own food.

"Watch it with the crop spray!"

"Sorry. Anyway," He continued unperturbed, "there is a reason for everything and I know that all we have to do is find out what that reason is. It's like, well you know, there is no such thing as a coincidence."

"Right, more of that stuff. Weren't you the one who tried to warn me away from this type of stuff?" I said with a frown trying to turn the whole thing around.

"Yeah, but," He started, the irony hadn't been lost on him, "I was right wasn't I? I mean you could have been so happy in your ignorance of this whole thing had you just listened to me."

He looked at me with an I-Told-You-So look and His head cocked to one side.

"But I did get involved and I am here."

"Exactly! So, it was meant to happen. You were supposed to ignore me and I was supposed to attempt to jump you."

"As it so happens I believe you." I said.

"What?" Snapped a surprised Paul.

"That night that Sam caught you and I before we dived into the muddy waters."

"OK. So, what was the reason?"

“She came over that night to kill me and if it hadn’t been for the fact that it soon turned into a livid jealousy and confusion over what She saw and walked out She would have done just that. I wouldn’t be on this plane right now explaining it to you if you hadn’t been about to do what you wanted to do.”

“Diving into the muddy waters huh? I was going to get my way with you was I?”

“Paul, I think you’ve missed the fucking point a wee bit there.” I said frustrated.

“Sorry, I know what you’re saying and you are starting to sound like me. Scary the way that you can make something that makes no sense at all sound logical.”

“It’s a gift.’ I said deadpan. “So, you say there are no such thing as coincidences.” I urged as the attendant whisked away the empty tray with a smile.

“That’s right.” He said wiping His mouth with a moist towelette. “It’s the same as saying there is a reason for everything you know. Coincidences don’t exist. Everything happens the way it is supposed to happen. It’s like trying to find enough money to fill your car with enough petrol to get you to a job interview.”

“Huh?” I saw the irony, but I didn’t see the connection.

“OK, so you don’t have any money for petrol, so you miss the interview. You think it’s a fucking shame ‘cause you need the job ‘cause you need the money. Truth is that you weren’t supposed to have that job for some reason. Perhaps it’s because the building blows up or something, I don’t know. But the next day you get the opportunity to go to a different interview, but you still have no money. Now you mope around long and hard trying to find the money all to no avail and suddenly around the corner you bump into a friend that has just got into town that day and you haven’t seen for years.”

The story seemed to be going nowhere and He'd lost me, but I tried to stay with him.

“Right. So, far I’m following.” I lied.

"OK, so this guy suddenly remembers that He owes you money and hands you the exact amount that it would take to get you to the interview and back. Coincidence or what?"

"So, did you get the job?" I said with a smile.

"Don't you get it? You think that it is a coincidence, but it's a sign. You were meant to go for the job. What's more the friend that you ran into is the guy that is interviewing you and you get the job!" He said with and enthusiastic grin.

"OK I believed all that crap up until the whole thing with the friend being the guy interviewing. It's a little far fetched for me I'm afraid."

"That's because you don't look for the coincidences."

"You just told me there is no such thing."

"OK, what I meant was you don't look for that type of thing. The signs." He said trying to think of the right words to use.

"Still don't believe it." I resigned.

"It's true. And I still have that same job!"

"You're the guy who needed the money."

"You doubt that?" He said with a smirk.

"Actually, no. No I don't."

The captain came over the intercom to announce we were about to land and could we put our trays and our seats in the upright position *cetera*. Wellington, here we come.

***

"OK, now what?" Asked Paul, looking at me for leadership, but I had none to give.

We were standing in the arrival lounge of Wellington airport. I was looking around wondering what to do.

“Firstly,” I said snapping out of my daze, “we go and get our luggage.”

Paul just looked at me and shook His head.

“Yeah, but,” He answered as we made our way down to the baggage claim, “what then?”

“I don’t know, but I’m sure we will find out.”

I don’t know where I was getting my confidence.

“Are we just going to stand around and hope for something to happen to tell us what we’re going to do next?” He said as a joke.

I looked at him right in the eye.

“Something like that, yes.” I said with a smile.

“What are you, kidding? You have no plan at all about what we are going to do.” He looked at me blankly.

“Well, do you?”

“No, but I’m following you remember.”

“Would you believe that? Our bags are the first off, here they come now.”

“So, what are we here to do exactly?”

“Following our noses.” I said picking up the first bag. “Here grab this, yours is next.”

“With all due respect, King, I don’t know if I trust your nose!”

“Thanks for the vote of confidence. I guess you’re just going to have to trust me aren’t you. After all, Paul, who was it that told me that there were no such things as coincidences?” I responded indignantly as I picked up Paul's bag. “You have to realise that I have been following this stupid universe around since I met Sam and this is where I am now. Here, grab your bag. There have been some very weird things that have happened since I met Her. I guess I’m just giving myself a chance with it all now.”

“You can’t seriously believe all this stuff do you? I mean the things I told you are just conversation fillers. You know, things to make you think.” He said.

“Paul, if there is one thing I have learnt since I've been on this case is that all of this airy-fairy stuff actually does exist. It’s not just something to talk about to get tingles up your spine.” I said turning to go outside. “There have been too many examples of the supernatural recently to ignore it. You can’t be that naive, can you?”

“Naive? You think I’m naive? Who’s the one who is standing around waiting for something to happen?”

“I’m not standing around, I'm walking towards the door and I guarantee you something will happen before we reach the aforesaid door.”

“You’re out of your mind King, how can you garant…”

“Excuse me sir.” Said a voice from behind us.

I turned around and saw a staff member standing there with my wallet in Her hand.

“Yes?” I said flashing a smile at Paul.

“One of you left this in the plane. I was hoping you hadn’t left yet.” She said with a smile holding up my wallet.

“My god! Yes, that’s mine.” I said reaching for it.

She pulled away.

“Sorry, you need to prove that it’s yours. Could I see some ID please, Sir?”

“I would love to, but all my ID is in that wallet.” I said to Her pointing to what She was holding.

Sometimes I wonder where the airlines get these people.

“Your boarding pass will do fine.” She said, looking at me as if I was stupid or something.

“Ah, yes.” I said rooting around in my overnighter, “Of course. Sorry.” I handed Her the pass.

“No problem. Here you go.” She said handing over my wallet.

"Thanks."

"Is there anything else I can do for you gentlemen?"

"No thanks. We're fine now." Said Paul.

"You wouldn't happen to know when the next full moon is would you?" I asked jokingly.

"Tomorrow night at six thirteen PM." She said with a smile

"How the hell did you know that?" We asked in unison.

"Don't you know? It's the first time in over three thousand years that all the planets, including He sun, are lined up on the opposite side of the moon."

"I don't follow." I prompted.

"OK, imagine this. There is a line of planets starting from planet X, going right down to the sun."

"Following."

"So, they are all in a straight line except for the Earth, which is on the opposite side of the Sun. After the Earth is the moon. All in a straight line, so if you looked at from space it would look like everything is revolving around the moon."

"Cool, but wouldn't that mean that we wouldn't be able to see the moon?"

"In theory yes. I'm not too sure about the scientific stuff, but apparently we will just be able to make it out, something to do with the sum of all the light or something like that."

"Surely this has happened a few more times over the last three thousand years years." Said Paul, surprising me with His interest.

"Yeah, but never on a Wednesday."

"Right." I said. "I see."

"Well, you know. Wednesday."

"Yes," said Paul, "the day after Tuesday."

She gave him a look of frustration and took a deep breath to explain.

"Do you know why it's called Wednesday?"

"Not really, no." Said Paul.

But this was something I should know. It's something that I used to know and it did sound vaguely familiar.

"It means the day of Woden. Woden is the Germanic word for Odin; the day of Odin, Odin's day." She said with a smile.

I looked at Paul in astonishment.

"OK, so it falls on a day named after the Norse Father of the Gods, which happens once every seven days. So what?"

"You didn't hear about the scrolls then?" She asked.

"What scrolls?" Paul Replied.

"Not so long ago," She started explaining, "archaeologists uncovered a buried scroll in Norway. It's hundreds of thousands of years old. It was on the news, did you hear about it?"

We both shook our heads.

"OK, so this scroll, and this was only found about three years ago, told about when Odin was banished from the realm of the living to Asgard because of some things He had said and done. I'm not too sure what, but anyway this scroll tells of the day when He claims the world back as His own. It goes on to say that when this astral thing happens on the day of the celebration of Odin, then Odin will come back to the mortal realm with a human and claim Her as His queen."

"What about Frig?" I butted in.

"Who?" She said, screwing up Her face.

She was kind of cute.

"Frig, the wife of Odin?"

"How should I know? I'm only telling you what I saw in the news."

"OK, sorry. Go on." I said.

"Well, that's about it really. That's what is happening tomorrow night." She finished.

"Thank you for that, believe me, you have been a big help."

"You're welcome." She said with a smile and wondered off.

"See! This is what I am talking about. Everything happens for a reason and this woman just gave us everything that we needed to know." I said to Paul as we walked out of the airport.

"She didn't tell us where to find Sam."

"That will come to us. Everything will come to us. You said it yourself, well someone said it, we are all part of the one. So, whatever we need will come to us. We just have to be patient and wait for it."

"Who got reincarnated and made you Buddha?"

"What's the time?" I asked ignoring the comment.

"Seven forty-five in the AM." Paul replied.

"OK, so we have little under thirty six hours to find Sam and get to the bottom of this. Lets go."

"Where? Where the hell are we going? We have no clue as to where Sam is! We don't know what we are looking for and we don't know what to do! Face it, we don't know squat!" He said coming to a stop at the Taxi rank.

"Oh yea of little faith. Let's just go! We don't have much time, it will all come to us."

"OK, Yoda, where are we going?"

"Hop in." I said as I opened the door to the nearest Taxi. "To town please."

- 39 -

8:00 AM

I was just starting to believe all this stuff about every moment being part of every other moment and the coincidences and everything to do with everything being part of everything else. It was all very confusing, but once you grasped the basic concept that nothing is as it seems it all sort of slots in nicely and you find that you have no control over anything. The secret to it, as I was starting to find out, is everything happens for a reason. There is some sort of divinity working here. Some sort of destiny thing, I don't know what it is, but it seems that if you let go and watch as things start to happen around you, it all makes perfect sense. Most of the time it doesn't make sense until everything has happened and you can look back, but every once in a while things unfold before you that you feel were going to happen anyway. I have all these ideas flooding into my head from everywhere. I was thinking these thoughts that I had no right to think. Things that seemed almost impossible now seemed so real to me. I could doubt nothing. I knew that somehow Sam and I would get back together. I knew that whatever it was that was happening now it would all be OK. There were just things that seemed as though they could never happen, never be true, yet they would happen. There was just no way that I could say things as they are will stay the way the are because of hope. Hope does nothing. Things that we hope for are just selfish desires that never come true because when we say we want these things, we are telling the universe that we want them, so we will always be of want for them.

I heard something a kin to a gun shot which made me jump then felt the gut-wrenching, bumpity-bump of a flat tyre. The barrier came down between us and the driver.

“Sorry lads, seems as though we’ve got a puncture. Look, I’m sorry about this, I’ll call another cab to come and get you. OK?” Said the driver.

“That’s fine,” I said, “we’ll take it from here.”

“What are you talking about, King? We don’t have much time to do anything, let alone walk into to a town we know nothing about. Let the man call us another taxi and we can take it from there.”

“Good in theory, but what are we going to do once we get into town? Trust me, there is a reason for everything. Like this flat tyre.”

“You’re starting to scare me now. I know the reason that we’ve got a flat tyre…”

“Do you want me to call another taxi or not?” Asked the driver a little impatiently.

“…We ran over something sharp is why.” Said Paul.

“All I ask is that you trust me.”

“And what happens when the world ends?”

“Then you won’t need the other taxi.” Answered the driver.

“Shut up!” Paul and I shouted together.

“Sorry.”

“I know what you’re thinking…” I started.

“So, you know that I think you’re mad?”

“…Let’s just get out of the taxi here and see what happens, OK?”

“You’re the boss. I guess we wont be needing that taxi, how much do we owe you?” Paul asked the driver.

“Mate, we never charge on a flat tyre.”

“Well, thank you. Have a nice day then.” I said as we both got out.

We started walking down the road and I began to feel this sinking feeling in my stomach, like we had just made a wrong move. The thing is it felt like the right thing to do at the time, so how could I doubt myself after everything I had just been telling

Paul. But with so much road a head of us and no clue as to where we were even going, I was more than a little worried. On an impulse I stuck my thumb out.

"What the hell do you think that's going to do?" Rasped Paul.

"Get us a lift." I said deadpan.

I was still trying to think about what we were going to do and how we were going to do it.

"More like get us killed. Do you know how unsafe it is to get in the car with a stranger these days?" Paul said with a shrill. "That's if someone actually does stop for you. If you wanted a lift why did we refuse another taxi? There are so many…"

"Shut the fuck up."

"What?"

"You heard me. I don't think I can take any more of your constant ridicule and complaining. Do you have to find fault in everything? I feel like just leaving you here. In fact, if you don't shut up, that's exactly what I will do. Now you are with me on this and you do what I do, or you go and sulk somewhere where I am not. Got it?"

There was silence as we walked on. I was totally convinced that I was going to have to deal with this all the way into town, and I wasn't even sure how far that was.

- 40 -

8:39 AM

The road was a hard one to travel. There was a grass verge that we were walking on, but it was damp and slowed us down, so that we had to exert energy just to move. The traffic was whizzing by us at a leisurely seventy odd km and no one was stopping for us. I can't blame them, quite frankly, as Paul said, no body stops for hitch-hikers any more. Too many murders. The days of picking up stunning woman and getting Penthouse type favours, which to my recollection has never happened to anyone I have ever known, have long gone. The sun had come out from behind the clouds and the smog was lifting, it was going to be a hot one. I didn't know how close I was to giving up right then and there, but just as that thought entered my mind I heard the sound of a car horn behind us that made me jump. I was snapped out of the world in my mind that I had escaped to. Gone was the whining from Paul, and gone was the pressure in my feet from walking and the headache that Paul had given me.

"Here it is."

"Here what is?" Asked Paul turning around to look where I was looking.

"Our next move. Told you something would happen."

The car slowed down and stopped just past us. Paul and I looked at each other, me smiling and him shaking His head.

"I just don't believe it." He said simply.

I cantered up to the passenger window. The window whirred down and I poked my head inside to talk to the driver.

"I thought it was you," said the driver with a huge smile, "I said to myself it couldn't be, not down here. But it is you!"

"My god, Sophia!? What are you doing down here?"

"Get in and I'll tell you." She said.

Paul got in the back, so I climbed in the front and introduced the two. I don't think things could have got any more bizarre had I wanted them to. On a hunch I decided to walk and this is what happened. The question I kept asking myself is when did all these coincidences start?

Did it start when we had the flat, so we had to walk? Did it start when I got this particular taxi, or did it start when that flight attendant stopped us? If She hadn't stopped us we would have got a different taxi, and left earlier, and it wouldn't have got a flat. But then again, had I not left the wallet on the plane…and it goes on down the track. Now I can't even guess as to what would happen next. Sophia put the car in gear and started to drive of leaving me in total awe of what was happening.

"You're a tinny bastard. You know that?" Those were the first words I heard from Paul for about fifteen minutes.

"Yeah, I'm starting to think that myself."

"I mean, to be picked up by someone you know in a town you have never been to before is beyond amazing" He continued.

"How do you know I've never been here before?" I asked.

"You've never been to Wellington, King?" Inquired Sophia.

"Just a guess." Answered Paul. "You don't know where you're going or anything, so, you know."

"Well," I said to the both of them, "it just so happens that you're right. I have never been here before. I just never had the opportunity I guess, but I'm here now."

"So, what's next."

"I don't know. Sophia, you still haven't told me what you're doing here."

"Witches convention."

"What?" I said looking at Her as if She just told me She's from outer space.

"A witches convention. They hold a national gathering of all the New Zealand Witches around this time each year. It's a chance to catch up with friends, and get the goss, some info, and the occasional spell." She said.

"Don't tell me you all sit around naked at a camp fire with a cauldron of bubbling stuff." Asked Paul.

"Well, as a matter of fact, that's not to far from the truth."

"And I take it you're a Witch." He asked.

"Indeed. I don't know that I am a witch as you may think, though. It's a long story, perhaps I can fill you in a bit later. Do you know where you are heading?"

"Not a clue." I fielded.

And I still didn't. This was going to be a ride-by-the-seat-of-your-pants type adventure, as I was slowly finding out. It seemed to me that when ever I didn't know where to turn, the answer found me.

"You can come to the convention if you like."

"Um, I think I'll pass on that." Said Paul. "I don't fancy being turned into a frog or a pig or anything like that."

"Tactful, very tactful." I directed this at Paul. "I for one would be delighted to come, Sophia. The further into this investigation I get, the more I seem to be interested."

"Great. What are you going to do Paul?"

"I don't know, but swallowing poison and dancing around a dead virgin isn't my idea of fun."

"It's not like that at all. I think you would really enjoy it, but it's your choice." She said.

"The main reason we are down here is to find a friend of ours. Samantha…"

"Isn't that the one who wanted you dead?" Sophia interrupted.

"…err, yes." I replied. "What do you know about that?"

"Let's just say that I heard it through the grapevine. There is something very strange with that girl."

"There is nothing wrong with Her. She's fine, it's what is inside Her that makes me worry." I defended.

***

The next few hours passed like seconds, seemingly getting no closer to what we were looking for, not that I had any clue as to what that was. I found myself in the back of nowhere, somewhere in Wellington, sitting in a circle of self-professed witches. Each one of them eyeing me up as if they knew something about me. Of course, that could just as easily have been my paranoia.

I have this dream where I'm on an elevator and it just keeps going up and up; it's like they could see this dream. The night was cold and I couldn't really see the faces of those that scrutinized me. Just the feeling. We had dropped PJ off in town, so He could try and find something, anything. He said He would try the relatives place, and a few other places that She may have gone; He was happy to take this on as His little piece of detective work. We hadn't heard from him in quite a while when all of a sudden my mobile rang and scared the crap out of me.

"King, it's me." I recognised the caller ID before I answered the phone, so this was no surprise.

"Hi PJ - what have you got for me?"

The house that Sophia had brought me to bore a striking resemblance to the one Sam described when She first came to see me. The light was starting to fade and the air was chilly on the wide-open lawn where we sat. Sophia introduced the owner of the house as Kathryn, and She was the one that was glaring at me right now.

"On second thoughts, PJ, can this wait? I'm kind of in the middle of something here."

"Not really; it's about Sam."

"Look, I'll get back to you in about ten minutes." I ended the call and smiled at Kathryn.

"Everything OK, Mr. Kingly?" She asked.

"Please, call me King."

"That's kind of conceited isn't it?"

"Not you too." I defended.

"We prefer" She continued unabashed, "to have all cell phones turned off, Mr. Kingly."

"Well I prefer" I mocked, "to call them mobiles and for people to call me King, but we can't have everything we want can we?"

I really wasn't making friends here, but I was trying to save the world. As this thought hit me, so did a gust of wind so strong that it knocked me over. This sudden burst of freaky wind snapped me back into reality, and I sat there on the ground for a good couple of seconds to clear my mind and make sense of what just happened. Were these real Witches? The weight of the situation rolled over me like a truck. I clumsily got back to my feet.

There were four other people besides the three of us, they were introduced to me, but I was still adjusting to the fact that I was standing naked in front of six other naked people, four of which were women, to remember their names. This wasn't what I was intrigued with though, what had captivated me was the way these witches thought about the world. We were all standing in a circle trying to raise energy, and what they were saying was amazing. Somewhere deep in my brain it all clicked. The life we lead has so many restrictions, too many restrictions, placed on it that anything natural that we partake in can be seen as the complete opposite, and in fact could be called dirty. This rang my bells and it started to solidify some of my theories in my case. It was always going to be me fighting this battle, it could only be me. I just wish I knew why that feels so right, and I wish I knew why we all had to be naked out here.

"Because there is something about who you are." Said Sophia as if reading my mind.

"What?" I snapped. She was starting to freak me out.

"She's right you know." Announced the taller of the two men. "There is something more to you than you know. I can feel it."

"I'm not sure I understand what you're saying."

"Lets just say that you knew. You know. You just don't believe it." Added Kathryn. "You have to let yourself be aware of who you really are. Don't be scared, you will remember."

"Remember what?" I asked.

They were talking very cryptically when all I wanted was a straight answer.

"We can't tell you exactly what it's all about. We can only tell you, or describe, what we feel." This was Sophia again.

She had an amazing body, which was very distracting for me, but I was listening and taking in what they were telling me. It all sounded very familiar in an airy-fairy way, then I remembered what I was there for and suddenly looked at my watch.

4:50 PM

I excused myself from the circle to the moans and groans of the other participants.

"I have to make a call. This is very important. Trust me," I said looking at Sophia, "if I could stay I would." I added.

"Please just give us the grace of letting us close the circle first." Pleaded Kathryn.

The energy that Witches deal with can be very volatile, this I can attest to being blown over by a very isolated and suspicious gust of wind. The energy needs to be protected, so a circle is opened to contain this energy. It's nothing spectacular, but there is a definite change in the surrounding air when they did their thing. Closing the circle, as I was about to find out, is something completely different.

"Watchtowers of the North, we thank you." Was the chorus of voices.

"Watchtowers of the East, we thank you." There was, just then, a marked rise in temperature.

"Watchtowers of the South, we thank you." The air was starting to feel electric and I was getting worried.

"Watchtowers of the West, we thank you."

I must say, I was beginning to get used to all of this weird shit happening and I admit to looking forward to what was going to happen next. I was not disappointed. Suddenly the air started to haze over with a blue tinge. Sophia smiled at me.

"It's all right, you're going to like this."

For once I put my faith in Her and trusted what She said. I breathed a sigh, which had been pent up for sometime, and watched as little blue sparks flicked here and there. On the occasion one of the sparks would touch me, but all I could feel was a soft surge of energy. Something that will stay in my memory as the moment I believed. This was the reality I had been told about. Once morc my belief was confirmed as all the spooky stuff became non-fiction rather than science fiction. The sparking increased and all feelings of awkwardness and shyness about me being naked left. I could see the plan. The world saving, non-selfish, special project afoot and working. The time was ticking by, but I wasn't worried. The blue charge was growing in brightness, and static, and it was as if we were in a blue bubble of protection. As the energy built it gravitated towards the top of the sphere creating and energy spot. Swirling shadows and reflections played their way across my chest bringing me higher with euphoria, and I didn't want it to stop. The gathered energy above was reaching what seemed like critical mass.

"Um, what's going to happen?" I asked.

"Shh." Sophia hissed. "You'll see."

And with that She held my hand and gave me a smile. My body shrilled with excitement as the energy built up in what I can only describe as being orgasmic. The energy spot exploded through the skin of the bubble and like a laser beam shot off into the skies above and disappeared. If I stopped to figure out what was going on here I think I would have to check myself into the funny farm. What the hell is it all about? I mean what drugs am I on to accept this as normal goings on? My legs gave out and I fell to the ground.

5:00 PM

My mobile rang again, this time I could answer it safely without anyone getting annoyed with me.

"King here."

"King, no time to talk or explain. I have Sam with me and we're on our way. Where are you?"

"Honestly, Paul, I don't know. But I will put you onto someone who does." I looked around for help in the shape of Kathryn.

"I need a favour," I said to Her, "could you tell my friend how to get here?"

I walked over to Her and offered Her the phone; She took it with a shrug.

"Hello?" She spoke into the phone.

For about a minute I heard Her giving directions to the house before She hung up and handed the phone back to me. I turned to Sophia.

"Sophia, I need to talk to you." I lead Her by the hand over to a clearing and spoke to Her in hushed tones.

"You seem to know, or at least understand, what's going on here.' I said.

"Kind of." She said with a shrug.

"Well, I need your help. We don't have much time."

"To save the world?" She said sarcastically.

"Exactly."

"So, what do you want me to do?" She asked.

"First, I want you to explain to these guys," I said, pointing to the others, "what is going on. I'm sure you will do a better job at that than I would. I want you people to do whatever it is you do best to try and protect everyone; especially Sam."

"I can't guarantee anything, but I'll try."

"That's all I'm asking." I said and gave Her a kiss on the cheek.

I was still naked and feeling a little vulnerable, so when everybody started to get themselves dressed I hurriedly did the same. They started the preparation for god only knows what, while I patiently waited for what I could only now describe as bait.

"Mr. Kingly."

Kathryn was waving to me from the stairs to the house. She started towards me almost excitedly.

"Everybody should be ready in about ten minutes." She said.

"Thank you."

"You know, I think what you're doing is a big thing."

"Look, I don't have time for any tender moments right now. Any minute the woman that I love, or at least the body of the woman I love, will come through that door and there will be hell to pay, or not, I really don't know what's going to happen."

She stared at me for a moment or two looking a bit hurt.

“I’m sorry, I didn’t mean to offend you, but I meant what I said. What I need from you,” I explained with a sorry look in my eyes, “is help. I can’t do this on my own.”

“You have my support, Mr. Kingly. Let’s just hope you don’t need it.”

I dug into my pockets and found my cigarettes. In quiet contemplation I put the filter end between my lips and lit the tip. I inhaled deeply while watching Sophia make Her way towards me as Kathryn left my side.

I can remember when I was very young, my Mother read me stories. Some would be dramatic and some would be silly, and some were down right scary. They all shared one thing in common; they all had happy endings. This was no fairy tale and nothing that would get any kid, no matter how sadistic, to sleep. My own nightmare was drawing to a close and those stories came rushing back to me. Over and over in my head I could sense my own mortality, and for the first time in my life it was someone else that mattered. The world, as they say, was on my shoulders. I also felt, for the first time in my life, that I may not make it out the other side.

“What are you thinking?” Inquired Sophia, who had reached my side.

Things had become a little quieter for the time being and the moment was a calm and peaceful one.

“Just wondering what’s going to happen next. I feel like I’m in WW2 and just about to go over the top.”

All was silent apart from the odd voice here and there of one of the Witches. All fables of old crones and broomsticks bit at my brain and tried to encourage thoughts of hate to these people, but as Sophia and I stared out onto the lawn all I could think about was how nice these people are.

“What’s up with Her?” I heard one of the guys shout out.

I looked over to where He was looking and saw PJ and Sam walking down the stairs towards me.

“There’s some bad mojo there that’s for sure!” Said the other.

“Excuse me, that’s my friend and colleague!” I exclaimed.

“Colleague huh.” Said PJ with a smile.

“No offence man,” said one of the girls, “but there is something wrong with that chick.”

“I can feel it too.” Said Kathryn.

“And me.” Said Sophia.

“You’re telling me, but you should try sharing a car with Her!” Added PJ loudly, “She ain’t right, King. We gotta do something now! It’s starting to scare me I can’t lie.”

“Sam, are you OK?” I asked Her.

She didn’t even acknowledge me, just kept on walking. They were right, this wasn’t Sam. There was some sort of bustling within the ranks. I didn’t much like the smile She was giving me. A cool southerly picked up, and from there things just got bizarre. It wasn’t Her, but I couldn’t help it. She had me fully in Her talons of life and I had to give in. Then, out from nowhere, and I mean nowhere, no puff of smoke, no taxi, just there on the steps, stood Billy. If I hadn’t seen it with my own two eyes I wouldn’t have believed it myself. But it happened. It has taken a few months to draw the negativity out of the woodwork, but now it’s out. It’s all over the place and I was terrified. Through everything I had been through up to this time, this has to be the bit where I truly felt like shitting my pants. I was seeing things that I never thought I would see. All around us grew black, all but the area around Billy and those familiar chills ran up and down my spine. The Witches huddled together and started to chant something that I couldn’t make out. I didn’t understand all the ins and outs of good and bad energy, but it didn’t take a genius to figure out that this was no picnic. There was an evil look in Billy's eye and She started screaming. I mean She could have brought the walls down She was so load. It was like a thousand people dying, some unearthly, ungodly scream that made my ears literally bleed. Then She started to talk.

"Ereh eeshi."

It was like no language that I have heard. She was in plain view of everybody and nobody moved. Completely naked from head to toe. She turned away from our accusing stares and spoke loudly;

"Ooh dairteeb sah eesh – ooh dairteeb sah eesh."

She was standing at the top of the stairs then almost floated down backwards and over to me. I put myself between Her and Sam like a Father protecting His daughter, and I was ready for anything. She stopped and stood there facing me and just looked at me with bloodshot eyes that seemed to take on a glow of their own. Samantha followed suit coming closer to the three of us with the same horrific eyes. My breathing became heavier and heavier, harder and harder as She finally stopped next to Billy. I looked Billy right in the eyes, we still had more than twenty-four hours before all hell broke loose so, I decided to call Odin on His word.

"What the hell do you want? Wait, it doesn't matter."

I guess the plan just seemed to fall together as I turned back to Sam and kissed Her.

- 41 -

THE SHADOWLAND

From the start of this whole ordeal I have prided myself with not ever wanting to give up; until now. My body was weak, my heart and soul were weak, and I just didn't know what else to do. It was so faint that I almost didn't hear it. A voice, well, less than a voice. It was like a feeling; something. An echo of a feeling, but it was there. I wasn't sure at first, but then I heard it again.

"You knew. You know."

All I could do was shake my head and try to clear some of the fog that invaded my mind. I was alone and afraid. Something had happened. I had done something that I shouldn't have done. The guilt ravaged my mind and I could see the end of the world, but something else must have happened. This was not the end. Where was everybody? Where were the gods and fallen worriers? Where were the Witches and my friends? Where was Sam? What have I done? What did I do? Have I started all over again? All my wits had abated me and the only sense I had left that I could rely on was the feeling of the cold, wet ground that I found myself slumped on yet again.

"They'll be here soon and it'll all be over."

"Oh, God! What have I done?" I whimpered.

To Be continued…

www.ingramcontent.com/pod-product-compliance
Lightning Source LLC
Chambersburg PA
CBHW020613310726
48979CB00008B/1459/J

* 9 7 8 0 4 7 3 1 6 8 0 4 9 *